An evil lurks among them

I'm right here, but they can't see me. They're too caught up in their stupid little lives. Too bad. I'm their worst nightmare. They've had fair warning. It's showtime!

"Teens who think this is just a chick-lit book will find more than they bargained for . . . [This] book delivers." —*Booklist*

"Gripping suspense" —*School Library Journal*

"Clever, full of personality and deliciously spooky" —Teenreads.com

pretty little devils

A NOVEL BY

NANCY HOLDER

razOr
bill

Pretty Little Devils

RAZORBILL

Published by the Penguin Group
Penguin Young Readers Group
345 Hudson Street, New York, New York 10014, U.S.A.
Penguin Group (USA) Inc., 375 Hudson Street, New York, New York 10014, U.S.A.
Penguin Group (Canada), 90 Eglinton Avenue East, Suite 700, Toronto, Ontario,
Canada M4P 2Y3 (a division of Pearson Penguin Canada Inc.)
Penguin Books Ltd, 80 Strand, London WC2R 0RL, England
Penguin Ireland, 25 St Stephen's Green, Dublin 2, Ireland (a division of Penguin Books Ltd)
Penguin Group (Australia), 250 Camberwell Road, Camberwell, Victoria 3124,
Australia (a division of Pearson Australia Group Pty Ltd)
Penguin Books India Pvt Ltd, 11 Community Centre, Panchsheel Park,
New Delhi – 110 017, India
Penguin Group (NZ), Cnr Airborne and Rosedale Roads, Albany,
Auckland 1310, New Zealand (a division of Pearson New Zealand Ltd)
Penguin Books (South Africa) (Pty) Ltd, 24 Sturdee Avenue, Rosebank,
Johannesburg 2196, South Africa

Penguin Books Ltd, Registered Offices: 80 Strand, London WC2R 0RL, England

10 9 8 7 6 5 4 3 2 1

Interior design by Yvette Mangual

THE LIBRARY OF CONGRESS HAS CATALOGED THE HARDCOVER EDITION AS FOLLOWS:
Holder, Nancy.
Pretty little devils: a novel / by Nancy Holder.
    p. cm.
Summary: Life seems rosy for the Pretty Little Devils, the most popular girls' clique in high
school, until its members begin to experience threats and assaults.
ISBN 1-59514-030-1
[1. Cliques (Sociology)—Fiction. 2. Interpersonal relations—Fiction. 3. High schools—
Fiction. 4. Schools—Fiction.] I. Title.
PZ7.H70326Pre 2006
[Fic]—dc22

                                                    2005023867

Razorbill Splashproof paperback ISBN 978-1-59514-152-1

Manufactured in China

pretty little devils

Sylvia: "Damn it, Carolyn, I can still hardly hear you. Thank God you only have one more month on that loser phone. It doesn't get any reception."

Carolyn: "I know. I cannot wait. Can you hear me now?"

Sylvia: "That might be funny if I actually *could* hear you."

Megan: "Same here. I thought three-way calling was supposed to make this *easier*."

Sylvia: "Moving on. Listen, Breona threw down again. At the mall. It was another Josh incident. She said he wants to go back to her, but he's staying with me because I 'put out.' 'Put out.' Who even talks like that?"

Megan: "You have got to be kidding me! What a slut! She is dead!"

Carolyn: "So dead. But you know she was lying, Sylvia. Josh would never say that."

Megan: "Totally lying."

Sylvia: "It was like she was begging me to lose it right there in the mall, you know? It was in the food court. I was standing in line at Boudin's and she just came over. She was smart to pick a public place. You guys know what I can do when I'm pushed."

Carolyn: "She's so déclassé."

Megan: "*Vraiment*. Did you talk to Josh yet?"

Sylvia: "*Excuse* me? There is nothing to talk to him about. She's lying!"

Carolyn: "God, Megan, you don't believe her, do you? You don't think Josh would actually say something like that about Sylvia?"

Megan: "It's just . . . I don't know, I wonder how she can lie like that in front of everybody. Josh should know she's lying about him to people."

Sylvia: "You have a point. Josh should know his reputation is in danger."

Carolyn: "Except . . . it'll look like you don't trust him if you talk to him about it."

Megan: "Then one of *us* should talk to him."

Sylvia: "Maybe Ellen should. She's so *nice*. By the way, Ellen is our second agenda item, after we take care of this."

Megan: "Yeah, because she was wearing that retarded outfit again—"

Sylvia: "Megan, *second* agenda item."

Carolyn: "Right. Back to the first. Breona is such a ho."

Sylvia: "Well, it's just stupid anyway. The way she deals with guys is dysfunctional. If I ever thought Josh really was staying with me because I—because we—"

Megan: "She's so wrong. How can she think she can get away with this?"

Sylvia: "That's my point. She can't. By the way, she talked about the *incident* too. You know which one I mean."

Megan: "Oh my God."

Carolyn: "That skank. She really is looking for trouble."

Sylvia: "Absolutely. But, as you say, no one will believe her. No one believed all the other gossip about your little entanglement.

It died down over the summer. With the pictures."

Megan: "Was Stephan there when she mentioned it?"

Carolyn: "Megan, get over Stephan. He just brings it up to get a reaction out of you."

Megan: "Whatever. We need to discuss how we're getting back at Breona."

Sylvia: "Give me your best ideas tomorrow morning. Before school. We are seriously weakened as a group if Breona thinks she can just say whatever she wants without any repercussions. Now, on to the second item. Let's talk about Ellen."

Megan: "She's been a total humiliation lately. That dress—"

Sylvia: "One bad outfit I could forgive. But that hair . . . This is the beginning of junior year, ladies. We have to take ourselves seriously, or no one else will. When Ellen started falling all over that guy at the movies—"

Carolyn: "She does act a little dorky on occasion. . . ."

Megan: "A *little*? His friends were *laughing* at us. She didn't even notice."

Sylvia: "Ladies, ladies. I don't want to get rid of Ellen. She's been really loyal, and she's a good friend to all of us. But it is a bit of a problem."

Megan: "It's like you always say, Sylvia. We are known by the company we keep. If we hang with losers, *we're* losers. We've worked hard to get where we are. We all take pains to look good, to be popular. What we do reflects on all of us."

Sylvia: "No. No dumping Ellen. It is not an option. We don't want people saying we turn our backs on our friends.

It would be terrible publicity. Breona would jump all over it. And she would probably invite Ellen into her group just to get to all our secrets."

Carolyn: "Ellen would rather die than betray us."

Sylvia: "Well, it's a situation, definitely. She's losing ground. Maybe she's working too hard, babysitting *too* much. We could cut back on her jobs. . . ."

Megan: "Then *we* would have to do them. I've already got tons of homework, and Mrs. Sprague said I have to get some more extracurriculars if I'm going to get into a decent college."

Carolyn: "Like your brother?"

Megan: "Back off, Carolyn!"

Carolyn: "God, Megan, what's your problem? Your brother goes to a serious school. Does that, like, freak you out or something?"

Sylvia: "Megan? Are you keeping something from us? Because friends share."

Megan: "No. It's nothing. I didn't understand what she meant."

Carolyn: "So you thought the worst?"

Sylvia: "Both of you chill out right now. My God. Do you even remember what we were talking about? I say it's time to ask a new girl in. That way we can dilute the Ellen factor."

Megan: "Are you serious? It's always been the four of us."

Sylvia: "Are you questioning me, Megan? Who has kept this group going all this time? Me. And what I say goes. Oh, look, Ellen's logged on. Let's go to the chat room, *mes petites*. Now remember, be kind. Ellen is still one of us."

THIS IS A PRIVATE CHAT ROOM FOR INVITED MEMBERS ONLY

Members in chat room:

PLDSLY

PLDEL

PLDCARO

PLDMEG

PLDSLY: *Bonjour,* El! Home early?

PLDEL: Still at Hernandez. Using their laptop.

PLDCARO: *Bonjour, toutes!*

PLDMEG: *Bonjour!*

PLDSLY: Clever U, El. Don't forget 2 charge 4 lateness.

PLDEL: Suki warned me ahead of time might B late.

PLDSLY: Late = late. Suki agreed 2 7 PM. On schedule.

PLDEL: OK.

PLDSLY: We let 1 slide, they all do it.

PLDEL: Sorry. :(

PLDSLY: N/p. Listen, El, Breona attacked me at the mall. Re Josh. It was bad.

PLDEL: OMG, that's terrible! She hurt U? :(

PLDSLY: Not physically. Not a scratch. Though she did have her claws out. LOL.

PLDEL: What'd she say?

PLDSLY: SOS. Josh couldn't wait 4 me 2 go 2 France, only came back 2 me cuz I give him benefits.

PLDEL: OMG. UR kidding! :(

PLDSLY: No worries. I ripped her a new 1. She wuz crying by time I left. :)

PLDEL: Go, Sylvia!

PLDSLY: Of the past. We move on.

PLDCARO: But Josh needs 2 know she's lyin' about him. Some1 needs 2 tell him. Not Syl, cuz it'll look like she doesn't trust him.

PLDEL: Don't worry, Syl, I can do in Art2.

PLDSLY: GR8. I'll call U later, fill U in.

PLDEL: KK, but before 9 OK, cuz my dad.

PLDCARO: Just put cell phone on vibrate. More fun anyway, LOL.

PLDEL: LOL, but big trouble if he finds out.

PLDMEG: El, UR a wimp.

PLDSLY: Meggers, B nice. :(

PLDMEG: Sorry, S.

PLDSLY: N/p. El, I'll call B4 9. So, new school year goin' on. PLDs gotta look good. Love streaks, Meggies. New salon?

PLDMEG: Still at Tuberose.

PLDCARO: In the mall, right?

PLDMEG: Please. Who goes to mall 4 hair? White trash!

PLDSLY: El, UR place is in mall?

PLDEL: Yes.

PLDMEG: Oops. Sorry, El! My bad X2.

PLDSLY: El, mebbe try Meg's? Also, gel . . . over.

PLDEL: Hair not good?

PLDSLY: U've done better. Every1 remember, we R in spotlight. That dress Friday . . . *mais non, cherie.*

PLDEL: ?

PLDMEG: No offense, it makes U look fat.

PLDEL: OMG!

PLDSLY: We can't give Breona any reason 2 attack us. Solid

fashions, solid rep. We R Pretty Little Devils!

PLDMEG: *Mais oui!*

PLDCARO: *Mais oui!*

PLDEL: OMG, Suki home. Gotta go.

PLDSLY: *Au revoir!*

(PLDEL has left the chat room)

PLDMEG: So, do you think she got it?

PERSONALBLOG

HAPPY2BME

SHE'S SUCH A STUPID BITCH. SHE THINKS SHE'S TOTALLY

HOT, BUT SHE'S GOT NO IDEA WHAT CONSEQUENCES ARE.

YEAH, WE'LL CHANGE THINGS. WE'LL SEE WHO MAKES THE

CUT. ONE BY ONE. THEY'LL ALL FEEL THE BLADE. *LAISSEZ LES*

BON TEMPS ROULER!

CHAPTER ONE

By the end of the first week of school, everyone had their designated seats in the cafeteria. Hazel Stone's spot was at the third table from the diversity mural on the west side. There, the diffuse light from the thick windows cast a halo over the heads of her so-called friends—Lakshmi, Ginger, Jamie, and the embarrassingly named LaToya.

Friends . . . they were more like friends by default. Joy had been the one they had in common, and Joy had moved to San Jose during the summer. As soon as she'd left, Hazel had tried her hardest to break away. It hadn't taken.

She had gotten a job and steered clear of the phone, preferring to blog on her LiveJournal or watch *Osbournes* reruns with her little brother, Corey. Hazel had spent more time that summer with Corey than she had the rest of their lives combined, and if her parents had been the kind of people who actually commented on what was going on around them, they would have told her they were pleased.

They wouldn't have been pleased if they'd known what else

had happened during the summer, but she was not going there.

Lakshmi spotted Hazel and waved expectantly. Hazel cringed as the four girls smiled and beckoned her over, as if they had to invite her or something. It would never occur to them that she didn't want to sit with them. It didn't matter that Hazel had pretty much avoided them for the entire summer.

She had pretty much hidden herself away from everybody, feeling guilty and unsure about what she was doing. She would start to think, *Okay, I've made the break*. Then her mother would answer the phone and unknowingly accept an invitation from the Lakshmi contingent on Hazel's behalf. Her mother was clueless, as usual.

Unable to explain that she was trying to dump "those nice girls," Hazel would find herself at the movies or the mall. Thus she would be reconnected with Lakshmi's group, and all her careful isolation would be thrown out the window.

Hazel didn't feel she was asking for much. All she wanted were *real* friends—friends who were interesting and intelligent, friends who understood her. Lakshmi and the others were just treading water until they got out of school, content to stay in the background, idly worshiping the popular kids. Graduation was their only goal.

Hazel had bigger dreams—way bigger. She wanted high school to count for something. She wanted to be one of the girls people remembered when they opened their yearbooks. Not just some other "Who?" in a sea of unrecognizable faces. This was the year to make it happen. Senior year would be too late. The time was now.

And this was a defining moment. Or at least it felt that way. Here she was, halfway through October and still trapped. She knew she needed new friends. And not just good friends, but great ones. And if she worked it right with the right group, she might even have a shot at the object of her total desire, the new guy, Matty Vardeman.

She stole a glance at his table. Despite being new, he was already on the varsity football team, and he sat with some of the first-string guys, like Stephan Nylund, Brandon Wilde, and Josh Douglas.

Stephan was stocky, with red hair and a goatee. He was some kind of tackle or something. Brandon and Josh were the team quarterbacks—friendly rivals—and Josh was Sylvia Orly's boyfriend. He was tall, blond, and very wiry. He laughed a lot, and he was very smart. He would have to be, to keep up with Sylvia.

Brandon was bigger, with chestnut hair and a pair of very thick eyebrows. Unlike Josh, Brandon was a total jerk. Last year he had humiliated a girl in Hazel's geometry class by pretending to ask her out, then telling her he was kidding when she stammered out a yes—as if he would ever go out with someone so beneath him.

Hazel felt sorry for the girl. Then she felt sorry for herself. For her, Matty was just as unreachable.

But God, she thought, *he is hot*.

Matty Vardeman sat at the far end of the table, leaning back casually in his chair. He was wearing a gray sweater that looked thick and expensive, maybe hand-knit, and a pair of black jeans. He favored dark clothes, and he looked good in them. The other guys had on their green letter jackets and jeans. Matty usually just carried his jacket, but when he did wear it, his shoulders looked enormous.

She had noticed him on the first day of school. He was Matty, not Matt—and he was a miracle of quirks. Push the quirk meter one more click on the dial, and he would be ugly. But somehow, all of his face's strangenesses came together into one amazing picture. He had a long, straight nose, flaring cheekbones, and deep-set eyes that were dark chestnut in color. His eyebrows were heavy and also dark, like his wavy hair. No spiky tips for him; instead, it was a little long—more Ashton Kutcher than Chad Michael Murray, to use Lakshmi's fan-girl vocabulary.

He was smart, too, Hazel knew. His classes were all AP or honors. He carried a sketchbook wherever he went and some-times spent study hall or lunch working on a drawing.

His birthday was March 16 and he was from Virginia. He had a soft southern accent that made Hazel smile.

His father was in the navy and his parents had moved to Japan. He had come to Brookhaven to live with his sister and finish out his junior and senior years. Hazel had heard he was really pissed off about having to leave Virginia, but whenever she saw him, his full lips were curled in a faint smile, as if everything secretly amused him.

He was a little reserved and still a little apart from the other guys. He sat at their table and hung with them, but Hazel could tell he wasn't one of them. Not yet.

Hazel had tried everything to get him to notice her. She had memorized his schedule and had "just happened" to wander by his classes so many times that one of the boys in his precalculus class had asked her what the homework was. Despite the fact that Hazel sucked at drawing, she'd taken to carrying a sketchbook as well. She hoped if she appeared to be into art, it might pique his interest. Nothing seemed to have any effect.

"Hazel!" Lakshmi shouted over the din, half rising from her chair as the others waited for her to come and sit down. LaToya gazed at her over her soda cup, sucking on a straw.

Hazel sighed. She just didn't know how to do it, how to go through with cutting them loose. Putting on a little smile, she made eye contact, walked steadily to the table, and put down her tray.

They all had on knockoffs of the current fashions: short blazers, white shirts, and light wash jeans. But somehow on them, it looked like trying too hard.

Hazel had gone preppy, with an oxford shirt, knee-length denim skirt, and black ankle boots. Blue went nicely with her auburn hair, which she'd added a tiny bit of henna to. She had blue eyes, and she knew she wasn't ugly. But looks weren't always enough.

"Hi," Lakshmi said, grinning at her as the others made a show of clearing a welcoming place. "Didn't you see us?"

"Oh, I—I . . ." Hazel stuttered. "I just got distracted for a sec. I thought I heard someone call my name."

"Guess what!" Lakshmi said. "Breona and Sylvia had a fight in the mall last night. The security guards had to come and pull them off each other. There's a deep scratch on Breona's cheek and she's going to sue Sylvia."

Jamie nodded. "She's going to get plastic surgery. Because of the disfigurement."

Hazel's attention immediately ticked to the cheerleader table, where Breona sat with her new, spiky haircut. Her brown sugar complexion was flawless; her dark almond eyes glittered as she talked with the other cheerleaders, all of them in tight kelly green sweaters and gold cheer skirts that showed off their skinny, muscular bodies. There was a Band-Aid on her cheek. But it hardly covered a plastic-surgery-worthy wound. Lakshmi was good for gossip, but sometimes she tended to overdramatize.

Not that the Breona-and-Sylvia war needed dramatization. The two queen bees had always hated each other. They were the two most popular girls in school, and the source of their conflict was always Josh.

The gossip went that last summer things had come to a head. Even though he was officially Sylvia's boyfriend, Josh had hooked up with Breona two weeks after Sylvia had gone to France with her family. Sylvia came back and Josh pretended everything was fine. But of course Sylvia found out the truth. From what Hazel had heard, Josh was lucky to be alive.

"It's all over the school," Lakshmi gushed as she plucked a couple of french fries off Hazel's plate. "Everybody's talking about it."

Hazel watched as Lakshmi popped the fries into her mouth and chewed.

Lakshmi had a skin problem. Hazel had tried to tell her not to eat greasy food, but Lakshmi was very fragile on the subject. She would start crying and insisting that Hazel thought she was ugly.

She *wasn't* ugly, but her skin could definitely use some help.

Lowering her voice, Lakshmi leaned forward and added, "Sylvia's got to go to anger management classes. Court-ordered."

Lakshmi's face was flushed with excitement: the thrill of having serious information—the coup of being in the know—was almost too thrilling for her.

"Who told you all this? Your mom?" Hazel asked. Mrs. Sharma worked in the school's office and told Lakshmi all kinds of privileged information. It was wrong and tacky, but Lakshmi and her mom thought it was a way to raise Lakshmi's social Q, and it gave the rest of the group something to talk about.

Lakshmi nodded and Hazel shifted her attention to Sylvia's table.

There they were, the PLDs—the Pretty Little Devils—rivals of the cheerleaders as the most popular, stylish, lucky girls at Brookhaven. Party rumors aside, the PLDs *got it*. They talked about universities and internships and summers abroad. They made appearances at school events but weren't all "rah-rah" about it. They were just the right combination of interested and too-cool-to-care. Hazel would have given anything to be friends with them—if only she knew how.

Sylvia was dressed all in black, and she looked incredible. Her blue-black hair fell in long, sexy waves down her back. Regal as a queen, she sat in the middle of three chairs. Megan Williams and Carolyn Bosch sat on either side of her. Megan was all girlie-girl in a tan corduroy blazer and light green pleated skirt. Carolyn was serious fashion in black-and-white check. Ellen Schmidt sat across from them in a soft pink poncho (not over?), like a contestant from *The Apprentice*. She was touching her hair, which was pretty bad, actually: a poorly streaked, hacked-off kind of a bob thing. Hazel wondered if the PLDs were getting on her about it. If they were, they were doing her a favor.

Lakshmi picked up her fish taco and took a big bite.

"We'll ask Breona about it in lab," she said, her mouth full of cabbage, cod, and mayonnaise.

"I wish I had a class with Breona," LaToya said to Hazel and Lakshmi. "It must be nice."

Hazel shrugged, at the same time that Lakshmi said, "Oh, it *is*."

Hazel stifled a laugh. It wasn't as if she, Lakshmi, and Breona actually *spoke*. But bragging like that was Lakshmi's style. Unlike Hazel. Hazel didn't remind the others that she *was* on Breona's radar, that now and then Breona actually said hi to her and complimented her on her clothes, little things like that.

"What's Breona like?" Ginger asked Lakshmi.

"She's very nice." Lakshmi gazed over at Breona's table. She started blinking, the way she did when she was all wound up. "She looks like Alicia Keys."

"Not even," LaToya said, snorting. "Breona is, like, half Korean."

"Chinese," Lakshmi corrected her. "And she *does* look like her." That triggered something else, and Lakshmi smiled at the others without taking her gaze off Breona. "Ooh, did you guys see Orli Bloom on *People's Choice* last night?" She picked at her face, and Hazel had to force herself not to bat her hand away. "Hot."

"Hot," Jamie agreed.

Lakshmi had five Orlando Bloom posters in her bedroom. Jamie had two. LaToya was an Usher fan.

Hazel agreed that Orlando was good looking, but she didn't fawn over him like he was a boyfriend. She tended to live in the *real* world.

Talk of Orlando continued. Hazel was frowning down at her meal, trying to stay out of the conversation, when a bizarre, discordant drone wheeled into the cafeteria. Heads turned, then people began laughing and applauding and getting to their feet. Hazel's table did the same, but all Hazel could see were craning necks and shoulders.

"Oh my God! It's a bagpiper!" Lakshmi announced.

There was a stir among the students; the cluster in front of Hazel's table parted as the piper, fully decked in Highlander plaid and a beret with a green pom-pom, marched into their midst. He was playing "Scotland the Brave."

Directly behind him was a delivery guy carrying two enormous bags with P.F. CHANG'S written on the side. P.F. Chang's was an upscale Chinese restaurant in Brookhaven Center. Hazel had never eaten there, but she'd always wanted to.

Sylvia raised a hand, waving at the delivery guy. He came straight for her table. Ellen got up and rushed toward him, grabbing up the bags. She made a show of how heavy they were.

Brandon bounded over from the jock table and picked up not only the bags, but Ellen as well, carrying her under his arm like a football as she laughed and batted at him. The guys whistled and clapped, Matty included. Sylvia smiled serenely. Hazel knew immediately—this was *her* doing. She watched as Sylvia lifted her cell phone out of her purse.

In the middle of all this, she's taking a call? Hazel wondered.

Then Sylvia looked down at the phone and started keying in. *Ah, texting.*

"What's going on?" someone bellowed from the other side of the caf. It was their resident old hippie, Vice Principal Clancy, in his million-year-old Dockers and Birkenstocks.

The geometry teacher, Ms. Miller, who also had lunch duty, stomped beside him in her too-young-for-her fashions—low-slung stretchy pants and a clingy top in berry colors.

"Oh God, they're going to get in major trouble!" Lakshmi said, blinking excitedly.

Clancy was closing in. Sylvia's cell phone disappeared. Carolyn and Megan took the P.F. Chang's bags, opened them, and began spooning heaps of noodles, egg rolls, and vegetables onto four plates. Josh darted away, then returned with another plate as Clancy and Ms. Miller headed for the piper like they were going to tackle him on the twenty- yard line.

At a signal from Sylvia, the piper switched from "Scotland the Brave" to "Brookhaven Spirit," the school song. As the notes played over the cafeteria, clusters of students began to join in:

Brookhaven Spirit, our school so dear,
our love for you travels far and near.
Our voices ring proud and loud and clear
with loyalty and spirit, Brookhaven Spirit!
All hail! Our school so dear!

By the time Clancy reached the piper, nearly every person in the room was singing with gusto. Hazel remained silent.

The two teachers looked around and Hazel could practically read their thoughts. No one was doing anything wrong, exactly. And more people were singing than would at a regular pep rally. Okay, a takeout food delivery? Not exactly in the handbook, but what could it hurt? After all, it was Sylvia Orly. Such an upstanding girl. Pride of the entire administration.

Mr. Clancy waved at the students as if they might possibly be glad to see him.

Sylvia stood on her chair and held an egg roll above her head like the Statue of Liberty holding her torch. "Here's to varsity," she cried, "and the game this Friday!" Then she stepped down and graciously offered egg rolls to Mr. Clancy and Ms. Miller.

People cheered and the jocks traded high fives. Matty just smiled; he turned his head just so . . . and for one moment, Hazel thought he might be looking at her.

Breona's table—the varsity cheerleaders—sat stone-faced. Jenna Babcock, Breona's best friend, put a hand on Breona's forearm, as if to say, *Down, girl.*

"That was awesome," Lakshmi gushed.

"Yeah," Ginger agreed. She turned from the scene and started winding spaghetti around her fork.

"We could order a pizza sometime," Lakshmi ventured.

"If *we* did that, *we'd* get in trouble," LaToya muttered. "We're not celebrities like the PLDs."

Hazel smiled weakly. Didn't she know it. "I'm going to get some more Diet Coke."

She picked up her half-full cup and headed across the squeaky tile floor to the food line. The bagpiper had distracted *everyone*, but Hazel finally snagged the attention of one of the servers and got her refill.

She swiped her card at the register and dodged around a couple of guys who were pushing each other for no reason. Then she saw Matty talking to Jenna, who was pointing back at Breona's table, moving her arms, maybe yelling at him.

Matty frowned at her and shook his head. He stuffed his hands in his pockets and turned away. Jenna stomped off.

Hazel looked back at the cheerleader table. Breona and three or four of the others were gone, and the rest were knitting their brows and anxiously whispering. What was *that* about?

Hazel turned her gaze back at Matty, who was now talking to Josh and shaking his head.

She must have stared a little too long because Matty turned his head again, and this time he *did* look straight at Hazel. Their eyes met. She caught her breath.

"Oh my God!" someone yelped.

Hazel shrieked as her drink cup was crushed against her chest. Freezing Diet Coke and ice cascaded down her shirt. Hazel looked up angrily to see who had run into her.

Her mouth dropped open as she realized—it was Sylvia Orly.

"Oh no! Oh, Hazel, I am so sorry!" Sylvia said, one hand across her mouth. "I wasn't watching where I was going. This is totally my fault." Sylvia seized the drink cup from Hazel's hand and began yanking wads of napkins out of the nearest dispenser.

"Oh, you're soaked. Here." She handed more napkins to Hazel. "I'd help you clean up, but I don't want to, like, paw you. Oh God, this will stain. You have to tell me how much this cost. I'll pay for a new one."

"That's okay, Sylvia," Hazel said, laughing despite the rush of attention and the ice-cold layers of clothing clinging to her chest.

"Don't be silly. I insist," Sylvia said.

"It's old," Hazel fibbed. "Really. It's no biggie."

Sylvia pursed her lips and narrowed her eyes. "You are so lying, Hazel. I saw it in Neiman's last week. You're sweet, but you have to let me make this up to you." She considered for a moment. "We're having a little soiree tonight at Charlie Pollins'. Officially, it's a babysitting job." She wrinkled her nose as if to say, *But we both know better*. "Maybe you could come by."

Hazel's lips parted. Was this actually happening? Was Sylvia Orly actually inviting her to one of the PLDs' infamous parties? For a second, she couldn't breathe. But she quickly recovered. "Sure," she rasped. "What time?"

"Eight. Charlie's dad is going to be gone till midnight. The fun doesn't really start until nine-thirty. We close down around eleven-thirty."

"Cool," Hazel said, trying not to sound too eager. "Thanks."

"Which in French is *merci*," Sylvia replied, grinning. She was fluent in French. Word was she taught all the PLDs to speak the language too.

"Do you know the Pollinses' address?" Sylvia asked.

"Um, no."

Sylvia whipped out her cell phone, glanced down, and chuckled at the screen. "Oops. Just a minute." With rapid-fire fingers, she texted something. Then she glanced at Hazel and said, "What's your cell number? I'll put you in."

Oh, great, Hazel thought. *Already I have to betray my total lameness.*

"I don't actually have a cell phone," she admitted. "At the moment."

"You are so lucky," Sylvia replied without missing a beat. "They're a total pain. With a cell, you never get a moment's peace. I curse the man who invented them." She smiled charitably. "Well, let's go to my table. I'll write it down for you."

In a daze, Hazel followed Sylvia through the cafeteria. She knew people were watching, could see heads pressing together, people taking stock of this turn of events. Her cheeks were hot. Hazel prayed they weren't bright red.

Matty was watching too. His head was cocked just so, and his lazy smile broadened the slightest bit when their gazes met.

"Good taste," Sylvia whispered, noticing the mini-exchange. "Hey, look whose lovely new clothes I massacred."

They had reached the PLDs' table. Hazel looked down at Megan, Carolyn, and Ellen. She nodded at them.

Ellen fluffed her hair and said, "Hey, Hazel."

"Hey," Hazel managed.

"So listen, to make up for my horrible faux pas, I'm inviting

Hazel to the flash mob tonight." Sylvia flipped open a purple note-book and held out her hand. "Who's got a pen?"

Ellen opened her bag and instantly produced a gel writer in coordinating purple.

Megan and Carolyn smiled at Hazel as Sylvia wrote out a street address and phone number in beautiful, unusual handwriting. She ripped out the piece of paper and handed it to Hazel with a flourish. She had a French manicure, and Hazel noticed three identical Claddagh rings on the middle three fingers of her left hand, each with a different-colored heart.

"No selling this on eBay, right?" Sylvia winked, then pulled out her chair and sat down. "See you tonight."

Hazel knew she was being dismissed. She smiled pleasantly and said, "Okay."

The other three PLDs waved, bright smiles on their faces. Hazel saw that all of them were wearing Claddagh rings. It must be a PLD thing.

Then Sylvia gave Hazel a sly smile and said, "Oh, and be sure to dress to impress. There may be another addition to the guest list." She nodded in Matty's direction.

Hazel's heart pounded. As she made her way back to her own table, she tried to send an ESP message to Lakshmi and the others to stop looking so freaked out.

"What was that about? What did she give you?" Lakshmi demanded as Hazel grabbed up her backpack. Lakshmi reached for the piece of notebook paper, but Hazel held on to it.

"Just her number," Hazel said, her voice catching a little. She fished her purse out and popped the paper into it. Lakshmi hungrily followed it with her eyes.

"She wants you to call her?"

"Uh, yeah." Hazel shrugged. "She wants to see about replacing my shirt."

She glanced over her shoulder toward Sylvia's table.

Sylvia was talking to Matty—and handing him a piece of notebook paper too.

Hazel quickly glanced away and sat down, nearly throwing herself into her chair.

"Don't you want to go to the bathroom to clean up?" Lakshmi asked. "You're soaking wet."

"I'm fine." To prove it, Hazel picked up a fry and dipped it in her ketchup. "Where did Breona go?"

"Oh!" Lakshmi leaned forward. "Clancy came and got her. Something's up. Definitely." The other three nodded excitedly.

"Definitely," LaToya echoed.

PERSONALBLOG

HAPPY2BME

BREONA SUX. SHE DESERVES WORSE FOR ALL THE CRAP SHE PULLS. WHAT SHE GOT THIS AFTERNOON—AND WHAT SHE'S GOING TO GET! THIS IS JUST PHASE ONE. ALL THE PRETTY GIRLS WHO THINK THEY'RE BETTER THAN ME? THEY DON'T KNOW WHAT THEY'RE IN FOR!

CHAPTER TWO

At eight-fifteen Hazel parked her Corolla across the street from the Pollins residence. It was a sad little ranch-style house made of mud-brown stucco.

Hazel sat behind the wheel, building up her nerve. A parade of the cool and unapproachable from Brookhaven sauntered through the arched doorway.

To get out of the house, Hazel had told her parents she was "studying." She didn't give out any details—and wasn't asked. Her mom didn't realize that she had gone a little boho, changing into her new gold pointy flats, an ankle-length green cotton skirt, and a black cami, or that she had put on more makeup than usual. Typical. Her mom was too into her own stuff to notice.

Hazel watched as Brandon walked across the street with Josh. They were dressed in the same outfits they'd had on at school. Thanks to the Diet Coke incident, Hazel had a good excuse for changing.

Her palms were wet and her cheeks were hot. She flicked on the dome light to check her makeup in the rearview mirror.

She gasped when she noticed a figure staring back at her.

"Hey, girlfriend!" Hazel laughed when she realized it was Trina Esposito waving through the rear window. They had gym together. Hazel unlocked her door and climbed out.

"What's up?" Trina asked warmly, coming over to the driver's side. She was dressed up too, in a leather jacket, silver heels, and black cropped pants. "Sorry if I scared you."

"No problem," Hazel answered. "I'm a total wimp. Sometimes I can't believe I get spooked so easily."

"I haven't seen you at one of these before," Trina observed. "Didn't think this was your style."

"Well, yeah," Hazel said. "Sylvia invited me."

"Cool," Trina replied. "So, Breona. What an idiot, don't you think?"

Hazel frowned. She wasn't following. Trina raised a brow. "You *do* know she got expelled today, right? For drug possession?"

Hazel couldn't contain her shock. *"What?"*

"It went down at lunch. Didn't you see?"

Hazel tried to remember what she had seen—Jenna talking to Matty, Sylvia talking to her, then Breona gone. "No, actually," she said.

"Got escorted out of the caf by Clancy," Trina said. "Right after the bagpiper thing. Not that many people knew what was happening, so I guess that's why it's not all over the school."

"Oh my God," Hazel murmured. "She's a senior. What's she going to do?"

"Don't know," Trina replied. "Sucks for her."

"Seriously." *What was Breona thinking?* Hazel wondered. *She knows Brookhaven has a zero-tolerance policy. Why would she risk bringing drugs into school?*

Trina and Hazel crossed the street together. Like the other arrivals, Trina opened the door without ringing or knocking. She smiled and waved at the crowd in the living room. For a moment, the faces were a blur. Then Hazel got her bearings. There were probably a dozen kids in the room; for that many, the noise level was low.

Sylvia was sitting on Josh's lap on one of the sofas. She wore a baby tee with the words MANGEZ-MOI written in sequins across the front and a pair of low-slung jeans. Her hair was piled on top of her head in a loose, sexy updo and she was drinking something amber-colored out of a square glass.

Beside her and Josh, a couple was making out like crazy. Hazel had no idea who they were.

"Hey, Sylvia," Trina called.

Sylvia turned and waved at both of them. "Treeeeena, *bon soir*. Haze, hello! *Mes amies*, Hazel is here!"

As if on cue, Ellen, Carolyn, and Megan converged on her with friendly smiles. "Hazel," Ellen said brightly, giving her a quick hug. "Welcome to my humble babysitting job."

"As if," Hazel replied, totally loving the warm reception. "Thanks."

Sylvia rose off Josh's lap. "Follow me. Let's get you something to drink."

Trina, Hazel, and the PLDs sailed through the room, Trina greeting other guests with hugs before everyone hung a left.

Their destination was obviously the kitchen. It was packed with kids sipping from paper cups. The only sign that this was a babysitting job and not some spring break party house was the refrigerator loaded with kid art. Among the crayon drawings Hazel noticed a photograph of a mother, a father, and a little boy holding a Siamese cat. He had a cute buzz cut and large, thick glasses.

"That's Charlie, the kid I'm sitting," Ellen said, pointing to the picture. "His mom died six months ago. Cancer."

"Oh my God," Hazel said. The woman looked far too young to have died of anything.

"Yeah. It sucks." Megan sighed. "So, what do you want to drink? People bring stuff, and Charlie's dad contributes to the cause without realizing it."

Ellen giggled. "Some of the parents we sit for have so much booze lying around they don't miss it if we take something here and there."

Hazel gazed at the counter. It was a glittering row of liquor bottles. The stars of the school were pressed hip to hip, pouring drinks and carrying on. A heady mixture of perfume, cigarette smoke, and alcohol hung in the air.

I'm here, Hazel thought. *These parties are for real and I'm here—as a guest of the PLDs.*

"We have a rule that everyone must drink in the kitchen," Sylvia explained. "It makes it easier to clean up. Spills, you know."

I guess the rules just don't apply to Sylvia, Hazel thought, glancing at the glass Sylvia had carried with her from the living room.

"Go ahead," Megan urged. "Pick your poison."

Hazel scanned the liquor bottles. She didn't do much drinking, but there were a few things she knew she liked. She reached for the bottle of Amaretto and got herself a paper cup from a stack beside the stove.

"You'll have to drink a lot of that to get a buzz on," Megan said. "This does the job quicker." She picked up a fifth of Jim Beam.

Hazel poured Amaretto into her cup. "That's okay—I need to pace myself."

"A girl who knows her limit," Sylvia noted. "I like that."

"Hey, who's the new chick?" a low voice asked. Hazel felt a hand slide over her butt. She jerked. The Amaretto splashed around her cup.

"Don't be fresh, Stephan," Sylvia scolded. "This is Hazel."

Hazel glanced over her shoulder at Stephan Nylund.

"Hey-zel. Lookin' good." His eyes scanned her up and down. "We're *going outside* for a while," he said, making quotation marks in the air. "Want to come?"

"Going outside?" What did that mean? Hazel looked to Sylvia for help, but she was pouring herself a drink. "Maybe later," she told him. "I just got here."

"Cool." He gave her another long, lingering gaze before sliding open the glass door. "By the way, Meg, how's it hangin'?" he shouted as he sauntered out.

Megan glared at his back and hissed, "Ignore him. He's such an asshole."

"You'd do well to follow your own advice, *ma petite*," Sylvia put in.

Megan clamped her mouth shut.

Hazel's eyes returned to the picture on the refrigerator. "So where's the little boy?"

Sylvia gestured with her head. "Up in his room. He gets these really bad headaches. He has to lie down a lot. Ellen will check on him in a little while." She threaded her arm through Hazel's. "But don't worry about him. Let me show you around. This is your first time at one of our parties. They're not like the keggers you're probably used to."

Lowering her voice to a purr, she added, "We're low-key, but we have a hell of a lot more fun."

"So I've heard," Hazel said.

Sylvia shrugged. "Gossip is so déclassé. People who have lives don't bother chattering about people who do."

"I couldn't agree more," Hazel replied.

Sylvia gave her an appraising look. Hazel stayed cool.

"Tell me, how did you wind up with Lakshmi Sharma as your best friend?"

"She's *not* my best friend," Hazel shot back, the vehemence in her voice surprising even her. "I inherited those guys."

Sylvia nodded. "From Joy. What the hell was she doing with them?"

"I don't know," Hazel admitted. "I wondered that myself."

"Well, you need to move on, girlfriend," Sylvia drawled. "They are going nowhere fast."

"I know that."

"And . . . so? What's stopping you? Are they blackmailing you or something?"

"Yeah. They're blackmailing me. Holding my pet goldfish hostage. Isn't that how everyone keeps their friends nowadays?" Hazel bantered.

Sylvia laughed. "You're spunky."

"And witty," Hazel added.

"I like that." Sylvia laughed harder. "I *knew* you were the right person to drench with Diet Coke."

"Actually, I planned the whole thing," Hazel continued, sensing she was on a roll. "It's the next step in my plan to achieve world domination."

"The world is a very big place. You'll need help." Sylvia winked. "Come with me—you can see how this half lives."

Sylvia walked her out of the kitchen, waving her hand and saying a brisk "Excuse me" to anyone who stood in their way. They headed into a hallway behind the living room, where she pointed to the nearest door.

"That's Mr. Pollins's study. Anything illegal goes in there." *Illegal? Like drugs?* Hazel covered her shock with a quick nod.

Sylvia chuckled. "You'll see. People wander in and out of the room all night."

Hazel shook her head. "How do you guys get away with all this?"

"We're very careful about cleaning up after ourselves, and the people who party with us know they won't get invited back if they're careless."

"Right." Hazel glanced down and realized she had carried her cup of Amaretto out of the kitchen. "Oh. Sorry!" she blurted.

Sylvia smiled kindly. "That's okay. You're new." She took the cup from Hazel's hand and sipped. "Our philosophy is basically maintain and don't leave a mess. Use your manners and don't cause problems and you can do pretty much anything you want here." Sylvia stopped in front of another doorway on the hall. "This is the guest bedroom." She turned the knob and strode into the darkened room. "You can probably guess what goes on in here."

"Hey! Occupied!" came a girl's voice. Hazel heard the sound of another girl stifling a laugh. She did a double take and then squinted at the two figures entangled on the bed.

"Carolyn?" she blurted.

"Out!" Carolyn snapped. "Haven't you two ever heard of knocking?"

"Come on," Sylvia said. She pulled Hazel out of the room, laughing as she slammed the door behind them.

"Wait a minute," Hazel said, confused. "If that was Carolyn, is she . . . I mean, was that—"

"Was Carolyn fooling around with another girl?" Sylvia finished. "Yes. Carolyn is gay. Do you have a problem with that?"

"No, not at all. I just didn't—"

"Good. It's not information we spread around, because it's none of anybody's business. You know what they say: what happens here stays here."

"Cool," Hazel said, taking a minute to absorb the information. "So, what about Charlie? The kid you're sitting?"

Sylvia shrugged. "He's this little science geek. He has weird electronics stuff all over his room. He stays in there and works on his projects," she said. "He would never tell his father about us. We've been his sitters forever. Before his mother got sick, even."

"Wow."

"Yeah. So he just doesn't mention it. And we all go home happy." Sylvia spread her arms. "Now you know the lay of the land, so to speak."

"Thanks," Hazel said. She craned her neck, peering into the crowded kitchen.

Sylvia crossed her arms and tilted her head. "Looking for anyone in particular?" she asked.

"Maybe," Hazel replied coyly.

"He'll be here," Sylvia murmured. "I invited him—just for you."

Someone cranked up Gwen Stefani on the stereo. The bass thumped so loudly that paintings shook against the wall. Sylvia rolled her eyes. "Gotta go check on that. We keep things quiet for the neighbors so we don't get busted." She air-kissed Hazel and said, "Mingle, *ma cherie.* Go on, have some fun."

Hazel worked her way into the kitchen, back toward the counter where she had spotted a bowl of guacamole and tortilla chips. She was about to scoop up some guacamole when someone bumped into her from behind. She dropped the chip into the bowl.

"Hey!" She laughed and whirled around. It was Brandon.

"Hey, yourself," he said. "Do you know where Ellen is?"

Hazel looked over his shoulder. "There," she said, nodding toward the doorway. Ellen caught her eye and came up beside them. She was frowning. Upset.

"What's wrong?" Hazel asked.

"Charlie's worried because we can't find his cat, Isotope," she said, her brow creased with concern. "Hazel, have you seen him?"

She shook her head. "No. Did he forget to shut his door or something?"

"He says he didn't. He's always so careful." Ellen sighed. "I've looked everywhere for that cat."

"You're such a good sitter," Brandon said. He wrapped his fingers around Ellen's tiny wrist. "Come on. Maybe he's out back. I can help you look for him."

Ellen gave him a pained look, but her cheeks went pink. "He doesn't like strangers."

"I'm not a stranger," Brandon insisted. "I'm here all the time."

Hazel took in Ellen's slightly embarrassed expression.

Whoa. Is something going on between Brandon and Ellen? she wondered. *Everyone knows Brandon is bad news.*

Ignoring Brandon's hand, which was still on her arm, Ellen turned to Hazel. "Isotope is an indoor cat. If he got out . . ." She made a little face. "Charlie doesn't need any more grief. He just lost his mom."

"Yeah, I heard." Hazel shook her head. "It's a Siamese, right?"

"Seal point. But yeah. Same look."

"If I see him, I'll grab him for you."

Ellen smiled gratefully.

Brandon searched inside his letter jacket for a pack of Marlboros. He slid one out and put it to his lips.

"I could use one of those," Carolyn said, coming up from behind. She snatched the cigarette from his mouth and then put out her hand. Brandon sighed, handing over the lighter, and pulled out another cigarette for himself. Carolyn gave Hazel a mischievous grin while she lit hers.

"You'll have to excuse me for snapping at you back there," she said with an exhale of smoke. "You guys just took me by surprise."

"Oh, um, yeah. No problem." Hazel waved her hand like it was nothing. "Sorry we burst in like that."

Brandon squinted at Hazel, trying to place her. "Are you new?" he guessed.

Hazel blinked. Maybe she wasn't popular, but she hadn't been completely invisible for the past two years . . . had she?

"No, I'm not new. Are you blind?" she shot back.

Brandon gaped, surprised, and waited for her to continue.

"She's Hazel," Ellen filled in the blanks. "Hazel Stone."

"I'm in your geometry class," Hazel reminded him. "We see each other every day."

"Oh. Sorry." Brandon sounded almost apologetic. Then he turned to Ellen. "Listen, I do want to help look for the cat."

Carolyn snickered. "I bet you do."

"No, I'm serious," he insisted. "Charlie's a good kid."

Ellen sighed. "Fine. Come and help me." She looked at Hazel and Carolyn. "You coming too?"

"Sure." Carolyn linked arms with Hazel and they went out the back door. One whiff and Hazel understood the allure of "going outside": this was where everyone went to smoke, probably so there wouldn't be any telltale odor in the house. Hazel had to hand it to the PLDs. They partied, but they were very careful about it.

Brandon and Ellen moved on ahead, greeting a group beside a barbecue. Stephan offered Brandon a joint, but he shook his head.

"Come on. You don't want any, man?" Stephan asked.

"Naw, I'm cool," Brandon insisted. Stephan glanced at Ellen, who had her arms crossed and was peering into the bushes against the house.

"Aw, I see how it is," he said. He giggled and made a whipping sound.

"Shut up, man," Brandon said weakly before steering Ellen away to look for the cat.

Beside Hazel, Carolyn groaned. "God, I wish Stephan would just go home." They sat down on a bench, just out of range of the group. Carolyn glanced around. "Where's Megan, anyway?"

"I don't know. Why?"

"I want to tell her to stay away from Stephan. *He's* getting loaded and *she's* got PMS and they *do not* get along."

"Why not?" Hazel asked.

"Long story. Too long for tonight." Carolyn grinned at her— a slightly tipsy grin. "You having fun?"

"Yeah. A lot." Hazel smiled back. They were silent for a moment, then Hazel said, "Did you hear Breona got expelled for possession today?"

Carolyn smirked. "Hear about it? Who do you think called it in?"

Hazel's astonishment must have been obvious. Carolyn laughed and nudged her with her elbow. "Hey, zero tolerance. She was the one who brought them to school. You can't blame us for reporting her."

"Wow," Hazel said. "That's . . . harsh."

"I know, but she deserved it. She's a total dork." She shot Hazel a look of warning. "Just don't tell anyone it was us."

"Of course not," Hazel said.

Carolyn exhaled. "All I can say is thank God she's gone. She has been a total pain forever."

Ellen and Brandon emerged from the side yard, still hunting around the bushes and calling for the cat. Carolyn shook her head. "And those two . . . those two are trouble waiting to happen. Brandon is such a user. And Ellen's so sweet."

No kidding, Hazel thought.

She was about to say as much when she saw Ellen's face crumple. It looked like she was about to cry. Brandon pulled her close, stroking her back and whispering something. Reassuring her.

"Maybe he's not all bad," Hazel ventured.

"Pfffft!" Carolyn rolled her eyes at the thought. "Well, enough about them. Let's have some fun." She pulled Hazel over to the group still huddled by the barbecue. She extended her hand and Stephan passed her a tightly rolled joint. She took a long drag, then offered it to Hazel.

Hazel froze. The others were smiling—rosily, expectantly.

She wanted to fit in, but she didn't want to smoke. Would they bounce her from the party just because she didn't indulge?

Sylvia seemed to prize strong character more than anything. Hazel was willing to gamble that they'd be cool with her choice.

"Not tonight," she said.

"You sure?" Carolyn asked.

Hazel nodded and Carolyn handed the joint to Trina.

Hazel breathed a quiet sigh of relief. Crisis averted.

She glanced around the yard, half searching for the missing cat and half taking in the scene around her. Absolutely all the cool kids were here and finally—*finally*—she was among them.

Some of the kids even waved hello to her. Had they noticed her at school? Probably not. But now that she was here—now that she was invitation-worthy—all that seemed about to change.

For the first time, Hazel felt like she was on the way up. It was a good feeling, one she hoped wouldn't fade as soon as the party was over.

Hazel gazed upward. The night was chilly, the sky bright and clear. Brookhaven offered stars, something most San Diegans didn't get to see because of all the city lights. Tonight, this party was the center of the universe.

"I think Isotope is just hiding from all the strangers." Carolyn cut into Hazel's thoughts. "Might as well call off the search."

Hazel nodded. They broke off from Stephan and the others and Hazel began to mingle, moving through the swirls of conversation. She danced with a guy named Mark and then with Carolyn. Someone passed out monster chocolate chip cookies. Hazel had two. Later in the evening, she found herself with Trina, telling her an old story about Breona getting in trouble in chem lab.

"Ms. Carpentier found the notes she and Jenna Babcock had been writing *in* class. They were writing them in their notebooks so it would look like they were comparing findings or something.

There was one that said, 'Carpentier is a crazy bitch today.'"

Trina started cracking up. "Oh my God!"

"She was so busted. Ms. Carpentier sent her to Clancy," Hazel went on.

"Maybe she was busted, but have you noticed? She always bounces back. This time won't be any different. She'll be back in school before you know it," Trina proclaimed. She took a sip of her drink. "She's like a virus. You think you've gotten rid of her, but she just pops back up."

"A virus?" Hazel laughed.

"Yeah." Trina snickered. "The flesh-eating kind. And the only thing more dangerous than the Breona virus is Breona mixed with Sylvia Orly. Put them together and you get a supervirus—capable of wiping out everything around it! I don't know what those two have against each other, but it can get ugly."

"Seriously," Hazel agreed. For a moment, she thought about telling Trina that the PLDs had narced on Breona. Then Hazel remembered: she'd promised Carolyn she'd keep her lips sealed, and she wanted to keep her promise.

"What's going on out here?" a deep voice called. Hazel turned toward the sliding glass doors.

Oh. My. God. She blinked. There, walking out into the back-yard, was Matty Vardeman.

He looked amazing in his letter jacket, black jeans, and a black T-shirt. His faint smile was too incredibly sexy, and his dark eyes were dancing with amusement as he took in his surroundings.

"Whoa," Trina said under her breath. "New-guy alert. He is so hot."

Hazel licked her lips, aware that her mouth had gone dry. She could hear her heart pounding. Then Matty looked straight at her. He brightened and came toward her.

He stood facing her. "Hey."

"Hey," she managed.

"I'm Matty."

I know, she almost said. But she maintained. "Hazel," she introduced herself.

"And Trina," Trina said.

Matty nodded politely. Then his gaze returned to Hazel.

"So," he said.

Trina cleared her throat. "I'm going to get something to drink. You want anything?"

"I'm good," Hazel said. "How about you?" she asked Matty.

He held up a bottle. "I'm fine with water." Trina took off, and Matty nodded at some familiar faces. "Cool party," he said.

"Yeah," Hazel agreed. She glanced over Matty's shoulder to see Sylvia standing in the doorway. She gave a little wave.

Sylvia's eyes glittered. She pointed at Matty's back and mouthed the words, "You're welcome."

Hazel fought hard to hide her grin.

"This time of year, it's getting cold in Virginia," Matty said. "Out here, it's practically like summer."

"I've never been to Virginia," she said. "I've heard it's pretty, though."

"It is. Green grass, rolling hills . . . but what I think I'll miss most are the crazy thunderstorms we get in the spring. I used to sit out on our front porch when the rain was coming down, and the thunder would get so loud." He drank from his water bottle. "You've always lived in Brookhaven?" he asked.

"All my life," she said.

"It's not a bad place; I just didn't ask to move." He sighed. "And living with my sister sucks."

Someone called his name and he waved.

"Well, at least you've made friends," she pointed out.

"Yeah. I mean, the guys on the team are cool, but I haven't found anyone I really click with yet. You know?"

His southern accent was insanely endearing.

"I totally understand. I'm that way too." *Not that I'm feeling that way right now,* Hazel thought.

"Really? But you've lived here forever!"

Hazel shrugged. "That doesn't mean I've made any real connections. The kind that count. The kind you have forever."

He squinted at her and gave a playful grin. "Maybe you're too deep for Southern California."

"Thanks a lot!" She laughed.

"No, I mean it," he said sincerely. "You seem a little more . . . in touch than most of the people I've met."

"Thanks," Hazel said, with a straight face this time. They both went quiet and Hazel felt his dark eyes swallowing her up.

The silence was broken when Trina returned.

"Hey, guys." She had an extra water bottle in her hand. "Brought this for you," she told Matty.

"Thanks," he said.

The three of them made small talk about classes and teachers and then about their favorite shows and bands. Hazel tried to keep up her end while inconspicuously drinking Matty in.

He was into Green Day. Trina liked Maroon 5. Hazel confessed her secret nerdy thing for the Beatles.

"I think that's just sweet," Matty said.

"Hey, did you see what happened to Breona today?" Trina ventured. "Seriously harsh."

Matty scowled. "I think there is something seriously wrong with that girl."

He seemed about to elaborate when Megan walked up to Hazel and touched her elbow. "Got a minute?" she murmured.

"Sure," Hazel replied. She looked at Matty. "Back in a few."

Megan grabbed her by the sleeve and steered her toward the opposite side of the yard. Along the back, a weathered wooden fence rose above some untrimmed bushes and woody geraniums. Carolyn and Ellen were huddled together in the midst of them, looking very freaked out.

"Problem," Ellen murmured.

"It's Isotope," Carolyn said under her breath. "Come here and see."

Carolyn stepped among the geraniums. She pulled back a couple of runners and pointed.

The moon shone down on something white and furry—and very, very still.

"Oh no," Hazel whispered.

Then Carolyn bent down, picked up the dead cat, and threw it hard at Hazel.

Hazel screamed. She batted at the body, knocking it to the ground at her feet.

Breathing hard, she stared down at the poor creature.

Matted fur, dirty paws, and . . . glass eyes?

Oh my God, Hazel thought, relieved. *It's a stuffed animal. Only a stuffed animal.*

Megan and Carolyn burst into gleeful shrieks. Ellen covered her mouth, her eyes glittering.

"That is so not funny!" Hazel protested as they doubled over. "You guys, that's really twisted!"

"Relax. You've been pranked!" Carolyn announced. "Everyone gets pranked at their first PLD party."

Hazel shook her head as different feelings battled inside her. The whole thing was kind of mean-spirited. But the girls were laughing, tossing the stuffed animal back and forth.

Everyone gets pranked at their first PLD party. Did that mean they accepted her? That she was really a part of the cool crowd now?

Hazel looked at the stuffed animal, a rabbit, with its crossed eyes and buckteeth. How could she ever have mistaken this for a dead cat? She definitely needed to lighten up.

Megan and Carolyn walked back to the house, still laughing. Ellen trailed behind.

"It was just a joke, really," she explained. "And it's a good thing. We wouldn't do that to someone we didn't like."

"It's cool," Hazel assured her. "I just have to know—was the whole thing a setup? Does Charlie even *own* a cat?"

"Yeah, he really does. And he really is missing." Ellen touched her arm. "Are you sure you're okay?"

"Sure," Hazel said. "It was just a joke."

Ellen smiled. "Good. I wouldn't want you to be mad or anything."

Carolyn was right. Ellen *was* really sweet.

She stayed on the deck as Hazel moved inside. She didn't see Matty in the kitchen, so she waited, leaning against the counter and helping herself to some more guacamole. She chatted with a few other girls before wandering into the living room.

There she found Trina making out with a guy in a nearby armchair. Hazel was curious. Who had Trina pounced on? She lingered for a moment, but as long as the two were lip-locked, there was no way of telling. Time to move on.

Megan and Carolyn sat on the rug, examining a shelf full of DVDs. Sylvia and Josh were curled up on the couch.

Sylvia turned to Hazel. "Hey. I heard you found Isotope?" She picked up her square glass and peered at Hazel over the rim while she drank.

"Yeah," Hazel replied. "That was, um, pretty extreme."

Sylvia smiled. "But brilliant for a last-minute prank, don't you think?"

"Cool!" Megan exclaimed, interrupting. "They *do* have *Scream*."

"We could watch that," Sylvia said. She turned to Hazel. "You in? Scary movies are part of the PLD party tradition."

"Sure," Hazel told her. She glanced around, wondering where Matty was.

As if she could read her mind, Sylvia pointed down the hall. "He went to talk to Charlie. Nice guy."

Hazel warmed. Comforting the kid who lost his cat? That was nice.

"Thanks." Hazel turned to go, then said suspiciously, "This isn't another trick, is it?"

"Go down the hall and find out," Sylvia urged her in a mock-creepy voice. "Wahahaha." She put her arms around Josh's neck, pretending to chomp him like a vampire. He laughed back, grabbing her around the waist and doing the same.

"No worries," Hazel said, making a cross with her forefingers. "I'm armed."

She went on down the hall, scooting around a couple engaging in serious PDA.

At the end of the corridor was a door marked CHARLIE'S LABORATORY. A little picture of Dexter from TV decorated the bottom of the sign. Hazel knocked, and the door swung open. An electronic voice said, *"Enter, carbon unit."*

She smiled and did just that. Inside, she found a little boy in flannel pajamas and enormous, thick glasses sitting on the edge of a twin bed. A comforter featuring galaxies and rocket ships was bunched around him. There were electronic parts, wheels, gears, and disassembled toys everywhere.

"Mind if I come in?" she asked.

"Hi," the little boy said. "I'm Charlie. This is Matty."

"I'm Hazel."

Matty sat in a straight-backed chair beside the boy. He seemed to be sketching something in the black three-ring binder in his lap.

"Hey, Hazel," Matty said, looking up at her. "Check it out." He held up the binder to display a drawing of a Siamese cat.

"Wow." Hazel gasped. "That's really good."

"Matty is going to help me make reward posters for Isotope. That's my cat."

Hazel melted. "That's so sweet. But maybe he's not missing. Maybe he's just hiding because of the party."

"Maybe," Charlie said. "But you can't be too careful."

She remembered Charlie's mother and nodded. "You're probably right."

"How's this?" Matty asked Charlie, tapping the sketch with his pencil.

Charlie squinted, thinking. "He has darker markings around his eyes."

Hazel and Charlie looked on as Matty shaded the almond-shaped eyes.

"Yep. That's Isotope," Charlie said wistfully. "It looks exactly like him."

"Don't worry, Charlie. I'll scan it in. Then we'll type the rest of the information and create a poster," Matty said. "What's your e-mail?"

Charlie told him. Matty wrote it on a blank sheet of paper. Then he looked up at Hazel. "What's yours?"

She couldn't contain her smile. He handed her a piece of paper and the pencil he had been using. She wrote down PURPLE-HAZE and the rest, adding, "That's my IM name too."

"Got a cell?" Matty asked her.

"I'm between phones right now," she lied smoothly.

Matty slipped the paper into the pocket of his jeans as he stood up.

"Okay." Matty turned to Charlie. "Looks like I'm done here. Good night, kiddo. I hope your head feels better."

"Good night," Charlie said. "You won't forget to scan in the picture, right?"

"I'll e-mail you a jpeg as soon as I get home," Matty assured him. Hazel followed him out the door and eased it shut behind her.

"I have to go soon," he said, staring deep into her eyes. "But we could talk for a little while. Unless you want to watch the movie."

"I've seen it a million times," she confessed.

Matty led her past the living room and outside. In the silvery moonlight, she saw Ellen and Brandon sitting together, deep in conversation. Matty gave Brandon a nod. Then he steered Hazel over to a couple of chairs.

They talked for what seemed like minutes but must have been much longer. Hazel memorized all the little details that came out during their conversation.

Matty's favorite color was blue. His favorite artist was Picasso. He had a dog named Clyde when he was a kid. He hated asparagus. His sister was a waitress and they didn't get along.

"Of course, all the phone calls haven't helped matters between us," he said.

She was about to ask him what he meant when Stephan Nylund staggered up.

"Yo, Matty, you leaving soon?" he asked, running a hand through his red hair. "I caught a ride over with Brandon, but I gotta go and he wants to stay."

Matty checked his watch. He swore under his breath. "Man. I'm gonna be late. What part of town do you live in?"

"Over by the mall," Stephan said. "On Lemon."

"Cool. That's near me."

They headed inside. Hazel accompanied them through the darkened living room to the front door. Stephan opened it and walked on ahead.

Matty lingered with Hazel on the porch. "So, see you tomorrow?"

She wasn't exactly sure what he meant, but she liked the question anyway. "Sure."

"Okay. Well, later." He leaned forward. . . .

Oh my God, he's going to kiss me! Hazel felt her cheeks flush in anticipation. But then Matty pulled back, as if he wasn't certain that was the way to go. He smiled down at her. "You know, you have the prettiest eyes."

He turned and walked down the path, toward a dark blue PT Cruiser.

Totally amazed, Hazel watched him go.

As he and Stephan got into the Cruiser, she waved. The headlights winked on and off, and then the car pulled away.

When she came back inside, she realized that the movie was almost over. Having seen it so many times, she knew exactly where they were in the plot. She perched on the arm of a chair to watch the ending—a total gore-fest—and realized the person sitting in the chair was Trina, disentangled from her smooching partner.

"Oh my God, Hazel. Matty is so into you," Trina whispered in Hazel's ear.

Hazel giggled. "You think?"

"Duh."

Hazel grinned and then stifled a yawn.

"I should head out," she whispered. She waved good-bye to Trina, then walked into the kitchen. There she found Sylvia, Megan, and Carolyn leaning against the counters, talking in whispers. Hazel hung back, not wanting to intrude, but Sylvia spotted her, catching her gaze with her laser blue eyes.

"Hey."

"Hey. Thanks for inviting me," Hazel said. "I had a great time."

"You're welcome. So." Sylvia raised her eyebrows. "Matty. Sparks?"

Hazel smiled shyly. "Maybe."

Sylvia sipped from her square glass. "I love playing matchmaker."

Ellen walked with Brandon into the kitchen. Sylvia ticked her glance over to them, shooting Brandon a hard, appraising look.

"Let me guess," Sylvia said coolly. "No sign of the cat?"

Ellen shook her head. Brandon put his arm around her shoulders and gave them a squeeze.

"Don't worry, he'll turn up," he murmured reassuringly.

Sylvia frowned deeply. "It's time to wrap things up. Brandon, be a dear and get rid of whoever is left in the living room. You know your way out."

"Okay." Brandon gave Ellen one last squeeze. He grabbed his jacket and headed for the living room.

Sylvia tipped her head sideways, pressing the rim of her glass against the line of her jaw. "That one," she said softly, "cannot be trusted."

Hazel turned to stare at Sylvia. "What do you mean?"

But Sylvia had already moved on.

"Come sit with us at lunch tomorrow, Hazel. We need to talk."

"Lunch? With you?" Hazel stopped short. Being invited to the party was one thing; being seen at school with the PLDs was so very much another.

"Okay," she said, keeping calm. "What are we going to talk about?"

Sylvia shook her head. "Tomorrow." She turned to the rest of the group. "Well, ladies, say *bonne nuit* to Haze."

"Bonne nuit," Ellen said sweetly.

"Bonne nuit," Megan replied, lifting a beer to her lips.

Carolyn blew Hazel a kiss. *"Bonne nuit,* Haze."

"Good night," she said to the group.

"Uh-uh-uh." Sylvia wagged her finger. *"Dis-nous, 'Bonne nuit.'"*

"Bonne nuit," Hazel said shyly.

"Not a bad accent," Sylvia told her. "You've got potential."

The pretty little Devils chat room

Members in chat room:

PLDCARO

PLDMEG

PLDSLY

PLDSLY: H is perfect!

PLDCARO: H is cool. *Oui.*

PLDMEG: Still like just us 4.

PLDSLY: Ellen factor, remember?

PLDMEG: OK. I guess *oui.* But El's not here 2 vote.

PLDSLY: It's cool. She luvs H. She already told me.

PERSONALBLOG

HAPPY2BME

THE PLDS LIKE BEING SCARED? WAIT TILL THEY FIND OUT WHAT I DID.

POOR KITTY, KITTY THAT WILL NEVER COME HOME. IT WAS A GOOD WARM-UP, BUT IT'S TIME TO WORK MY WAY UP THE FOOD CHAIN!

CHAPTER THREE

"You were there, Hazel. I saw you!" Lakshmi whispered in the cafeteria the next day.

"Saw her where?" LaToya asked.

"At a PLDs' party," Lakshmi continued. "I was at my grandmother's house last night. On my way home I saw all these cars and everyone going into this house. Trina Esposito, Stephan Nylund . . . It had to be a PLD party. And Hazel's car was there—parked right next to Sylvia Orly's!"

"Oh my God," LaToya gushed. "Hazel, is it true?"

Hazel nodded. She felt guilty about being at the party without the rest of the group, but they were bound to find out eventually.

"They were hanging out in someone's backyard," Lakshmi continued. "And they were smoking pot!"

"Whoa!" Jamie gasped. "Hazel, did *you* do it?"

"No, I—" Hazel stared at Lakshmi. "Wait. How do you know about that?"

Lakshmi shrugged. "I saw your car. I wanted to find out what was going on. I snuck around the back and peeked over the fence." She turned to the others. "You guys, the *entire* football team was there!"

"That's so amazing," LaToya gushed. "Hazel, why didn't you tell us Sylvia invited you?"

Hazel frowned. "She told me to keep it a secret."

"Well, how was it? Was it as wild as everyone says?" Jamie asked eagerly.

"Yes . . . and no," Hazel answered.

"You have to get us invited to the next one," LaToya insisted.

Hazel just stared. It was kind of sad, really. Lakshmi, LaToya, and Jamie had no clue. The chances of them actually being invited to a PLD party were slim to none.

"I'll see what I can do," she fibbed. "In the meantime, Sylvia asked me to sit with her and the PLDs at lunch. Is that cool?"

"The coolest," Lakshmi said. Her smile seemed genuine, a mixture of pride and happiness for one of her closest friends.

Jamie and LaToya nodded like bobbleheads. Their awe knew no bounds. "Go on. Tell us all about it later, okay?"

"Of course," Hazel said, unsure if she was lying or not.

Tray in hand, she made the long walk over to Sylvia's table. As usual, the PLDs were looking fine. Sylvia was dressed in a sweet, blue-flowered, ruffled skirt and a blue stretchy top. Megan had on tan capris and pointed metallic flats very much like the ones Hazel had worn to the party.

Hazel had ransacked her closet for the perfect outfit, coming up with a black skirt and kimono top. The skirt was just a bit too long. But she had good black boots, so that helped.

Hazel couldn't help noticing that people were watching her as she made her way toward the PLDs. At every table, heads turned and kids nudged each other, taking in the new development.

Then Hazel saw that Matty's eyes were on her too. He gave her a nod, almost as if he were offering her encouragement. Her face went hot.

"Hey," she said as she reached the PLDs' table.

"Bonjour," Sylvia greeted her. "Have a seat."

Hazel set down her tray and pulled out the chair next to Ellen's. The four PLDs shifted, leaning forward.

Sylvia folded her hands. "Get home okay?"

"Yes, thanks. I mean, *merci*," Hazel corrected. "Did you find the cat?"

"No," Sylvia told her, her full lips pouting for all they were worth. "Poor kitty."

"It's okay," Ellen cut in. "I'm sure he'll turn up."

"Well, it was a great party," Hazel said.

"Just a typical little soiree," Sylvia said airily. "Nice to see that Matty Vardeman accepted his invitation, no?"

"Yes. Thank you for that."

"He's looking straight at you," Sylvia informed her.

Hazel shrugged. "Lots of people are looking at me." As if Matty's attention made no difference. Sylvia's smile grew.

"Speaking of invitations," Sylvia continued, "we've been thinking about inviting you to something else." She paused dramatically. Hazel's eyes darted to each one of the PLDs' faces. Her stomach gave a little flip.

"God, Sylvia, cut the drama. You're going to make her nuts," Megan said.

Sylvia shot Megan a glare before continuing. "Here's the deal. We've been talking about adding another person to the PLDs. How would you feel about joining our little group?"

Hazel blinked in astonishment. Was she dreaming? This wasn't just beyond comprehension, it was . . . too good to be true.

"Sylvia," she began in the calmest voice she could muster. "Is this a joke?"

"Why would we joke? You're smart, you've got style and attitude, and we think you're cool. You'd make a perfect PLD. There will have to be a probationary period, of course." Sylvia paused. "And you'll have to earn your place."

"Like an initiation," Megan supplied.

"It sounds crass, but Megan's right. It *is* like an initiation. We have stages." Sylvia raised a finger. "Stage one is party conduct. You passed that."

"Stage two—prank," Carolyn said, holding up two fingers. "She passed that."

"Then you'll have to do a babysitting job," Sylvia said, "which is a no-brainer. I mean, who hasn't babysat by the time she's a junior in high school?"

"So that's it?" Hazel asked. "That's all it takes?"

"Well, there are some other things. But you'll find out about those later." Carolyn gave an impish grin.

"We have a chat room and everything," Ellen cut in excitedly. She grabbed Hazel's hand and gave it a squeeze. "You'll love it."

Sylvia bit her bottom lip as if she were hesitating to deliver bad news. "You *will* have to get a cell phone."

"Um, I don't know if my parents will—" Hazel began.

"Oh, don't worry about them. I'll just buy one and you can pay me back with your share of the sitting money."

"Really?" Hazel asked. "Wow. Thanks!"

The sitting money. The parties. The status. It was all beginning to sink in.

Just days ago Hazel had been wishing for the chance to belong to a group as cool as the PLDs. Now they wanted her as one of their own.

"So, do you think you'd like to give it a go?" Sylvia asked with mock innocence. "It's not too horrible an idea?"

Sylvia knew Hazel would be an idiot to say no.

"Oh, I suppose it'll help me pass the time," Hazel replied, using the same nonchalant tone Sylvia used. "That is, if I don't get too tired of all of you."

"Well, *mes amies*?" Sylvia prompted.

Megan, Carolyn, and Ellen produced little wrapped gifts, which they placed on Hazel's lunch tray.

"Welcome, Haze," Sylvia exclaimed. "We're happy to have you."

"Oh," Hazel said, thrilled. The others smiled at her, obviously pleased.

"Allez," Sylvia said, gesturing to the presents. "Go on. Open them."

"That one's from me," Ellen said, pointing to a rectangular box wrapped in purple foil.

Hazel quickly unwrapped it. Inside was a miniature plastic bottle of lavender body lotion.

"Thank you," Hazel said sincerely. She uncapped the bottle and smelled the lotion. "Oh, it's nice."

Ellen nodded. "I buy it all the time."

Hazel's hand ranged over the other gifts as she wondered which one to open next. She chose a purple bag, its handles tied with curly ribbons. There was something hard wrapped in white tissue paper inside. She drew it out. It was a purple candle.

"Short notice," Carolyn said, as if apologizing for her gift.

"I love it," Hazel assured her. She smelled it. "Lavender?"

"Spring rain," Carolyn corrected. "Purple and lavender, it gets kind of old." She looked at Ellen. "No offense."

Ellen shifted a tiny bit. "No problem."

"Mine's kind of twisted." Megan picked up an oblong object about the size of Hazel's palm, wrapped in purple tissue paper.

"You? Twisted? That would be new," Sylvia joked. Megan gave her a little bat on the arm, and everyone laughed.

Hazel pulled the tissue paper away. It was a replica of a human brain, made out of something purple and squishy.

"The brain!" Ellen cried. "Oh my God, Megan. You're giving away your brain?"

"I stole it from my brother a long time ago," Megan explained to Hazel. "Because it's purple, which is our color. Also, because I used to use it on the kids I babysat. I would tell them it belonged to someone who misbehaved. It's yours now. And trust me—you're going to need it."

Everyone cracked up.

"It's true. A lot of the kids we sit are monsters," Sylvia said. "But their parents realize it, so they pay us a lot of money."

"Hey, Sly, what about your present?" Carolyn asked.

"I'll give mine to Hazel after school."

Hazel's head reeled. As if being a PLD wasn't present enough!

She glanced around the lunchroom. Lakshmi and LaToya caught her eye. They smiled and each gave Hazel a thumbs-up.

Hazel quickly turned back to her lunch, pretending not to have seen them.

Ellen slurped the last of her Diet Coke. "Out of soda," she announced. "Anyone else?"

Carolyn shook her head. "No thanks, but go ahead. We've got time before the bell."

Ellen headed toward the serving line. Hazel watched as Brandon left the jock table and joined her there.

Cosmic soda coincidence? Probably not, Hazel thought.

The two of them chatted as they went through the line. Brandon stooped slightly, listening carefully to every word Ellen had to say. Hazel was caught off guard by the gentle expression on Brandon's face. He didn't seem like the same guy who had destroyed that girl in geometry last year. Maybe Ellen brought out something different in him.

"They are so not right for each other," Sylvia mumbled to herself.

"Really?" Hazel said. "I think they look kind of cute."

Sylvia snorted. "You don't know Brandon like I do."

She glared at the pair—like a cat watching the quick, scurrying movements of a mouse.

Then Josh appeared behind her, and the storm clouds parted.

"Hey, sexy." She beamed at him and gave him a kiss.

He reciprocated, then took in the packages surrounding Hazel. "You guys have presents? Is there a birthday?"

"We're celebrating Hazel's induction. She's in the club." Sylvia smiled broadly.

"No way! Good for you," Josh congratulated her. "These guys could use some fresh meat."

"Don't be disgusting," Sylvia said lightly.

"Well, where's *my* present?" he whined, nuzzling her cheek.

"You'll have to earn one. Just like Haze."

Sylvia turned again to stare at Brandon and Ellen. They were laughing now. Brandon had his arm around Ellen's shoulders. Sylvia's lips pressed together to form a grim line.

"I know!" Sylvia looked at the group and clapped. "Why don't we learn the word for the day?"

Hazel had heard about this. For fun, Sylvia taught her friends dirty words in French. Then they worked them into regular conversation, making everyone wonder what they were talking about.

"Why don't we wait for Ellen?" Hazel asked.

"She looks busy," Sylvia scoffed. "Today's word is *salope*. It means 'whore' in French, only it's more shocking than if we say *whore* in English."

"Context?" Carolyn ventured.

"Breona is a *salope*," Sylvia provided.

The girls giggled and Josh turned slightly pink.

"Hazel, on the other hand," Sylvia continued, "is as far away from a *salope* as one can get."

"*Oui*," Carolyn agreed. "She has good hair, good style. Hazel rules."

"You want her," Megan sneered.

"Shut up, Megan," Carolyn snapped.

"Now, ladies." Sylvia put her arm around Hazel. "We all want her. Everyone is in love with Hazel. She's our one true love. Someday we'll move to Canada—French Canada—and marry her."

Sylvia and Carolyn beamed at her, and, as silly as it all sounded, Hazel was flattered.

The bell rang and Hazel gathered up her presents. The PLDs walked out of the lunchroom in a pack—first Sylvia, then Megan and Caroline, then Hazel and Ellen. All of them turned heads as they went. Josh came up beside Sylvia, and Matty fell into step with Hazel.

"Hey," Matty said.

"Hi," she said softly. He tentatively put his arm around her and Hazel leaned into him. As they passed by a group of senior girls, Hazel noticed them whispering, shooting her envious glances.

This is what it's like being a PLD. You get the most attention, the hottest guys. And I'm one of them now! Hazel realized, amazed. *I'm one of them and there's no way I'm ever going back!* She gazed up at Matty and smiled.

"Jenna Babcock's skirt is way too short today," Carolyn said. "She looks like a total *salope*."

"Mais oui," Sylvia replied. "And good usage, *ma cherie*."

"Wait," Ellen ventured. "Is that a new word?"

"Bien sûr," Sylvia replied.

"Bien sûr," Carolyn said.

"Well, what does it mean?"

Sylvia only laughed. Ellen looked from Carolyn to Megan. They both shrugged.

Finally, Ellen turned to Hazel. "Do you know what it means?" she asked.

"Of course she does," Sylvia informed her.

Ellen suddenly looked panicked. "What did I do? Is it my hair? I'm getting a new cut, I swear."

"Don't be silly," Sylvia drawled. "But if you want to know what the word means, maybe you should ask Brandon."

She chuckled as Josh wrapped both his arms around her waist and murmured, *"Salope,"* in her ear.

Ellen stopped dead in her tracks. She wore a strange expression.

Was it sadness? Concern?

"Ellen?" Hazel asked. "Are you okay?"

"Sure," Ellen whispered. She stared as Sylvia and the rest of the group strolled away with Josh.

No one looked back.

After school the PLDs met Hazel at her locker. "We're going to Starbucks," Sylvia said. "Time to give you our last gift."

The group settled around a table by the window. Hazel offered to order everyone's drinks, but Sylvia waved her hand. "Don't be silly. When you're a PLD, the drinks come to you."

As if on cue, one of the counter people—a good-looking college guy—approached the table. Sylvia flirted with him for a minute or two, leading him on just enough to give him a tiny bit of hope. Soon after, each of the PLDs was gifted with the Frappuccino of her choice.

Hazel took a sip. It was a small thing, she knew, but real evidence of the kind of influence a group like the PLDs could have.

Everyone chatted for a while, eager to let off steam about school before getting down to PLD business. Hazel stirred her Frap with her straw. She glanced up when the door opened.

And swallowed when she saw who walked in.

Lakshmi.

What was *she* doing here?

Hazel knew Lakshmi wanted to be in with the popular crowd—maybe even more than Hazel did—but didn't she know how pathetic she seemed, following the PLDs around like a puppy?

Lakshmi caught sight of Hazel. Her face broke into a broad smile. She waved and started to approach.

Oh God, Hazel thought. *Don't come over here. Not now.*

She frowned at Lakshmi and shook her head subtly—almost imperceptibly—hoping she would get the hint.

Lakshmi stopped, confused. Then realization dawned. She changed course and made her way to the register to order her drink.

Whew, Hazel thought. *That was close.*

"And now, Haze, it's time for your final present," Sylvia

announced. She pulled out a small, rectangular package in purple wrapping and placed it in front of Hazel.

"You guys know you didn't have to do this," Hazel gushed. "All the gifts were so unexpected."

"Just open it," Sylvia commanded. "This one is the most important of all."

Hazel unwrapped the package and found that it contained a small purple notebook. It had been carefully decorated with stickers, mostly of purple flowers. The center of the cover read:

PURPLEHAZE

PLD HANDBOOK

Hazel opened it. There was a sparkly pen topped with a purple feather lying on the first page, which read, RULES.

"It looks silly, but we wrote these up in middle school, so we tried to make yours look like a little replica of the originals," Sylvia explained. "We've made a few amendments, but the rules are basically the same ones we started out with."

The others nodded, Carolyn chuckling as if at a private joke.

Sylvia held up a finger. "Rule number one?" She looked at the three PLDs.

"PLD loyalty," Ellen quickly replied. "Before guys and anyone else."

"That's our most basic rule," Sylvia said. She looked back at Hazel and leaned forward on her elbows. "Think about a herd of animals. Gazelles. Predators pick off the weak ones, the ones on the outside. The ones who stay close together survive."

"We've been through a lot," Megan elaborated. "We've tried to have outside friends, and it just doesn't work. We stick together, and it makes us solid." The others nodded.

"That means you're free of those hangers-on," Sylvia whispered, "from this point forward."

She didn't need to explain. Hazel knew she was referring to Lakshmi, who was now seated a few feet away, pretending to read a gossip magazine.

"The second rule is, you have to uphold the PLD standards," Sylvia went on. "We have to look good, be united. Support each other. There are people who would like nothing better than to see us fall flat on our faces. Which is why we need to let each other know if we're slipping."

She placed a hand on Ellen's shoulder. Ellen's cheeks colored.

It was a harsh rule, Hazel knew, but it was true. Here at the top of the food chain, it was survival of the coolest.

"Here's some important info," Sylvia explained, flipping toward the center of the notebook. "Basic info. Our phone numbers, birthdays, locker combinations, stuff like that."

"Locker combinations?" Hazel echoed, a little uneasy.

"Sure. We leave things for each other," Ellen replied. "Like, when one of us is down, we surprise her with a little something to cheer her up."

"Oh. Um, that's nice." *Nice*, Hazel thought, *until the PLDs get you busted by Vice Principal Clancy.*

"Needless to say, you cannot lose this notebook," Carolyn pointed out. "If you do, people who are jealous of us could use it against us."

"And while we're on *that* subject," Sylvia continued, "I know you had a class with Breona. She's gone, but all her little friends are still around. You cannot speak to any of them under any circumstances, all right?" She gave Hazel a hard stare.

"No problem," Hazel said.

"Good. Moving onward." Sylvia turned a page to show an elaborate spreadsheet. Each of the PLDs' names was printed there, in a column. Sylvia's first, then Megan, Carolyn, Ellen, and Hazel. The days of the week headed the rows. Each day was divided into thirds, labeled AFTERNOON, EVENING, and NIGHT.

"This is how we keep track of our sitting jobs," Sylvia informed her. "I'm in charge. The parents call me to set up appointments, and I distribute these sheets every week. You're going to take the Darlings tonight. I already arranged it with Cynthia, their mom."

"Oh. Um, isn't that kind of short notice?" Hazel pointed out. Last night, she had barely made a dent in her homework, despite staying up till one-thirty working on it. She was still behind in her reading for econ, and she'd planned on catching up tonight.

Sylvia frowned. Hazel saw a flash of displeasure in her eyes. "Yes. Is that a problem?"

"No, no," Hazel covered. "I just . . . I need to make sure it's all right with my parents."

"Well, it has to be," Sylvia said pleasantly. "I already set it up. Okay, the details. The Darlings are twins."

"And not exactly 'darlings.'" Megan snickered. "You'll need the squeezy brain."

Sylvia gave her a cold look. Megan lost her smirk and said, "You'll be fine."

"We turn in our books once a week," Sylvia said. "On Mondays. I keep track of the sitting jobs and the pay. We usually just pool the money, but sometimes there are exceptions."

"Plus, there are fines," Ellen said.

"Fines?"

Sylvia nodded. "Of course. Like, if you show up late for a sitting job or whatever. All of us shouldn't suffer because one person acts irresponsibly."

Hazel took that in. "Well, I'll really do my best. I'm just—I'm grateful that you guys invited me."

"You seemed like PLD material," Sylvia said. "We think you're really going to work out."

"Um . . . there's one other issue," Megan broke in. "Do you like scary movies? Because they're kind of our thing."

"We started out renting them when we babysat. Now we play them at all our parties. It helps everyone . . . get a little closer," Sylvia explained.

"Oh. Sure," Hazel replied. "I'm totally obsessed with all the *Friday the 13th* movies. They're cheesy, but I love them."

"Yeah," Carolyn added, "the night we rented *Halloween*, like, six people paired up. That's when we knew we were on to something."

Hazel nodded. "I guess everyone likes being terrorized."

"Oh, you won't when you meet the Darling twins." Sylvia laughed. "You need to be there at seven. Sharp."

✛   ✛   ✛

PERSONALBLOG

HAPPY 2BME

HAZE'S GOT DARLING DUTY 2NITE. SHE'S IN FOR THE FRIGHT OF HER LIFE. POOR HAZEL. SO SWEET, BUT IT'S ALL GOING TO GO SOUR. COME OUT, COME OUT, HZL. IT'S TIME TO PLAY.

✛   ✛   ✛

Avenida Escondida—Hidden Avenue—divided Brookhaven into two sections, east and west. The west side of town was the ritzy part. The Darlings lived on a hill *overlooking* the ritzy part. Meaning they were even richer than the rich people.

Their house was a mansion. The floors were hardwood, and all the furniture was cutting-edge modern: everything was done in bold, bright, jarring colors. There were paintings on the walls that were taller than Hazel, all of them abstract—people with blank cube faces or swirly, desolate landscapes. . . . They creeped her out.

If Hazel was honest, the entire house creeped her out. The twins lived there with their mother, who was divorced, but the place was too big for just three people. It had an empty, isolated feeling. When Hazel walked on the wooden floors, her footsteps echoed hollowly back to her.

The front of the house was nothing but glass, and tonight fog had crept up the hill, slithering over the vast, manicured lawn.

A scene right out of one of the PLDs' horror movies, Hazel thought.

As soon as Hazel arrived, the twins had told her how much they loved playing "ghost in the graveyard," a game that required turning out all the lights in the house and then searching for each other in the dark.

Hazel was hiding, crouched behind the home entertainment system, nearly pressed up against the wall of glass. While she waited to be discovered, she watched the swirling fog and concentrated on keeping perfectly still.

"Where are you?" Katie Darling called in a spooky voice. Her flashlight moved across the window. Hazel watched as the silhouette of a gnarled tree caught in Katie's light. It waved in the wind like a skeletal hand—its bony fingers reaching out for her.

The light moved away and Hazel's hiding spot fell back into shadow. She sighed. Should she make it easier for them to find her? At least then the game would be over.

She glanced at her watch. It was only eight, and she was dragging. Nine was the twins' official bedtime. She had tried to get them to put on their pajamas and brush their teeth, but they'd refused. That was when all the lights-out games started. It seemed like everything they wanted to do was in the dark.

Pain shot through Hazel's calf. Her muscles were beginning to cramp, and she was getting sleepy.

That's it. Time to call it quits.

"Katie?" Hazel called softly. "Chrissie?"

There was no answer. No sound at all.

Gingerly she rose, half expecting one or both of them to jump out and spook her. She tiptoed through the cavern of a living room toward the hall that led into their bedroom.

She hesitated, then fumbled for the hall light. She heard a noise and moved her hand a little faster, searching for the switch.

A footstep sounded at the other end of the hall.

"Okay, I know where you are," she announced.

She found the switch and flicked it on. She glimpsed one of the small, dark-haired girls, standing in a white nightgown in front of a closed door.

Click. The hall light flicked out again.

"You guys," she said, trying to sound bored. "Stop playing with the light switches."

The girl at the end of the hall turned on a flashlight beneath her chin so that her features were illuminated from below. Her mouth hung slack and her eyes were glazed.

"I'm dead," she murmured.

There was a swishing sound behind Hazel.

She turned to find the other twin in the same pose, her face slack, in the middle of the living room. "I'm dead," she repeated. "I'm a ghost."

The girls shambled slowly toward Hazel, looking for all the world like clones of that evil spirit from *The Ring*. Cold, relentless, evil.

Hazel had no idea why it freaked her out. She fought to keep from becoming unnerved.

"Girls, it's time to get your ghost selves into bed," she said bravely. She turned the light back on. Immediately, it clicked off again.

"I'm dead," one of the twins moaned. "I'm dead and I'm coming for you."

"Oh yeah?" Hazel challenged. She headed toward her, taking bold, long strides. She was halfway down the hall when the girl shone her flashlight in Hazel's eyes and then flicked it off, leaving her seeing spots.

When Hazel reached the end of the hall, the twin was gone.

"I'm dead," she moaned from the living room. "You killed me."

Hazel followed the voice.

"Katie, Chrissie, this isn't funny," she called.

Then she looked toward the wall of glass and caught her breath.

A tall, hooded figure stood outside the house.

Hazel stared at the silent figure. Slowly, slowly, it lifted its head.

It raised its hand and pointed at Hazel.

She shrieked. The person was wearing a hockey mask, and he was carrying a long, silver knife.

"Chrissie! Katie!" Hazel screamed. "Come to me! Now!"

Behind her, voices chorused, "Surprise!" as all the lights blazed on.

Hazel whirled around. Megan, Carolyn, and Ellen were standing in the doorway with the Darling twins. Megan was doubled over with laughter. Carolyn applauded as the twins took bows.

Hazel struggled to catch her breath. Ellen came to her and threw her arms around her. "Aw, it's all right. It's a prank, Haze! Just a prank."

Megan clapped. "We got you good!"

The front door opened. Sylvia came across the threshold, the hood of her sweatshirt thrown back, the hockey mask in her hand.

She rushed toward Hazel, her arms open.

"Ah, *ma petite*!" she said, kissing her cheek with a noisy smack.

She wiggled the knife. The blade wobbled, clearly a prop.

"Friday the 13th." Sylvia winked. "Your favorite."

Hazel laughed, embarrassed and weak from relief. "You guys! That was twisted. I was really *scared*!"

"Then our work here is done," Megan said, high-fiving Carolyn.

Sylvia handed Ellen the mask. She let go of Hazel and went to the twins, bending over and tousling their hair. "Hey, monsters. Good job." She looked over her shoulder at Hazel. "Wouldn't you agree?"

"Oscars are in their future," Hazel affirmed.

Katie and Chrissie lifted their chins proudly.

"You two are just awful," Sylvia said affectionately.

"We're dead," one of them said.

"Were they giving you a hard time?" Sylvia asked.

"Oh no," Hazel managed, flashing Sylvia a weak smile. "Aside from the whole 'scare the babysitter into a coma' project, everything's been fine."

Sylvia chuckled and took Hazel's arm. "Note to self? You suck at lying. C'mon. We'll make you something to take the sting out of sitting these little monsters."

"We are not monsters!" one of them insisted as they trailed after Sylvia. "We're dead!"

The seven of them walked into the kitchen, which was a small city of brushed stainless steel. Sylvia opened the freezer, fished around inside, and brought out a bottle. Grey Goose vodka.

"Grab some martini glasses, won't you?" she asked Hazel. She pointed to a cabinet shimmering with glassware. "In there."

Hazel took a moment, then selected a large Y-shaped glass and held it up for Sylvia's inspection. Sylvia laughed. "Wow! You must be thirsty. We need five. Katie, get the vermouth. Chrissie, get the olives."

Megan, Carolyn, and Ellen took seats at the slate table in the breakfast nook. Hazel followed.

Sylvia poured vodka nearly to the rim of each glass. Seeing Hazel's surprise, she chuckled and splashed in a little more. "Relax. It's fine."

The girls returned with another bottle and the olives. Sylvia finished making the drinks and passed them around. Hazel was about to take a sip when Sylvia held her glass aloft.

"To Haze, everyone! A good sport and a great victim. Ellen? The traditional PLD toast?"

Ellen smirked. "To damnation!" she said in a clear, ringing voice.

"To damnation!" the others echoed. They clinked glasses.

Then Sylvia turned to Katie and Chrissie. "Okay, I'm throwing you in bed. Hazel, take a load off. The cavalry, she is here."

Hazel smiled gratefully but didn't want Sylvia to think she couldn't handle her first job. "It's okay," she told Sylvia. "I want to do it."

"About the bad lying?" Sylvia scolded. "You haven't gotten any better in the last thirty seconds."

The other PLDs giggled. Sylvia carried her drink as she herded the two girls toward their bedroom.

"Teeth and faces." Sylvia's voice trailed down the hall.

"We can't brush our teeth," Katie announced. "We're dead."

"You'll wish you were dead if you don't brush them, *mes petites*. Now, come on. You don't want to make Sylvia mad, do you?"

Chrissie and Katie squealed as if equal parts thrilled and terrified by the idea. Hazel sipped her drink—*Yow! It's all vodka!* She listened to the rushing water and the girls giggling in the bathroom.

"Told you you'd need the squeezy brain," Megan teased.

"You were right." Hazel took another, tinier sip. "I just didn't realize *how right* you were."

"I'm sorry if we scared you, Haze. It was kind of mean," Ellen apologized.

"Dude, don't be such a wuss," Megan said. "It was a good prank."

"We started pranking in middle school," Carolyn explained. "Around the same time we got into horror movies. You know, long nights sitting, nothing to do but watch TV or do homework. . . . I think Sylvia did the first one."

"On me," Ellen said. "She started knocking on all the windows."

"We used to have séances too," Megan said. "Remember that? They were kind of dorky, but we believed in them."

"I never did," Ellen insisted.

"Yeah, right." Carolyn snorted. "You used to *cry*."

Ellen frowned, embarrassed. She glanced at the clock on the wall. "I gotta go," she announced. "My dad . . ." She made a fist and breathed into it. "Who's got the breath mints?"

"I've got some in my purse," Megan offered. "Out in the living room. And actually, I should go too."

"Me too," Carolyn added.

They took their half-full martini glasses to the counter, dumped them out, rinsed and dried them, and put them back in their places.

"Well, your first job is almost over," Ellen said, smiling at Hazel. "You did great."

"Yeah." Megan slapped her on the back. "You definitely had a squishy-brain moment." She knocked on Hazel's head. "Huh, I think it's still in there."

Carolyn gave her a little hug.

Carrying her drink with her, Hazel followed them into the living room.

Sylvia emerged from the girls' rooms a moment later. "Okay, I ran the chain saw. They won't be bothering you anymore." She took Hazel's glass and measured how much was left. "You might want to dump this out now," she suggested. "It's important not to be too drunk when Cynthia comes home."

"Damn. I had such plans," Hazel quipped.

Sylvia made a check mark in the air. "Third initiation item: sitting job and near-stroke-inducing prank. You're almost done!"

"What's left?" Hazel asked, emboldened by her success . . . and the vodka.

"Wait and see," Sylvia teased.

"Okay. As long as no animals are harmed in the fulfilling of the item," Hazel said.

The four giggled appreciatively. They gathered their jackets and purses and filed out the front door. Hazel waved as they got in their cars.

She shut the door and leaned against it, taking another hefty swallow of her martini. Then she carried it into the kitchen to dump.

I'm so on top of this, she thought. *I was born to be a PLD.*

✛   ✛   ✛

PERSONALBLOG

HAPPY 2BME

HAZEL, DO YOU LIKE YOUR NEW FRIENDS? DO YOU LIKE SURPRISES? YOU HAVE NO IDEA WHAT'S COMING. NONE OF THEM DO. I'M JUST GETTING STARTED—GEARING UP FOR THE REAL THING. YOU'LL SEE WHAT BEING A POPULAR GIRL MEANS. . . . SOMETIMES, IT MEANS YOU HAVE TO DIE.

CHAPTER FOUR

Hazel was truly blessed.

Her econ teacher was out sick. Her AP chem teacher lectured too long and told everyone to turn in their homework the next day. Every assignment she had blown off yesterday, she'd gotten a lucky break on today. Thank goodness.

Ten minutes till my next class, she thought as she sprinted down the hall. *Just enough time for a stop at my locker.*

She spun her combination, opened the door—and cried out in surprise.

A huge spider hung inside the locker. It dangled from a web stretched across the opening.

Hazel took a deep breath and looked more closely. *It's a fake spider*, she realized, *courtesy of the PLDs.*

A drawing was stuck in the center of the spider's web. It looked like a skull and crossbones, only this was a hockey mask with two chain saws crossed beneath it. WE PRANKED HAZEL! was written in jagged letters above the mask.

Those guys. She giggled and rolled her eyes.

"You have the nicest laugh," said a voice behind her. A voice with a deep, southern accent.

Hazel smiled. *Matty.*

He had been hanging around nonstop since that first PLD party—e-mailing her and talking to her at every opportunity. Still, he hadn't asked her out. Hazel sensed that he was waiting for the right moment. She hoped he wouldn't wait too long.

"Thanks," she said as she folded up the web and the picture.

"What was that?" he asked, pointing to the items.

"Oh, just a little love note from Sylvia and the other PLDs." She hauled out her books and slammed her locker shut.

"Oh yeah." He grinned. "I forgot. You're one of the bad baby-sitters now."

"That's right. The baddest."

Matty leaned against the nearby locker. "I don't believe that. You're more angel than devil."

"Shh! Don't tell the others," Hazel joked. "They think I'm as rotten as they are."

The bell rang. Matty groaned.

"I gotta take off. My class is at the other end of the school."

"Run. Run like the wind," Hazel told him. She turned away, playing a little hard to get.

"See you at lunch?" he asked her.

"I'll be there."

"Cool." He looked like he was about to say something

more. Too late. The second bell sounded. Matty sighed and took off.

"We are completely ignoring her," Sylvia informed the PLDs at lunch.

"Who?" Hazel asked. "What's going on?"

"Over there." Megan nodded toward the cafeteria entrance. "Check it out, but don't be obvious."

Hazel turned and saw the entire varsity cheerleading squad striding into the cafeteria. There were fifteen girls total—and Breona Wu was among them!

She walked in the center of the group, her best friend, Jenna Babcock, by her side. All the girls wore kelly-green-and-gold uniforms, their hair and makeup flawless, like an army of glam.

Breona sat down at her usual place, about eight tables over from the PLDs. Jenna took the chair next to Breona. All the others filled that table and the two surrounding it.

"How'd she get back in?" Megan demanded. "What about the zero-tolerance policy?"

"Zero tolerance, my butt," Carolyn growled.

"Stay calm," Sylvia said sternly. "We'll figure something out."

The PLDs settled in, everyone refusing to look in Breona's direction. Hazel stole a glance at the jock table, which was to her left. Josh, Brandon, and Stephan were already wolfing down hamburgers. But Matty hadn't shown yet. Where was he?

"Tonight you're sitting Charlie, Hazel." Sylvia's voice

interrupted her thoughts. "That would be the little boy with the cat. From the last party."

"Right. Isotope." Hazel tried to build up her nerve to tell Sylvia that she really had to stay home, but before she had a chance, Sylvia continued.

"I was talking to Josh between classes. He brought up your Mr. *Matt*ise. Josh says he is very aggressive on the field."

"Ooh la la," Carolyn drawled. "Hot-blooded."

"Mmmm. *Très bien*, Mattise!" Sylvia smiled at her own cleverness and stabbed a piece of lettuce.

All Sylvia ate was salad, Hazel noticed. Maybe it was the secret behind her awesome complexion.

Hazel sneaked another peek at the jock table to see if Matty had arrived.

Ellen glanced over too, obviously mooning over Brandon.

Sylvia noticed, and her expression went grim. She rapped her fist in front of Ellen's tray.

"*Pardon moi*, what are you doing?" she asked.

Ellen blinked, as if waking from a daydream. "I—I was just—"

Sylvia sighed. "Ellie, we've been over this. Brandon is an asshole, okay? He has hanging-out privileges, but he is not nice."

Ellen shifted. "I don't know, Sylvia. He *seems* nice."

"They all *seem* nice," Carolyn said.

"Even Stephan seemed nice," Megan muttered.

"Well . . . he's nice to *me*," Ellen whispered.

Sylvia touched her fingers to her chest. "Don't be so naive, El.

Brandon is a user. If you let him, he will chew you up and spit you out. Trust me on this."

Hazel thought about the girl in geometry. "She's right, El."

Everyone looked startled. Sylvia raised an eyebrow. "And how would you know?"

Hazel blinked. Had she overstepped her bounds somehow? "He—he totally humiliated this girl in my geometry class last year. He pretended to ask her out and then he laughed at her when she said yes."

"No way," Ellen protested, stricken.

"It's true," Hazel insisted. "I was there."

"Well, thank goodness," Sylvia breathed. "For a moment, I thought you had firsthand experience with the matter."

"No, no," Hazel protested. "It's nothing like that."

"Good. Because that's the kind of thing PLDs share." Sylvia leaned forward, locking her electric blue eyes on Hazel. "I would hope that if you had been with any of the guys in our circle, you'd tell us about it."

"Of course," Hazel confirmed.

Of course, I would. Don't go getting so intense about it.

Ellen turned her head in Brandon's direction—again.

"Jesus, El," Sylvia hissed. "Did you not just hear what I said? Show some pride. If not for yourself, then for us."

Ellen opened her mouth to answer.

"Uh-oh," Megan cut her off. "Trouble, two o'clock."

Hazel glanced up and saw Jilly Delgado—one of the cheerleaders—sidling up to their table. Sylvia shot her a withering glance.

"Can we help you?" she asked.

"Breona knows it was you," Jilly said, glaring at them. "There will be payback."

She turned and walked back to Breona's table.

"God! We're terrified!" Megan called after her.

"Tais-toi," Sylvia snapped at Megan. "Don't give them any satisfaction. They're not even on our radar."

"Right," Ellen said. "Beneath our notice."

"Exactement." Sylvia looked hard at each of them. "Now is the time to show them who we really are. PLDs act. We don't react. Breona's going to try to get to us all today. You have chem lab with her, don't you, Haze? Don't let her pressure you. She'll try to tell you that she's the victim in all this. It's a lie. I want you to know that."

"But why would she—"

The others looked straight at Hazel, and she remembered that she was still on probation. Not officially one of them.

Maybe she'd be able to ask questions later.

"I'll be fine," she promised.

When Hazel got to chem lab, she found Breona waiting at her table. She shifted slightly when Hazel approached.

"Hey, Hazel," Breona said, pasting on a big smile. "Do you have the notes I missed while I was out?"

"No. Sorry," Hazel said coolly, navigating around her.

"I'm a little behind, you know," Breona continued. "I don't know if you heard, but I was kicked out of school *when someone planted drugs in my locker!*"

Hazel shook her head. *Sylvia said Breona would play the innocent victim.* She balled her fists inside the pockets of her black hoodie and looked away.

Breona rolled her eyes. "Oh, come on. Did they tell you to diss me? You aren't really a PLD, are you? You're just hanging out with them, under the mistaken impression that they're nice people. Right?"

Hazel kept her voice calm and steady. "Actually, I *am* a PLD."

"Oh my God! Hazel, do *not* hang out with them. They are totally evil. I know you didn't have anything to do with what happened to me, but—"

"I'm sorry, Breona," Hazel said. She pulled out her lab stool. Case closed.

"Okay," Breona muttered, her eyes flashing with anger. "But if you stick with them, you have signed on for some serious trouble, girlfriend."

Lakshmi hurried into the room. She glanced over at Hazel and gave her a little smile. Then she set her pack down and clambered onto her stool one table away.

"How's it going?" Lakshmi asked.

Before Hazel could reply, Breona leaned over. "Don't bother, Lakshmi. Hazel's just like the rest of those bitches. She's not allowed to talk to anyone who isn't a PLD."

Lakshmi blinked. "Oh?"

"That's not true," Hazel countered quickly. "I can talk to whoever I want."

"Oh. That's right. It's not that she *can't* talk to you. It's that she just doesn't *want* to talk to you. She thinks you're a loser. And so do all her little friends."

Lakshmi's mouth dropped open. "Hazel? That's . . . not true . . . is it?"

"No," Hazel said.

She tried to make the word believable, but her face gave everything away.

Tears brimmed in Lakshmi's eyes.

Then Ms. Carpentier looked up from her desk. "All right, people. Take your seats."

Everyone fell mercifully silent, but Lakshmi shot Hazel a dirty look before turning to the front of the classroom.

Hazel sighed. *I knew I'd make friends as a PLD*, she thought. *I hadn't really counted on making enemies.*

When Hazel arrived for her sitting job at Charlie's, Mr. Pollins, a chubby, middle-aged man, was rushing around getting ready for a night shift.

"Charlie will show you around," he said as he went into his study.

She suppressed a grin. Clearly Mr. Pollins was unaware that she had been in his home before—along with about twenty other high school kids.

Pale little Charlie was clad in pajamas and a bathrobe. He led Hazel into the kitchen. "Hey. Matty didn't send me the jpeg yet."

"I'm sure he will," she promised, hoping it was true.

She noticed an open can on the counter and a pot on the stove. "Do you want some SpaghettiOs?"

"No," Charlie answered. "I'm not really all that hungry."

"Is there something else you'd rather have?" she asked.

"No." He rubbed his forehead. "I'm a kid. We eat stuff like this."

Hazel chuckled at Charlie's matter-of-fact delivery. He continued to rub his temples.

"Headache?" Hazel asked sympathetically.

"Tension," he replied.

"Tell you what. Why don't you go on to your room and I'll bring you dinner in bed. Sound good?"

He nodded. "Thanks." He shuffled off to his room like a little old man.

Hazel dumped the can into the pot and lit the burner. While the SpaghettiOs were heating, she got some two percent milk out of the fridge and found an *Incredibles* cup in the cupboard.

Mr. Pollins came into the kitchen. "I'll be home very late. Please feel free to nap. And if you wouldn't mind answering the phone . . ."

"Of course. Whatever you say."

"Lock up after me, all right?"

She followed him to the door and secured the dead bolt.

As she returned to the kitchen, the phone rang.

"Pollins residence," she said, picking up the wall unit.

"You are a bad babysitter," whispered a muffled, obviously disguised voice.

"You guys," she said calmly. "I know this is a prank."

"I'm outside. I'm watching you."

"The drapes are shut," she replied, glancing at the window over the kitchen sink. "You must have x-ray vision."

"Maybe I do. Hey, here's a thought: do you think the door to the study is locked?"

"Because you left me a present in the study?" she asked.

"Check it."

She moved the pot off the burner and wandered down the hall to Mr. Pollins's study. She tried the knob. It didn't move.

"Yes," she announced. "It's lockay-vous."

"I mean the outside *door, bad babysitter. The one that leads from the backyard into the study. You know about that door, right? No, of course you don't. Because you are a bad babysitter."*

She cocked her head. "The outside door . . ."

"For all you know, I let myself into the study and I'm behind that door right now. And when you're not looking, I could sneak out of the study and creep up on you. I could kill you—and the kid."

"That would be pretty, um, drastic." She tried for a light tone, but her voice shook a little.

It's a prank, she reminded herself. *Don't let them get to you.*

"That's right, I'm behind that door. . . . I'm in the house right now!"

"You guys?" Hazel said shrilly. "This isn't funny, okay?"

"Hey, we're just seeing if it's all good over there," Sylvia's voice responded coolly.

"Oh God," Hazel breathed.

"Chill, Haze," Sylvia said. "You knew it was us, right?"

"Yeah. Well, kind of. Everything's fine." Hazel stumbled, fiddling with the knob to the study door again. "But the door . . . it *is* locked, and . . ."

"Sometimes Charlie's dad locks it before he leaves," Sylvia

explained. "You can't get back in without the key. But there is a door that leads into the study from the yard, and we always make sure that's locked."

"Well, I'll certainly never forget that again!"

"Good, *ma petite*. So anyway, next subject. We had a thought about Ellen's hair. Obviously she needs some guidance on this matter. Tell me, where do *you* go? Because your hair works and her hair is the same texture, so maybe your person could do hers."

"Does she know we're discussing this?"

"Don't worry, it's not like she's here, so you can speak freely. We have been trying to explain to her that her hair is, you know, a *problem*, but she's just not getting it."

"It *is* kind of bad." Hazel thought for a moment. "Yeah, I'll help. It's just—she's sensitive. Let's be subtle about it, okay?"

"Absolutely. Thanks, Haze."

✛   ✛   ✛

YOU HAVE ENTERED
The pretty Little Devils chat room
THIS IS A PRIVATE CHAT ROOM FOR INVITED MEMBERS ONLY

Members in chat room:

PLDSLY

PLDEL

PLDCARO

PLDMEG

PLDSLY: We're on the line with Hazel now. She sez UR hair's bad. Every1 staring at U, El.

PLDEL: Haze sez so?

PLDSLY: *Oui.* Real bad. Sez U can go to her place.

PLDEL: OK. Plz thank her.

PLDSLY: We're here 2 help. Friendz! :)

PLDCARO: Friendz! :)

PLDMEG: Friendz! :)

PLDEL: Friendz! :)

✛   ✛   ✛

PERSONALBLOG
HAPPY2BME

THE PLDs THINK THEY'RE SUCH GOOD FRIENDS. NONE OF THEM HAVE ANY IDEA WHAT REAL FRIENDSHIP IS. TOO BAD I'LL HAVE TO TEACH THEM . . . THE HARD WAY. I JUST HOPE I CAN HOLD ON.

THE CAT WAS GOOD, BUT IT'S NOT ENOUGH. I NEED MORE!

NO. NO. I HAVE TO HOLD ON. JUST A LITTLE TINY BIT LONGER.

✛   ✛   ✛

The next day at lunch, Hazel sailed into the cafeteria. She joined the serving line just as Sylvia and Josh sauntered in. They walked with their heads held high, completely aware that all eyes were on them, like a pair of movie stars. Sylvia's hand was tucked into the back pocket of Josh's jeans, her hair was up in a French twist, and shiny chandelier earrings dangled above her shoulders.

Josh was wearing aviator sunglasses and a white Lacoste shirt. On anyone else, it would look like trying too hard. On them, it just looked perfect.

Before parting, Sylvia pulled his sunglasses down his nose and he bent to kiss her.

Hazel sighed. Maybe someday she'd have a boyfriend. And together they would look as amazing as Sylvia and Josh.

She grabbed her tray, and someone tapped her shoulder. She turned her head, hoping . . . and there he was. She smiled calmly, though her insides were jangling happily.

"Hey, pretty girl," Matty said.

"Hey."

"Tell me what you think." He pulled out a stack of printer paper. "They're my posters for Isotope."

There was the sketch Matty had drawn, Charlie's contact information, and above it all a single line—REWARD: $100.

"A hundred dollars?" she said.

He shrugged. "I figure the kid is good for a loan."

"That is so nice of you," she said sincerely.

He put his finger to his lips. "Don't need to spread it around, remember. School gossip can get so out of hand."

"No kidding," she said.

They got their food. Matty walked Hazel toward the PLDs' table.

"You coming to the game tomorrow night?" he asked.

Hazel brightened. She set her tray at her place and opened her mouth to respond, but Sylvia beat her to it.

"The PLDs go to all the games," she said, smiling. "We always sit together."

Hazel shrugged. "I'll be there, then."

"Cool," Matty said. "I'll look for you in the stands. I'm sure you'll be easy to spot." He looked directly into Hazel's eyes, and she worked overtime not to blush.

"We *are* hard to miss," Sylvia cut in again.

"Well, then," he said with a suppressed grin, "guess I'll catch you later." He gave a final wave before making his way over to the guys' table.

Hazel settled into her seat. "He's sweet," she said with a sigh.

"I guess. But here's something really sweet," Sylvia replied. She placed a cell phone with a neon purple cover plate on Hazel's lunch tray.

"Oh my God," Hazel murmured. "Thank you."

Sylvia took the phone from Hazel's hands. "You're welcome, but it's not a gift per se. Let me run you through the functions. First, here's your ring."

She pressed a button and Alicia Keys's "Karma" trilled.

"Sylvia, that's the ring *I* wanted!" Ellen moaned.

Sylvia shook her head. "It's easily acquired. You can download it. Now, I programmed in all our numbers. I'm one, Megan's two, Carolyn's three, and Ellen is last but certainly not least at four." She smiled at Ellen. "Oh, and be sure to give our little El the name of your salon."

Ellen dragged her fingers through her bangs, clearly embarrassed. "I'll be right back," she said, slipping off to the bathroom.

Sylvia continued. "I'll just deduct your share of the sitting money until it's paid for. Now, this is your cell phone number. But please don't give it out to just anyone."

Hazel frowned. "Um, Sylvia, if I have to pay for the phone, shouldn't I be able to give the number to anyone I—"

But Sylvia wasn't listening. "Be sure to keep it on vibrate during school; otherwise it will be confiscated. You can send texts. It has a browser and games." She handed Hazel the phone back. "Welcome to the twenty-first century, *ma petite*."

"You guys! You guys! Oh my God!" Ellen stage-whispered as she ran back to the table. "Jilly Delgado is having a total freakout in the bathroom."

Sylvia rolled her eyes. "Jilly is such a drama queen. What's the crisis this time?"

"She's having a complete breakdown. Kathy Wilcox and Cara Dugan are trying to get her to pull it together," Ellen explained. "Something happened to her horse."

"Spirit?" Hazel asked with concern. The others gave her a look.

"I rode him once, when I was a little kid," Hazel explained. "Jilly has had that horse, like, forever."

"Did they say what happened?" Megan asked.

"No. Jilly was totally hysterical." Ellen glanced left and right. "She is obsessed with that horse. Like, *unhealthily* obsessed. Did you know that she's even got a picture of him in her locker?"

"Well, that's kind of freaky," Sylvia muttered, taking a bite of her salad. "I wonder what could have happened to him."

CHAPTER FIVE

Hazel decided to go to school early and wander down to the football field.

Sylvia had told Hazel that perhaps Matty needed a push, and with homecoming just a few weeks away, the time for pushing was now.

Matty had mentioned that the team had practice before first period. Maybe she'd be able to talk to him—to show him she'd been feeling the exact same way he had for the last few weeks.

But the field was empty, the freshly mown grass sparkling with dew.

Hazel waited, but no one showed. A little crestfallen, she went to her locker. She turned a corner—and found Matty in his letter jacket and jeans. He was standing at her locker door, trying to tape a green carnation to the front of it.

"What's this?" Hazel asked. "Special delivery?"

"Uh, hey. Morning," he said, turning at the sound of her voice. He flashed a quick smile as she glanced at the carnation. "This was supposed to be a surprise."

"So surprise me," Hazel said.

"We get these on game days," he explained. "From the cheer-leaders. I thought . . . well, here." He held it out to her.

"Thank you." She took it and gave him a hug, lingering in his arms a second more than usual.

"I went to the field to see if you were having practice," she said.

"You did?" He smiled and shifted his feet nervously. He seemed to be searching for something else to say.

Hazel turned toward her locker.

"Wait." He put his hand on her shoulder and drew her closer.

Hazel looked up at him and he planted a soft kiss on her lips.

He pulled back and gave a nervous smile.

"How about another?" she whispered. He closed his eyes and kissed her again. She felt like she could melt right into him.

Oh my gosh, Hazel thought happily. *I can't believe this is happening. Right here—with Matty Vardeman!*

"Hazel," Matty murmured when he pulled away, "I think you're really awesome."

"Thanks." Hazel blushed.

"I wanted to know. Would you, uh, go out with me?"

Hazel wanted to shriek with joy. Instead, she looked at her feet for a moment.

There were footsteps in the hall. A locker banged open. People were drifting in to start the day.

Reluctantly she pulled back. "Class," she said.

"Is that a yes?"

Hazel nodded.

He grinned at her, his eyes crinkling, his quirky-handsome mouth pulled up in that lazy half smile. "Just one more." He leaned in and kissed her again as the bell rang.

"I see a lot of tardies in my future," he complained happily.

"We can't have that," she replied. She wrapped her hand around his, giving it a final squeeze. "You should go."

"I know." He sighed. "I don't want to."

"I know," she replied, and they both chuckled.

"Okay. I'm going," he said.

He kissed her cheek, then he turned and walked away, looking so good in his jeans and jacket.

He turned back and grinned at her. "See you later?"

"*Scram!*" she joked.

Then finally he did.

Hazel drifted through her classes that morning, unable to focus on anything. Every time she closed her eyes, she could feel Matty kissing her.

She glided along, smiling a secret smile. No one knew what she was thinking about. *Who* she was thinking about.

Matty Vardeman. Hazel Vardeman. It was silly to think about. But it definitely sounded nice.

School was a tangled mess of information, exercises, and quizzes, but all she wanted was to revel in everything that had happened: her induction into the PLDs, Matty. If this was what selling your soul to the Devils got you, she was glad that she'd signed on the dotted line.

Matty met her at the lunch bell and they kissed some more before strolling across the quad to the cafeteria. The sky was clear; it was the kind of warm, sunny day people paid to live in Southern California for.

The other four PLDs were already at their table.

"You all always sit together. Maybe sometime it could be just us?" Matty asked as he and Hazel drew near, hand in hand.

"That would be nice."

She smiled, then wondered if that was some kind of official no-no. No one, not even Sylvia, sat elsewhere at lunch. Maybe it was one of the PLD rules.

They reached the table. Matty said, "Hello, ladies."

"Hi," Sylvia said sharply, not looking at him. Her gaze was fastened on Ellen. There was tension in her voice. This was not the time for leisurely chat.

"Um, later," Hazel said quietly. She squeezed Matty's hand.

"Okay." He paused a moment, then bent down to kiss her.

Loud smooching sounds came from the jock table. Matty smiled, then strolled over to his friends. Stephan hit him on the shoulder. Josh and Brandon touched fists with him.

It was official. Matty had made sure everyone knew that he and Hazel were an item. Nothing could bring Hazel down now.

"Heads up. Someone's in a mood," Megan drawled as Hazel took her seat. She gestured with her head at Ellen, who did not look up.

"Megan," Sylvia reproved, sitting back in her chair. "I told you, it's all good." She smiled directly at Hazel. "How are you?"

"Great." She held out her carnation. "Look."

"Ah. The cheerleaders give them to the guys. It's all very symbolic, I'm sure."

Hazel put it down on the table. "It is."

"Oh, Hazel. That's so sweet," Ellen gushed.

Hazel smiled her thanks.

"Well, it's Friday," Sylvia announced.

"Game day," Hazel concurred.

"And . . . ?" Sylvia turned her head. Her hair was pulled back in a ponytail, and Hazel realized what she was getting at: Sylvia was wearing the trademark PLD purple scrunchie. The four girls wore them every Friday. Another tradition upheld since middle school. They all had them on, even Ellen, although she'd had to hold back her hair with some clips to manage it.

With a flourish, Sylvia held up a purple scrunchie.

"Pour toi," she said to Hazel. Hazel reached for it, and Sylvia playfully pulled it out of her grasp. "This is your last chance, Haze. The scrunchie damns you for all eternity. So, you in?"

"Oui," Hazel said happily. She took the scrunchie and made a ponytail. She turned her head, displaying it. "How's that?"

"Perfect," Sylvia said. "To Hazel!"

Megan and Carolyn raised their drink cups. Ellen lifted hers as well.

Then Sylvia glanced down at her water bottle, which was empty. "Ellen? Be a dear and get me another, would you?"

Ellen's smile fell. She hesitated. Then she pushed back her chair and left the table.

94

"It's time for another soiree. I want Ellen to ask her dad about having it at their place," Sylvia said to Hazel. "She's dragging her feet about it. My patience is wearing thin."

"Oh . . . That's too bad," Hazel said, shifting in her chair.

So Ellen hasn't asked her dad about a party, Hazel thought. *What is Sylvia doing? Punishing her for it?*

Hazel turned to glance at the jock table. Brandon was in the center, clowning around with some of the others. At the sight of him, Hazel got the feeling that this was about more than the party.

"Let's talk about happier things." Sylvia cocked her head and scrutinized Hazel. "You and Mattise? Holding hands? A carnation. And a kiss? Public affection? Is that the way to go?"

Hazel's lips parted. She thought for a moment. *Sylvia* kissed *Josh* in front of everyone. What was wrong with her and Matty—

"I think it's a good move," Carolyn declared. "He's hot, and he's on the team."

"But is there anybody you'd rather have?" Sylvia asked Hazel. "Because once you start kissing in public, you're stuck. Although I guess the proper term is *committed*."

"I like him," Hazel murmured. "A lot."

"It would be hard to do better," Carolyn said. "And everyone else has hooked up for the year."

"Until the inevitable breakups," Sylvia added. "But he is one of the best."

"If you're into that sort of thing," Carolyn put in.

"Then it works," Sylvia decreed. On either side of her, Carolyn and Megan nodded. "However, Brandon does *not* work. Not for our Ellen." She scowled at Ellen's empty chair. "The sooner she gets that, the better."

Hazel frowned. Again, there was something strange about Sylvia's tone. It was as though she were trying to teach Ellen a lesson.

But if Ellen decided to date Brandon, was it really any of Sylvia's business?

The lunch bell rang and Hazel went to bus her tray. She caught sight of Lakshmi and the others standing in a clump beneath the diversity mural, scanning the crowd.

They're looking for me, Hazel realized. But Sylvia had been very clear: she couldn't be friends with Lakshmi anymore.

That was a sacrifice Hazel was more than willing to make.

She took a breath and avoided Lakshmi by using the side door. The PLDs followed her toward the quad.

In chem lab Hazel was donning her goggles when her cell phone vibrated. She fiddled with the end of her carnation while she checked the message.

It was from Sylvia.

PLDSLY2PURPLEHAZE: Plan change. C me L8r

"Okay, everyone." Ms. Carpentier clapped. "Let's begin today's experiment."

Hazel couldn't respond now.

Lakshmi appeared in the doorway. Hazel busied herself putting the phone back so that she couldn't catch her eye.

"Where did you get this?" an outraged voice demanded.

Breona Wu had rushed up to the side of Hazel's table. She grabbed Hazel's carnation so tightly that the stem broke.

"Hey!" Hazel cried. "That's mine!"

As she reached for it, Breona raised it over her head. Her eyes were slits, her lips pulled back so her teeth were showing. "These flowers are for the team! What did you do? Steal it?"

"Excuse me?" Hazel asked.

"Breona? Hazel?" Ms. Carpentier called from the front of the room. "Is there a problem?"

Breona shook the flower toward the teacher. "She stole this!"

Ms. Carpentier raised her brows. "Hazel, is that Breona's?"

"No," Hazel said. "It was a present from—"

"Matty Vardeman gave it to her," Lakshmi said loudly, half rising from her stool. "I saw them. At her locker."

Hazel and Breona both turned to stare at Lakshmi in surprise.

Hazel thought she and Matty were alone in the hall. Had Lakshmi been watching? God. What was that about?

"You—you are so lying, Lakshmi!" Breona screeched. Her face drained of color.

"No, I saw it," Lakshmi insisted. "He gave it to her." She turned to Ms. Carpentier. "It's Hazel's."

"But . . ." Breona's face crumpled. She covered her mouth with her hands and ran into the hall. The entire class watched her go.

There was silence. Then Brian Palmeri, the slacker in the back of the room, piped up. "Dude, what's her deal?"

"She's on drugs," Hazel shot back, furious and embarrassed.

Her statement was greeted with hoots and laughter from the rest of the class.

"Hazel! Would you care to visit Mr. Clancy?" Ms. Carpentier snapped.

"No. Sorry," Hazel apologized, carefully scooping up the carnation. Petals dropped from the ruined flower.

"All right. Then let's get back to work."

Carpentier got them started on a mixing exercise—adding copper sulfate and sulfur to water. Then she left the room, no doubt to deal with Breona's diva moment. As soon as she was gone, the class got rowdy.

Lakshmi leaned over her lab table. "By the way, Haze, that's so cool about you and Matty. Way to go!"

"Thanks," Hazel said. She tried to focus on her experiment, adjusting her heavy goggles as she held a test tube of blue liquid over a Bunsen burner. But she couldn't help wondering—how did Lakshmi know about her and Matty in the hallway?

Lakshmi leaned closer. Behind her own goggles, she was blinking excitedly. "I was trying to find you at lunch. Did you hear about Jilly Delgado's horse?"

"Yeah," Hazel said coolly. "Something happened to him."

"Something happened, all right. He was killed! Some psycho murdered him and cut him into little chunks!"

Hazel turned from her experiment. "What?"

"Someone hacked him up," Lakshmi repeated eagerly. "They found one of his eyes ten feet away from his body. His tail was missing."

Hazel shook her head. "Oh my God. How awful!"

"There's going to be a police investigation," Lakshmi added. "They need to find the perpetrator right away. They're clearly crazy—and you never know what someone like that will do next."

Hazel understood. She watched *CSI* too.

Footfalls sounded in the hall. Various conversations died away as Ms. Carpentier returned—without Breona.

"Uh, Hazel?" Lakshmi whispered. "We're all getting together tonight to watch a movie. I thought, if you're not busy . . ."

"Sorry." Hazel turned away. "I have plans."

Lakshmi sighed. "Yeah. I figured you would."

Hazel's last period was a study hall that met in the media center. She set her heavy backpack on the table before her and opened it.

She wanted to study, but her mind was whirling. So much was happening. And it was all so confusing.

Breona's meltdown, Jilly's horse, her first football game as a PLD . . . and as Matty's girlfriend. Sylvia, Ellen, Brandon. What did it all mean?

She shook her head. Now was not the time to figure it out.

Focus, she coached herself.

She cracked open her econ book. Supply, demand . . . she could do this.

After a few minutes, she felt someone standing just behind her. She turned her head to find Matty, smiling down at her and waiting to be noticed. She gave him a little grin and raised her brows.

"Hey," he said softly.

"Hey. I didn't know you had study hall," she replied.

"Actually, I'm in Photo II," he said. "I came in to do some research." He held up a magazine titled *Digital Photographer* that had a bunch of cameras on the cover.

"You're into photography?" she asked.

"Yeah." He glanced left and right, scanning for the study hall monitor, Ms. Engstrom. The coast was clear. He pulled out a chair and sat down.

"I was selling some of my work to the local paper back in Virginia. Country scenes. I caught a car accident too."

"Wow."

"Yeah. I was the first one on the scene of the accident. It was a total scoop. Extremely gross." He paused. "It was a fatality. They used it. They had to digitize out some of the details, but the editor said I had a good eye for composition." He ducked his head and grinned. "Or rather, decomposition."

"Ew." She grimaced.

"They paid me a hundred and fifty dollars for it too." He played with the dog-eared corner of the magazine. "I tried to convince them I could e-mail things from here. They said thanks but no thanks."

"Too bad," she said empathetically.

He shrugged. "Hey, it's no big. There's . . . other stuff to keep me busy."

He means me, she thought, pleased.

"I see you got your new cell," he said, pointing to the phone sitting in her backpack. "Can I have the number?"

Sylvia's caution sounded in her ears. *Don't give the number to just anyone. . . .*

Was Matty "anyone"? Would Sylvia be angry if Hazel gave him the number?

Hazel set her jaw. *Whatever,* she thought. *Sylvia may nose around in everybody's business, but she's not going to control me.*

"Sure." She wrote the number down for Matty on a scrap of notebook paper.

"Thanks," he said, slipping it into his pocket.

He glanced down at her textbook. "Economics? I took that. If you get stuck, I got an A."

Good grades too. She sighed. *Could he be any more perfect?*

"Good to know," she said. "Thanks."

Then his smile faded as he dropped his voice even lower. "Hey. Did you hear about Jilly Delgado's horse?"

She nodded. "It's horrible."

He toyed with the magazine, rolling it between his hands. "Poor thing's neck was severed almost clean off. There was blood everywhere. The stable hands who found it said they thought it was mud at first, it was so thick." He gazed into the distance—almost as if he were looking at something else. Something invisible to her.

Sickened, Hazel worked overtime not to see any of it. She crossed her arms, hugging herself. She'd been to Jilly's stable, Brookhaven Ranch, years ago for a birthday party. She'd ridden

Spirit. She could remember the way he chuffed and shook his mane. His steady gait and big brown eyes.

"And its left eye—"

"Matty, *stop*," she pleaded.

He tapped the magazine. "Sorry. It's just . . . maybe I do have a journalist's fascination with this kind of thing. There are a lot of strange people out there, Haze. And a lot of serial killers start out with animals."

Hazel felt a chill. "God. That's uplifting."

Matty sighed and gave her shoulder a squeeze. "I gotta get back." He looked at her with a penetrating stare. "I don't mean to scare you, but you should be careful, Haze. Stick with your girlfriends. Don't take chances."

"I won't. We won't." She frowned slightly. "It seems like we do just about everything together."

"Okay." He tucked the magazine under his arm. "I'll see you tonight."

Hazel had no idea how she was going to get anything done now.

Poor Jilly, she thought, shivering. *What kind of person would hack up a poor, defenseless horse?*

HAPTER
SIX

A t the game, the PLDs huddled together in the bleachers, sharing a big, scratchy blanket.

Despite the fact that the Highlanders were winning, Hazel felt like the PLDs were the main event—sitting front and center and drawing everyone's interest.

Hazel had to admit that she loved the attention. She cheered loudly and wagged her purple-scrunchied ponytail whenever the team scored.

Sylvia had brought popcorn, and the PLDs discreetly shared a flask filled with scotch. Hazel abstained. Sylvia had her booked for a babysitting gig after halftime. She didn't want to show up at Charlie's house smelling like a distillery.

She threw a Hershey's Kiss into her mouth instead.

Between plays, Daliah Firestone and Francesca Morano slid over to say hi.

Daliah and Francesca were popular girls, known for their style and their rep as stars of the drama club. Hazel would have given anything to hang with them just a few weeks ago. Now the tables were turned.

"Hazel," Francesca gushed, "I love your outfit. That shirt is totally cute."

Hazel glanced down at herself. She had on jeans, a long-sleeve T-shirt with a rhinestone cowgirl on it, and her black hoodie. Nothing special.

"And those jeans!" Daliah continued. "They're the perfect wash. What brand are they?"

Hazel had opened her mouth to accept the compliment when Sylvia cut in.

"Merci!" she said. "Our Hazel has the best clothes, doesn't she?"

Francesca nodded, obviously thrilled to have Sylvia's attention.

A roar sounded from the large crowd and everyone leapt to their feet. Hazel jumped up, craning her neck to see what she'd missed.

Carolyn nudged her. "Your boyfriend just completed a huge play!"

Hazel didn't know anything about football, but she knew Matty was a wide receiver. She spotted him high-fiving Josh. Then he turned directly to where she was sitting and pointed, his face breaking into the broadest smile. He gave a little wave, then returned to the game.

"Ooh, sweet!" Sylvia teased Hazel.

"Matty Vardeman." Daliah sighed. "He's *so* hot. You're *so* lucky!"

This is like a dream. The other girls don't just like me. They envy *me—they want to* be *me.*

That is what being a PLD is all about, Hazel thought.

At halftime, the cheerleaders took over the field. Breona Wu, who seemed to have recovered from her afternoon meltdown, was the star of the show. She vaulted into the air, balancing on top of a complicated human pyramid.

She tumbled down, then held up a cardboard sign with the number 43 painted on it.

Forty-three. Matty's number, Hazel realized. She stared at Breona as she whooped and hollered. *Was it that I had a carnation or that I had* Matty's *carnation that made Breona so insane?*

Hazel wasn't sure. When you were a PLD, there was just so much drama.

When Hazel showed at the Pollins house, she fed Charlie some mac and cheese. He went to bed in his roomful of gadgets, and she settled in the living room, delving into her homework.

She was engrossed in history when the doorbell rang. She set down her book, uncurled her legs from the sofa, and went to the door. She checked the peephole, fully expecting to see one of the PLDs on the porch.

Oh my God!

It was Matty, in jeans and jacket, his dark, curly hair glistening from a post-game shower. He must have seen her peering through the hole, because he waved.

Warmth rushed through her and she fumbled to unlock the

door quickly. When she yanked it open, he smiled at her hesitantly. "Hey."

"Hey." She opened the door wider, gesturing for him to come in.

"Sylvia told me you were here," he said. "She thought you might need some company."

"I do," she confirmed. He put his arms around her and kissed her gently.

"So, did you go to the after-party?" she asked as they broke apart and moved into the living room.

He nodded. "Yeah, but not for long. I drove Stephan over there. Did you know he used to go out with Megan?"

Hazel's mouth dropped open. "You're kidding! That's—I mean, she hates him."

"I think the feeling is mutual. He kept trying to convince me that she's gay or something. I told him it was none of my business."

Hazel stared at him. "Megan? Gay? No, it's—"

She'd been about to tell him that Carolyn was the lesbian, but Sylvia had said not to spread it around.

Matty took off his jacket. "That's what some guys say when a girl ticks them off. It's either that or that she's a prude. All I know is, she must have hurt him bad."

Hazel processed that. Or tried to. Of the two, Stephan seemed more capable of doing the hurting than Megan.

She shook her head. "I can't even picture them together."

"Me neither." He paused. "So how's Charlie?"

"Asleep," she said.

The telltale beeping of a computer game sounded from Charlie's room.

Matty laughed. "Asleep, huh? Let's go see."

He grabbed her hand and led her down the hall. Hazel tried very hard not to melt at the feel of Matty's strong fingers wrapped around her own.

Hazel knocked on the door. Charlie's high, small voice answered. "Come in."

Matty pushed open the door. *"Hello, carbon unit,"* it announced.

Charlie was sitting in bed, playing with his Game Boy. "Matty!" he cried, leaping up. "My dad and I put up the posters and I've had three calls about Isotope!"

"That's great," Matty cheered.

"None of the cats were him, though," Charlie said, lowering his voice. "Just cats that looked like him."

"Don't give up hope," Matty said. "I'll bet he just went roaming. He'll be home soon."

Charlie sighed. Then he held up his Game Boy. "Hey, do you want to play for a while? I've got Rayman 3."

"Awesome." Matty pulled up the same chair he'd used when he made his sketch.

"Do you guys want something to drink?" Hazel asked.

"Sure. Water is fine," Matty said.

"We have some Sprite in the refrigerator," Charlie said eagerly.

"Sprite it is, then," Matty amended. "Make it a round, please."

Hazel went into the kitchen and got three Sprites out of the fridge. She grabbed a bag of tortilla chips and a jar of salsa.

She balanced it all against her chest and turned toward the bedroom.

"Oh!" she cried. Matty was there, blocking her way.

"Charlie's a sweet kid, but I hope you know—I didn't actually come here to play video games." He slowly removed each item from her arms and set them down on the counter.

His fingers brushed her collarbone. Chills rippled across her chest.

He tilted his head, gazed at her with an adoring expression, and brushed his lips over hers. "Hazel," he whispered.

She put her arms around his neck and gave in. They leaned into each other. The feel of Matty's lips made Hazel dizzy. She struggled to maintain control.

It's okay, she thought. *This is good. This is real. It's not like what happened last summer.*

The memory of that night in August hit her like a bucket of ice water. She hadn't told anyone about it—and she didn't want to make the same mistake again.

She broke away. "Charlie's waiting."

"He's got his Game Boy," Matty protested, putting his arms around her again. "He doesn't even know we're gone."

"I know, but . . ." She smiled uncertainly. "It's . . . I just don't think . . ."

He huffed. His brown eyes narrowed.

Hazel panicked. Was he angry? Did he think she had led him on?

Then she remembered that she was a PLD. Would Sylvia care if Josh was mad at her? Not likely. Hazel had the right to say no. If *that* was all he wanted from her, then he was a jerk.

Matty recovered quickly. He smiled. "Sorry, Hazel. I don't mean to rush you."

"It's—it's okay," she murmured.

For about an hour they all sat in Matty's room, playing video games. Matty let Charlie win. Each time, Charlie jumped up on his bed, doing a little victory dance. It sent Hazel and Matty into fits of hysterics.

After a while, Hazel reached over and checked the watch on Matty's right hand. "Almost midnight."

Matty yawned. "Wow. I should go."

"Yeah, I guess you should," Hazel agreed reluctantly. He reached out a hand to help her up.

She walked him to the door and they kissed for a few more minutes. She didn't want it to stop. Ever. But he had to go.

"Lock this door, okay?" he instructed.

"I will," Hazel promised. She tingled as she watched him go through the arch and down the walk to his car.

"Lock it," he insisted again before getting in. He started the engine and pulled away.

No longer caring about seeming cool, Hazel watched until she could no longer see Matty's taillights. Then she shut the door and turned the dead bolt.

She padded back down the hall to find Charlie fast asleep. She put an extra blanket over him and shut off his light.

She walked back to the living room to study. As she crossed the threshold, her cell phone went off.

Could it be Matty? She dug the phone out of her pack and checked the caller ID. ID BLOCKED. She pressed the connect button and put it to her ear.

"Hello?"

"Are you alone in the house?" The voice was disguised, midway between a growl and a hoarse whisper.

"Hey, guys," she said merrily. "Guess what!"

"Because I'm in the study, waiting for you."

"Ha ha! Wrong!" she said triumphantly. "I checked the locks, inside and out. You are so lying!"

"But I'm dead. I'm a ghost. I'm incorporeal."

"No, you're Katie and Chrissie Darling," Hazel said, laughing. "Matty came by. Thank you for sending him over."

"You let him in the house?"

"Damn straight," she said proudly.

"Without a chaperone? You are a bad babysitter!"

"The evilest," she confirmed.

"You will pay!"

"No, I will get paid." She carried the phone into the kitchen, remembering then that she had left dishes in Charlie's room. She would have to clean them up before Mr. Pollins got home.

"No. You will get laid," the voice said. Then a crescendo of evil laughter preceded the dial tone.

Hazel giggled, appreciative of the prank. In their own twisted way, it meant the PLDs cared.

Then she tiptoed into Charlie's room, got the dirty dishes, and carried everything into the kitchen. She was drying the last of the three glasses when the landline rang. She grabbed the receiver off the wall unit and put it to her ear.

"Pollins residence."

"*Someone should warn you.*" Another disguised voice. Deeper this time.

"Wow. You guys must be bored. I know. I suck. I'm a bad babysitter." She put the glasses on the shelf, closed the cabinet door, and hung the dish towel back on the hook beside the door to the pantry.

"*You think I'm one of your friends? News flash. They're not your friends.*"

The caller snickered. The sound was rough—mean. It rendered Hazel speechless.

"*They would turn on you in a second if it came down to you or one of them. You should watch your back. Popular girls are only out for themselves. If they're ever threatened, they'll throw you to the wolves.*"

"Who is this?" she said, shaken.

The dial tone buzzed in her ear.

She hung up the phone and replayed the voice in her mind. Who did it sound like? She felt certain that she recognized it somehow.

The landline rang.

Don't answer it, Hazel told herself. But Mr. Pollins had instructed her to.

"Pollins residence."

"Time for some homework?" the growling voice asked. *"How about this: if a horse bleeds to death at a gallon a minute and a cat bleeds to death at a cup a minute, which animal suffers more?"*

Hazel's stomach clenched. Hard. "Hey, whoever? You're sick, and this isn't funny."

"I should know the answer. I killed them both. And I need more. I'm right outside the door. Guess who's going to be next?"

Hazel slammed down the phone.

It rang again. She stared at it.

She backed away, hunched over, with her arms wrapped around her body. This was beyond a prank. This was extreme.

But . . . it had to be the PLDs. Didn't it?

What if it isn't? a voice inside her asked. *What if it's the psycho who killed Jilly's horse?*

Hazel hurried down the hall to check on Charlie. He was asleep, snoring softly.

The cordless in the hall blared, and a loud banging shook the front door. Hazel jumped and let out a small shriek.

She put the cordless to her ear. The voice on the other end hissed, *"Charlie's sleeping, nice and peaceful. I'm right outside. What are you going to do?"*

Hazel's heart thundered as she crept toward the door. The brass knob rattled violently. Had she locked it? Yes, after Matty left. But would the bolt hold?

There was only one thing to do. She had to call the police. If she could just sneak a peek at whoever was outside first . . .

She took a ragged breath and moved slowly, cautiously toward the peephole.

Oh, please, please let it be a joke. . . .

The caller's words rang in her ear. *Guess who's going to be next?*

Hazel put her hand on the knob.

The door burst open—and she screamed!

CHAPTER SEVEN

Hazel leapt out of the way as the front door slammed against the wall.

"God! Oh God, Hazel! I'm sorry. I didn't mean to startle you." Charlie's father lurched forward to grab the door, holding out a reassuring hand. "It's just me, kiddo. My key was stuck in the lock for a minute. Just me. Don't be scared."

Hazel panted, struggling to catch her breath. She switched off the cordless and held it in both hands.

"Are you all right?"

She cleared her throat and tried to smile, having no idea if she actually managed it. She wondered how much she should tell him.

"There was a wrong number. I think it was kids pranking. But they were really trying to scare me—"

"Oh. Well, we can't have that. I'll try redialing and seeing if I can find out who they were. I'm sorry about that, Hazel. What did they say?"

She hesitated, and in that space, he asked, "How's Charlie?"

"He had a pretty good night. He's asleep now."

Mr. Pollins sighed. His shoulders slumped. "He's still awfully overwhelmed."

Hazel figured Mr. Pollins was pretty overwhelmed too. He looked tired. Bags formed under his bloodshot eyes. He yawned.

"These past few nights I've had to work late and I'm not as young as I used to be." He glanced over at her. "Did Charlie talk about Isotope?"

She nodded. He looked at her very sadly. "I don't know if I should tell him this or not, but I found Isotope."

Hazel's heart thudded. "Oh. No."

"He'd been dead a couple of days. I think he ate something. Snail bait, maybe. I put him in the trash. Don't tell Charlie. I need to do it myself."

"Snail bait?" she asked. "You mean he was poisoned. Not . . . injured?"

"Not a scratch. I can only hope he didn't suffer." He reached for his wallet. "How much do I owe you?"

Hazel was grateful that Mr. Pollins had insisted on walking her to her car. She set her cell phone in the cup holder between the two front seats. Then she slid in and started the engine.

"Thanks again." Mr. Pollins gave her a wave and went back into the house.

As Hazel pulled away from the curb, her phone lit up. She grabbed it out of the cup holder.

It was a text message.

YRSECRETPAL2PURPLEHAZE: Here, kitty kitty!

"You guys," she said, her voice wavering.

✢   ✢   ✢

PERSONAL BLOG

HAPPY2BME

HAZEL THINKS HER FRIENDS ARE SWEET? SHE'LL LEARN. THEY'RE SWEET AS SNAIL BAIT. OR SWEET AS HORSE MEAT.

I TRIED TO WARN HER. I'M RIGHT UNDER HER NOSE AND SHE DOESN'T EVEN SEE ME. IT'S NOT MY FAULT IF SHE GETS HURT. AND SOMEONE IS GOING TO HURT . . . VERY SOON.

THE FEELING IS BUILDING AGAIN. SO QUICKLY.

NO ONE AND NOTHING CAN STOP IT.

✢   ✢   ✢

Ms. Carpentier was not at all pleased.

It wasn't a good way to start a school week.

"Your grades in this class have taken a real tumble," the teacher scolded. She clasped her hands and leaned forward—probably something she'd learned in a seminar on how to relate to her students.

Hazel stood in front of her desk with her backpack on. Breona slouched beside her.

"Both of you are falling behind. Now, whatever is wrong between you, I want you to sort it out or go see the school counselor."

"Like couples therapy? Hate to break it to you, Ms. C., but I don't swing that way," Breona said, snickering. The sound was raspy, familiar. Hazel wondered: had she heard it before?

"Breona . . ." Ms. Carpentier rolled her eyes.

"Fine." Breona took a breath and turned to Hazel. "I'm sorry I called you a bitch and accused you of stealing a carnation that the cheerleaders bought—*for the football team only.*"

"Apology accepted," Hazel muttered.

"So." Ms. Carpentier leaned back in her chair. A self-satisfied grin curled the corners of her mouth. "Are we all settled?"

Hazel nodded.

"Good. Then get to class."

Hazel turned and hurried away. Only two minutes to get to next period!

She jogged through the halls, thinking.

Breona's weird laugh. That raspy snicker. Could Breona have made the calls to the Pollins house?

A month ago, Hazel wouldn't have thought it possible. Then again, she would never have thought Breona would have a meltdown over a carnation either.

But it wasn't just a carnation. It was Matty's carnation.

Is that what this is about? Hazel wondered. *Is she freaking me out to get back at me for dating the guy she wants?*

No. Don't go there, Hazel thought. *Matty's my boyfriend. Breona must know that. It would be crazy for her to think she has a chance with him.*

Hazel rushed through the busy corridor. Lakshmi trotted up beside her.

"Hey, Hazel, wait up! I have something for you." She pushed two sheets of paper at her.

"What's this?"

"Next week's chemistry quiz. I already wrote in most of the answers."

"Oh my God. Where did you get this?" Hazel asked, swallowing hard. She and Lakshmi had never been the kind of girls who cheated on tests.

"My mom was copying it for Carpentier in the main office. Take it. Maybe you could share it with your friends. You know, let them know where you got it?"

Hazel turned. Lakshmi was blushing.

Payback, Hazel realized. Lakshmi was looking for juice from this little favor. Too bad Sylvia would never do anything nice for Lakshmi in return. Maybe thank her. But that would be about it.

"Hey, thanks," she said warmly, opening up her backpack to deposit the test. "That is so nice of you." Hazel's purple PLD scrunchie was sitting on top.

"Here," she said, impulsively handing it over. "From us. Just don't tell anyone."

Lakshmi's eyes grew wide. "Oh, wow, thanks!"

The bell rang. Lakshmi waved the scrunchie over her head. "Thanks a lot, Haze. See you later!"

"Lakshmi! Don't wear it in school!" Hazel called after her. Then she turned and ran to class. *I'd better remember to get to Sav-on to replace that. If Sylvia finds out I gave my scrunchie to Lakshmi, she'll kill me.*

✛   ✛   ✛

Hazel's phone vibrated during sixth-period English.

PLDEL2PURPLEHAZE: Can U sit 4 me 2nite?

PURPLEHAZE2PLDEL: Whaddup?

PLDEL2PURPLEHAZE: Want 2 see Brandon. Itz a secret. Plz

don't tell Sylvia!

✛   ✛   ✛

The Darling twins stared dully at Hazel.

"We're dead," Katie informed her.

"Not tonight," Hazel said. "Pull that again and I'll tell Sylvia how bad you've been. And you don't want Sylvia mad at you, do you?"

The twins opened their blue eyes wide. They squealed in mock fright and ran to their bedrooms, slamming the doors behind them.

That's better, Hazel thought. *At least they'll be out of my hair for a while.*

Hazel took off her coat and strolled around the main floor. The last place she wanted to be was back at the creepy Darling house, especially after her weird night at Charlie's. Hazel's nerves were jangled for sure, but Ellen had begged until she folded.

And anyway, Hazel decided, what could be better than helping out a pair of star-crossed lovers?

Romeo and Juliet. Brandon and Ellen, she mused. *They were all in the same boat. Of course, Romeo and Juliet's story didn't turn out so well in the end.*

Hazel walked into the kitchen. The twins' mother had left a vegetable lasagna in the microwave. Hazel was supposed to open the salad packet and pour some shiitake mushroom dressing on it. That was the extent of "fixing dinner."

The doorbell rang. The twins burst out of their bedrooms and thundered toward the front door.

"Katie, Chrissie! Let me get it!" Hazel shouted. But before she could stop them, they unlocked the door and jerked it open.

Sylvia stood on the threshold, blinking at her in surprise.

"What are *you* doing here?" she asked, walking into the room.

"I'm . . . I'm taking care of the twins," Hazel answered.

"But this is *Ellen's* gig," Sylvia argued.

"I offered to take it for her. Because . . . um, something came up."

For a moment, Sylvia remained silent.

"No, no, no, Hazel," she said after a moment. "This is not something we do. We don't trade assignments."

The twins were intrigued, looking from one PLD to the other.

"The parents like consistency," Sylvia explained. "That's one of the reasons they come to us. They know what to expect. They call and I arrange the schedule. It's part of our service."

"Oh." Hazel knit her brows together, confused. "I'm sorry. I was just trying to help out."

Sylvia sighed and shook her head. "What am I saying? Of course you didn't know better. This is *Ellen's* fault."

The microwave dinged. Hazel went into the kitchen while Sylvia and the twins waited in the living room.

She popped open the microwave door and checked the lasagna. It was only lukewarm, so she added a few minutes. She dumped the salad into a white ceramic bowl, unscrewed the cap on the bottle of dressing, sniffed it experimentally, and poured it on.

She placed the salad on the spotless slate table in the breakfast nook. The Darlings had a maid service. Hazel had found that out the first time she sat for the girls. She had told Katie to help clear the table after dinner. Katie had said, "Oh, don't worry. We have people for that."

The microwave beeped. Hazel put on a pair of hot mitts and took out the lasagna.

"You guys?" she called. "Dinner's ready."

After a couple of minutes, the twins and Sylvia swept into the room.

"Oh! Tell me you're not having any of *that*!" Sylvia said, wrinkling her nose.

"I, well . . ." Hazel glanced at the tray, disappointed. She had never had vegetable lasagna. In her house, it would be considered "fancy."

Sylvia picked up two plates and said to Hazel, "Give them some milk. Then come with me. I have something cool to show you."

Hazel's stomach growled. Thankfully, no one else heard it. She poured two glasses of milk and set them down before the twins.

"Eat," she urged.

"We don't eat," Katie said. "We're dead."

"No. You're in huge trouble if you don't eat," Sylvia cut in. "We're back in ten, and if you haven't eaten half of that . . ." She drew a finger across her throat.

Katie and Chrissie quickly picked up their forks and dug in.

On their way down the hall, Sylvia whispered to Hazel, "Do you know what's in that stuff? Wheat paste. The same kind we used to glue construction paper together in elementary school."

"Ew," Hazel said, grimacing.

"Exactly. But come see something tasty."

Sylvia pushed open the door at the end of the hall. She wiggled her fingertips at Hazel as if to say, *This way.* Hazel followed her—right into Cynthia Darling's bedroom.

"Um . . . isn't this off-limits?" she asked.

Sylvia went straight to the Macintosh on the desk next to the closet. "Don't be silly. Watch this." She typed in a line and clicked the mouse.

As Hazel bent over her shoulder, the screen filled with the words BROOKHAVEN HIGH SCHOOL STUDENT RECORDS.

"Oh my God! Really?" Hazel asked, leaning closer.

"Really," Sylvia said. She hit enter.

RESTRICTED: ACCESS CODE REQUIRED.

"Oh," Hazel said, deflated. "Too bad."

"Pffft," Sylvia scoffed. She typed in a string of characters—they came out as asterisks—and hit return. The log-in screen dissolved, and a list of files blinked into view.

"I don't believe it! You're in!"

"*Mais oui!* So. Who do you want dirt on?" Sylvia asked. A list of names scrolled down the screen.

Hazel watched, stunned. These were students' "permanent records"—all the stuff the administration put in student files . . . and never let them see.

"Oh, look," Sylvia chirped. "Here's Breona's little friend Jenna Babcock."

She hummed to herself as she highlighted Jenna's name. "Cheer, cheer, cheer. Three-point-two GPA. Wow, she really is boring."

"Yeah," Hazel said, her eyes devouring the screen. She couldn't believe it. Was she really seeing this?

"Ooh, how about little Lakshmi Sharma?" Sylvia suggested. "Let's see. She's been in the a cappella group for three years. Boring! Hey, wait a minute. Who was your friend from last year? Was it Joy?" Sylvia tapped the screen with her acrylic nail. "Joy Krasner?"

"Yes," Hazel affirmed. "But she moved. . . ."

Sylvia scrolled back up the screen. "Nonetheless . . . here she is." She highlighted Joy's name. The single line opened up into a file. Together they scanned Joy's grades, which were pretty good. Her extracurriculars were cool too: drama club, film club. . . .

"Oh, look here. She was seeing Clasen," Sylvia pointed out.

Ms. Clasen was the school psychologist.

. . . Joy is still struggling with her bulimia. . . . Episodes consistent with original diagnosis . . . The San Jose Center for Eating Disorders has received her intake summary. . . .

Sylvia looked from the screen to Hazel. "Did you know Joy was going to the loony bin?"

Hazel shook her head as she read on. . . . It didn't make sense.

Sylvia opened a new window and typed, SAN JOSE CENTER FOR EATING DISORDERS into Google.

San Jose Center for Eating Disorders, located in East San Jose, is a residential treatment facility dedicated to providing effective, quality care for children, adolescents, and adults. The average length of stay is three months, although some patients remain on-site for up to twelve months.

"Oh my God," Hazel whispered.

"Wait. You mean you really didn't know about any of this?" Sylvia pressed, sounding mildly incredulous.

"We haven't been writing. I sent her some e-mails, but she didn't reply. I thought . . . new school, moving on. . . ." She covered her mouth. "Poor Joy."

Sylvia sighed and pushed away from the keyboard. "Poor communication," she said. "That's not the way friends treat friends, Haze. Friends tell each other *everything*."

Hazel nodded as she continued to read. She crossed her arms over her chest, taking in the pictures of low buildings trailing with bougainvillea, the smiling portraits of the staff. Joy was in a place like this?

Her old blog had been titled JOYFULLGRL. She had always seemed so happy.

"Oh God. I never knew," Hazel confessed. "We hung out all school year and I didn't have a clue."

"That wouldn't happen with us," Sylvia informed her. "Sure, the PLDs are hard on each other. We tease each other a lot, but we're totally solid. We let each other know things. We are each other's support. We have to stay tight."

"I guess I didn't realize how rare it was. Or how important," Hazel said.

"We are the most popular girls in school," Sylvia stated without a trace of bragging. "Breona and her cheerleaders think they are, but that is so stupid, because after high school, they are going to go nowhere. This is their finest hour, and they don't even know it."

Sylvia perched on Cynthia's bed. Her eyes shone. "Why? Because we're smarter than they are. We're the ones in the middle of the herd. Just us. Just the PLDs. Other people are going to come and go. But we're going to have each other. Real lives. And real friends—forever. When you have a crisis, you can come to us. When something wonderful happens, we want to hear about it first." She paused. "But you have to share, Hazel. Let your friends really know you."

Sylvia held out her arms. "Look at me. I'm an open book. Ask me something."

Hazel blinked at her. "Like what?"

"Anything. Like, something I wouldn't tell just anybody. Something I would only tell a *friend*."

"Um . . ."

Sylvia gave her dark hair a shake. "See? You're too shy to ask me. You don't think you have the right. But you can ask me *anything*. So go ahead."

Hazel thought about the games of truth or dare she had played at sleepovers.

"Okay. Are you a virgin?" She blushed uncontrollably, but Sylvia snickered, unconcerned.

"I lost my virginity when I was fourteen. In France." She looked expectantly at Hazel. "What about you?"

"Oh. God, I . . ." She rubbed her forehead. "I, um . . ."

"Remember, it's about trust." She gave Hazel a slow grin, reached down, and opened the bottom drawer of the bedside table.

"This will help." She pulled out a bottle of Cointreau.

"Whoa!" Hazel exclaimed. "Do all the parents stash this much alcohol around?"

"More or less. Some message for the kiddies, huh?" Sylvia opened the bottle and took a hefty swig. Then she wiped off the lip and handed it to Hazel.

"Um, I . . ." She looked down at the bottle.

"Oh, go ahead. There aren't any glasses in here anyway."

Hazel hesitated. Sylvia took the bottle, put it to Hazel's lips, and gave it a little tip. The thick liquor splashed into Hazel's mouth. It was good—orange-flavored. She drank some more.

Sylvia smiled at her. Then she reached into the drawer again and brought out a joint.

"Shut up!" Hazel cried.

Sylvia winced. "Haze. No one says, 'Shut up' anymore."

"I know. It's just—we can't smoke that." She gestured to the joint. "She'll know."

"You're right." Sylvia dropped it back into the drawer and shut it. "And *I* know you have a secret, Hazel. Something you're not telling me. But if you want to be a PLD, you have to share."

Hazel met Sylvia's bright blue stare. She thought about Joy—how she didn't know anything about her, despite the fact that they were supposed to have been close. She didn't want that to happen again. She wanted real friends. Friends till the end.

She grabbed the bottle of Cointreau, took a swig, and made a decision. "All right. I worked at a stable over the summer. There was this guy."

Sylvia waited. "Like, a ranch hand?"

Hazel nodded. "He led trail rides. His name was Andy. He was maybe in his mid-twenties. He bought beer one night. We had a little too much to drink—well, I did anyway. . . ." She let her words trail off.

"That was the first time?" Sylvia asked.

Hazel nodded again.

"Did you regret it?" Sylvia gazed at her sympathetically.

"It all happened so fast." Hazel's voice cracked. "God, I sound like an after-school special."

"Oh, Haze." Sylvia sighed, pulling her into a hug. "You're so incredibly sweet."

Hazel melted against her shoulder. It was such a relief to finally tell someone the truth. She had held it in for so long.

"I can't believe I did it. I wish I could take it back," she muttered.

Sylvia pulled away and looked into Hazel's damp eyes. She pushed an errant piece of hair away from Hazel's forehead. "Yeah, I get that. But it could have been much worse. I know you're upset. But this isn't as bad as you think. If you didn't get pregnant and you don't have a disease, let it go. Move on."

She cocked her head. "You've been pretty sheltered, haven't you? Your parents . . . I don't think I've ever seen them around Brookhaven."

"My parents?" Hazel guffawed. "My parents haven't been anywhere. The other night, my mom said something about how people in Scotland should learn to speak English."

Sylvia chortled. "Oh my God! How clueless is that?"

Then the mood shifted back. "Listen, I'm glad you told me," Sylvia said earnestly. "It's a sacred trust."

"Thank you. I'm glad I told you too," Hazel replied.

Sylvia returned to the computer and pulled up the screen with the student files again. She dropped down to WU, BREONA.

"Let's see here . . ." she murmured.

Intrigued, Hazel bent over Sylvia's shoulder. Sylvia pushed the bottle of Cointreau toward her, and Hazel had another drink.

"Hmm, this is interesting. Seems Breona is having some problems. She's on *antidepressants*."

"Whoa," Hazel breathed.

"That might explain why she's such a bitch." Sylvia paused for a moment, thinking. "Wait. No, it doesn't."

Chuckling softly, Hazel took another swig of Cointreau. If you opened your mouth when you drank it, the evaporation was like a little flame going off. It was an interesting feeling.

"Hmm, nothing about her drug bust. The paperwork must not be complete."

"Wait a minute," Hazel said, her thoughts slowing—growing fuzzy. "The drug bust. You guys called in antidepressants?"

"Well . . ." Sylvia shrugged.

Hazel frowned. "Come on. You said friends share."

"Maybe we put a few extra little things in her locker."

"What?" Hazel nearly choked.

"Oh, please, Breona's drug use is well known. We didn't put

anything in there that hadn't been in there before."

Hazel stared at her. "So you planted the drugs, and then you called it in?"

"Yes. And with good reason." Sylvia pushed the chair away from the monitor and folded her hands across her lap. "Let me tell you why I hate Breona. Because everyone thinks it's just about Josh, and that's not true."

Hazel settled back onto the bed to listen.

"Breona and I started out as friends," Sylvia began. "In fifth grade. We were the smartest girls. And the prettiest. We were in all the same activities. We told everyone we were best friends forever." She smiled faintly. "But that wasn't enough for Breona. She was jealous. She didn't want anyone else hanging out with me. If they tried, she'd throw a tantrum or be mean. She started actually hitting the other girls. I didn't do any of it, but I got blamed right along with her. I spent more time sitting in the principal's office waiting for my mom to pick me up than I did in class."

"Yow," Hazel said. "That sucks."

"Hugely. I told my mother what was going on. Thank God she believed me. She said I couldn't play with Breona anymore. That was more than fine with me. Then Breona went nuts. She wouldn't leave me alone. She kept calling my house and coming by, begging me to be her friend." Sylvia looked at Hazel. "*Serious* boundary issues."

"No doubt," Hazel said, taking another swig of Cointreau. She felt pleasantly dizzy.

"Things kept escalating. My parents talked to her parents. My mom suggested therapy, and *Breona's* mom went nuts."

"No way. *Really?*"

"Really. We just wanted them to stay away from us. Life went on. Fifth grade ended. We were zoned for different middle schools—proving there *is* a God." Sylvia ironically made the sign of the cross. "I thought I was free of Breona Wu."

Her voice dropped. She took a deep breath, a dainty sip of Cointreau. . . .

"And then my dog," she said finally. "His name was Asterix."

"What happened to him?" Hazel asked.

"I don't know." Sylvia's eyes welled. "He disappeared. I couldn't prove that Breona had anything to do with it. Even though I *knew*. People said he must have gone out the side gate. But we *always* closed that gate."

A single tear slid down Sylvia's cheek. Hazel had never seen her look so vulnerable.

"Oh, Sylvia, I'm so sorry," she murmured. "That's . . . that's just awful."

"She kind of haunted me after that. I'd get calls, but there would be no one on the other end. She'd make up terrible stories about me and tell them behind my back. I lost a few friends from it. She could be so convincing."

Sylvia took a hefty swallow of the Cointreau. "And now we both go to Brookhaven. And nothing I have ever done to her can begin to compare to what she's done to me." She pushed a dark tendril of hair away from her forehead. "No one knows about this except the other PLDs—and now you. I hate her, Hazel. I really, *really* do."

"I don't blame you," Hazel replied, taking Sylvia's hand. Then she thought of something.

"Sylvia," she began. "I've been getting these weird phone calls . . . not the ones from you guys. They're different. Really scary. And when Breona saw my green carnation, she went totally insane. She called me a bitch and ran out of class."

"Oh God." Sylvia pressed her fingertips against her forehead.

"There's more. Charlie's dad found Isotope. He might have been poisoned."

Sylvia gasped. "That poor little kid."

Hazel took a deep breath. "And now . . . with Jilly's horse. I wonder. . . ."

"It has to be Breona." Sylvia exhaled slowly. "We have to be very careful. All of us. God knows what she's capable of."

"Sylvia?" a child's voice called impatiently. "We finished our dinner. We're supposed to take our baths tonight."

Sylvia sighed. "Duty calls." She hit the function keys to shut Cynthia's computer down. Hazel stretched and put the cap back on the Cointreau bottle, replacing it in the drawer. She straightened up the papers around the keyboard.

"I'll show you how to check the files yourself," Sylvia promised, standing up. "You need to arm yourself, Hazel. School is like war. You know that now, don't you?"

"Of course I do," Hazel replied.

"Of course you do," Sylvia agreed. She cupped Hazel's cheek. "It's okay. You're okay now. You're with us."

"Thanks," Hazel said. And suddenly, sharply, she did feel a little bit better.

"C'mon, I'll help you give these monsters their baths," Sylvia offered. "But if they pull that 'dead' crap again . . ." She gestured as if she were pushing someone's head underwater.

"What are we going to do about Breona?" Hazel asked. "She's an accident waiting to happen."

"Breona will keep at us until she gets a reaction," Sylvia continued. "That's her style. Don't worry. I'm thinking about payback. In a big, big way."

Hazel laughed, but a funny feeling burrowed under her scalp.

Must be all the liquor, she thought. She turned from the bedroom, closing the door behind her.

HAPTER EIGHT

The next morning Hazel was driving to school when a text message came in on her phone. At a stoplight she pulled the phone out of her purse to check it.

YRSECRETPAL2PURPLEHAZE: Wnt 2 plA, sxC?

She giggled. Sexy? Was it from Matty? Someone behind her beeped and Hazel glanced up. *Whoops.* The light had changed.

She replaced the phone and drove. When she got to the next light, she wanted to write something back, but there was already another message.

YRSECRETPAL2PURPLEHAZE: Wnt 2 di? Sum1 is going 2. mayB U!

Hazel caught her breath and gingerly set the phone on the seat.

Alicia Keys's "Karma" blared at her.

Hazel picked up the phone to check the ID and her finger jerked, depressing the connect button before she realized that she had just put the call through. Grimacing, she held the phone to her ear.

"Hello?" she said.

"The horse was cool," said a muffled voice. *"You'd be cooler."*

"That's not funny," she said. "Who is this?"

"Someone you know. Someone you trust. And you shouldn't."

"Breona?" she said, trying to sound annoyed.

"Who do you think it is? Breona Wu? Or one of your so-called friends? You shouldn't trust them. You shouldn't trust me."

Hazel disconnected. The phone immediately played again.

"Shit," Hazel muttered. She made the connection and put the cell to her ear. "Okay, listen. I've had enough."

Hazel heard someone breathing. She was about to hang up when a voice said, "Hazel?"

"Matty?" Hazel asked.

"Hi!" he whispered. She could barely recognize his voice. "I'm at practice. I just wanted to talk to you. I didn't get a chance to last night."

"I know. I had to sit for the Darling twins again." She hesitated. "Did you just call me about a minute ago?"

"No. Why?"

"No reason," Hazel covered.

"Are you going to the game tonight?"

"I think so."

"Great," Matty cheered. "Sylvia told me there's going to be a party at Ellen's after the game."

There is? Sylvia hadn't told *her* that. Hazel guessed Sylvia had finally pressured Ellen to the breaking point. The party was on.

"Are you showing?" she asked him.

"Do you want me to?"

She smiled, pulling into the school lot. "That'd be cool," she replied.

"Then I'm there. Whoops. Coach is on the prowl. Later, Hazel."

He disconnected.

That night Hazel stood in the corner of Ellen's living room, nursing her beer. This was more of a kegger than the other PLD parties Hazel had been to. The music was up and there were more people. Hazel preferred the smaller, quieter gatherings.

Hazel knew Ellen didn't have a mom, but she wasn't sure if she had died, or left, or what. Ellen's house was very much like a bachelor pad, with black leather couches and red lacquer bookshelves and a coffee table. There were animation cels in red frames on the walls and a rec room dominated by a pool table and an old-fashioned jukebox that played real 45s—old-fashioned singles.

Ellen had confessed that some of the 45s had been stolen during the last party she threw. That was why her father had said she couldn't have any more parties.

At least until now, Hazel thought. *When Sylvia commanded that it be so.*

Sylvia gathered the PLDs in Ellen's kitchen. "A toast to us." She poured Jim Beam into five shot glasses. The others touched their glasses to hers.

"To damnation!" Sylvia said joyfully.

"To damnation!" the others chorused.

Everyone threw back.

About an hour into the party, the football team finally showed up.

Brandon strode into the kitchen, carrying an enormous stuffed monkey. It was bright blue and about five feet tall. It was creepy looking, with its big, blank, happy face and blindly staring eyes.

"Oh my gosh! It's Monkey Boy!" Ellen trilled, kissing first the monkey and then Brandon.

"Monkey Boy?" Hazel asked.

"It's my pet name for him," Ellen confided. "Because he's about as sophisticated as a monkey."

"Sweet." Hazel chuckled. "Is it your birthday?"

"No," Ellen said happily, kissing him again.

"It's *not*?" Brandon joked. He put his arms around Ellen and hugged her tightly. "I just saw him and I knew El had to have him."

A bold move! Hazel thought. *Go, Ellen. Who cares what Sylvia thinks? You guys get yours.*

As if she had read Hazel's mind, Sylvia approached. She walked up to the enormous blue monkey, flicked its nose, and gave Brandon a pointed look.

"What's this?"

"Monkey Boy. And he's adorable," Ellen said, giving him a kiss on his perpetually upturned mouth.

Sylvia sneered. "Whatever makes you happy, *ma belle*." She turned and clapped. "*Alors, mes petites!* Tonight we're watching *I Know What You Did Last Summer*. Everyone go into the rec room and find a comfortable place to sit."

The partyers followed Sylvia into the room. Brandon and Ellen walked toward the jukebox.

"Nobody steal anything!" Sylvia called out. There was scattered laughter, but Ellen looked embarrassed.

Then Matty joined the party. He sidled up to Hazel and put an arm around her. "Hey, sexy. I guess I got here just in time."

He looked hot, dressed all in black. His eyes were so dark they practically hypnotized her.

Someone put in a DVD on the wide-screen TV. As the movie began, people scrambled for seats. Hazel and Matty grabbed an upholstered chair, which Matty pushed up against one of the couches. Ellen sat on the couch with Monkey Boy in her lap. Brandon was beside her; Megan flanked her on the other side.

Matty made a show of putting his arm around the creature and Hazel both. The girls giggled.

"Don't touch my boyfriend!" Ellen hissed at Matty.

"Hey, are you messing with my girlfriend?" Brandon said, grabbing Monkey Boy around the neck and bopping Matty on the head.

"Shh!" Sylvia snapped.

Brandon let go of Monkey Boy, and Ellen petted the creature's fuzzy blue fur. It stared straight ahead, its crazy cartoon face utterly devoid of expression.

"That thing is creepy," Matty whispered to Hazel.

They touched heads, grinning.

The movie started. There it was, the hit-and-run that started it all. Hazel shifted, a little bored. She'd seen this movie a couple of times already, and she didn't think it was that good.

"Watch," Ellen whispered to Hazel and Matty. "Soon Sylvia will announce that we should have watched *Diabolique*."

Hmm, cocky, Hazel thought, approving. *Maybe now that Brandon's gone public with their relationship, Ellen will stand up to Sylvia a little more.*

"I finally gave up and ordered *Diabolique* online," Sylvia announced. "It should be here in a few days."

No one dared shush her, but Ellen and Hazel had to stifle their giggles.

After a few more minutes, Hazel shifted again and hid a little yawn. Matty murmured, "Want to go out back?"

He gave her a hopeful smile and she nodded. They both tiptoed out of the room.

Outside, the air was brisk but not too chilly. Ellen's yard smelled of night-blooming jasmine. There was a Jacuzzi and a large gas barbecue and, beyond them, a vast stand of bamboo.

Matty walked her into the tall stalks. It was very dark. She couldn't see him. But she could smell him and feel him as he put his arms around her. She closed her eyes and he lowered his mouth to hers. . . .

He kissed her, hard, as his hands pressed her against the length of his body. He was so urgent, so needy, Hazel wondered if he'd devour her entirely. He kissed her again. And again. Then he pulled her gently down to the ground. He kept kissing her, cradling her head while his hand worked its way up the front of her hoodie.

She had no idea how long they made out. Her back ached and her wrists were sore, but she didn't care.

Finally, he exhaled slowly. He sat up, coming back to earth. "Want a beer or something?" he asked.

"That'd be great. Thanks."

Matty kissed her on the lips, lightly, and sighed again. He got to his feet and said, "I'll be right back."

He made his way out of their bamboo hideaway.

Hazel heard another set of footsteps nearby, shuffling through the undergrowth. She peered through the darkness, but she could see only shadows.

"C'mon, Brandon." It was Sylvia.

"Sly, it's just not cool, okay?" Brandon argued.

"Why not?" Sylvia asked, pulling him close.

Brandon groaned. "You—you have Josh."

Sylvia snorted. "Josh is a cheating pig. And besides, that never bothered you before. What bothers you now is that you have sweet little Ellen. She has no idea what a bastard you are. You'll just use her and lose her, like all the others."

"No," Brandon said. "It's not like that."

"Oh, come on. People don't change." Sylvia ran her hands through Brandon's hair, down his chest.

"I *am* changing. I'm not going to do that to her."

Hazel heard the uncertainty in his voice. It made her wince. Maybe Sylvia knew him better than he knew himself.

Yeah, Sylvia, who is being unfaithful to her boyfriend and who's hitting on the guy Ellen likes . . .

"You're full of it, Brandon. You know what you are. I should tell Ellen—"

"You leave her alone!" Brandon hissed. He pushed Sylvia away. "You power-tripping bitch. Maybe I'll tell Josh—"

"Oh, please. Like he would believe you."

"Hey, I know things about you that other people don't, okay?" Brandon challenged. "I've been cool up till now. But you mess things up with Ellen, and—"

"Don't you ever threaten me. You're a lowlife, Brandon, and you know it. Your father pumps gas and your mother—"

"You shut up!"

"Watch it, babe! I will *so* cut you down to size. You know I can. And you know I will."

Brandon left, his footsteps fading. After a few seconds, Sylvia made her way back to the house as well.

Hazel stayed silent, trying to make sense of what she had heard.

Then Matty returned. "Hazel?" he whispered.

"Matty, I need to go inside for a second."

"Sure thing."

They left their bamboo hideaway. Matty went to the rec room to watch some of the movie. Hazel found Sylvia reapplying her lipstick in the bathroom.

"Hey, babe," Sylvia said, looking at Hazel in the mirror. "Want some lipstick?" She offered Hazel a tube of red.

Hazel took it and smoothed it carefully over her bottom lip. "Sylvia?" She paused. "I'm confused about something."

"What could that be?" Sylvia asked, picking up her beer from where she'd rested it on the edge of the sink.

"You told Ellen to stay away from Brandon because he wasn't a nice guy. If that's the case, why are you hooking up with him?"

Sylvia laughed. Hazel didn't.

Sylvia took a breath and said, "Okay. I think he's hot. I have a thing for him *physically*. But I can handle that. Separate it. It wouldn't be that way for Ellen. He'd use her and break her heart."

"And you're sure that's the reason?" Hazel asked, handing back the lipstick. "There's nothing else? Nothing more *personal*?"

"I am." Sylvia smiled and turned to face her. "You're still such an innocent, Hazel. So upset about your ruined virginity—worried that someone might find out, someone like Mattise. But that's okay. Once you've matured a little more, you'll understand."

Hazel's face burned as if Sylvia had slapped her. She gaped at her, wondering—was that a threat?

"Later," Sylvia said, drifting past her.

When Hazel came out of the bathroom, the movie had ended. People were gathered in little groups. Hazel found Ellen, who was eating some popcorn beside the barbecue and laughing with Megan and Carolyn. Monkey Boy was propped up beside her. She pretend-fed it some popcorn, then put her beer bottle to its lips.

"Hi, guys," Hazel said.

Matty smiled, unaware of her distress.

"So. Did the ending change?"

They giggled. Megan's laugh was extreme, and Hazel realized she was wasted.

"Have you seen Brandon?" Ellen asked.

"Not for a while," Hazel said guiltily. She had no idea what to say to Ellen about what she had seen. Or if she *should* say anything, ever.

Stephan Nylund sidled over to the group. He smelled like a liquor store.

He gave Megan a salute and said, "Hey, Williams, how's it hanging?"

"Fuck off," Megan said.

"Whoa, you sure don't talk like a lady," Stephan said. "Which is not surprising, you being a dyke and all."

"Just *leave*!" Megan snapped.

"Oh, struck a nerve, did I?" He staggered around a little.

Hazel looked at Matty, who slowly shook his head. "Hey, man," he said, putting his hand on Stephan's arm. "Chill."

Stephan stared down at Matty's grip. "Don't you freaking touch me," Stephan slurred.

Then Brandon walked up. "Hey, what's going on?"

"Megan's a dyke," Stephan said, "and I'm going to kick Matty Vardeman's ass."

"Whoa! Stephan, you've had too much to drink." Brandon turned to Matty. "Don't worry. I'll get him home."

"You know it's true," Stephan insisted. "You're the one who said Megan's so butt-ugly no guy would ever do her."

Brandon turned bright red. "Shut up, man."

Ellen looked stricken. "Brandon, you did not say that."

"He did!" Stephan insisted. "Josh was there. Yo, Josh!" Stephan hollered across the yard.

"El?" Megan's voice was shrill. "Are you going to let him get away with that?"

"Let's go," Brandon said, tugging on Stephan.

Stephan leered at Megan. "Hey, I'm not the one who went all Ellen DeGeneres on—"

"Shut up!" Megan screamed. *"Shut up, shut up, shut up!"* Heads turned.

"Hey," Hazel broke in. She took Megan's arm. "Let's find somewhere else to be."

"You shut up about me!" Megan slurred. She pushed Hazel away, took a swipe at Stephan, and missed.

Stephan doubled over in helpless laughter.

And then, with the world's worst sense of timing, Brandon grinned. He covered his mouth with his hand, stifling a chuckle.

Sure, Megan was making a scene, but Stephan was way out of line. Sylvia was right, Hazel guessed. Brandon had some asshole left in him after all.

Hazel threw a look at Matty and pulled Megan toward the house. Carolyn walked beside her.

After a couple of seconds, Ellen came too. She carried Monkey Boy firefighter style, holding him tightly as she walked with her friends.

The three PLDs walked Megan into Ellen's room. Ellen set Monkey Boy down on a pink satin pillow.

Ellen was stuck in the froufrou-ruffles stage of girlhood, Hazel noted. All Laura Ashley and white curlicue wicker. It was kind of endearing.

As soon as they sat down on the bed, Megan burst into tears.

Carolyn bolted up. "I can't deal right now. I'm going to find Sylvia." Hazel nodded and turned her attention back to Megan.

"He is such a loser," Megan said, weeping. "I just hate him."

"What is his deal? Did you guys really go out?" Hazel asked.

Ellen paled and waved her hand as if to say, *Don't ask her that. Too late*, Hazel thought.

"It got so ugly," Megan began. "Stephan and I were dating. Then at a party I got drunk, me and Carolyn . . . and I wondered what it was like. Stephan found us and said he'd spread it all over school. *God*. I thought he was going to tell everyone."

"It's okay, Megan," Hazel said. "No big."

"No *big*? Stephan is holding the whole thing over my head! He's acting like I have this secret life or something."

"So what's the big deal if he says you're gay? We know it's not—"

"You *do* know about Megan's brother, right?" Ellen asked.

Hazel shook her head, looking to Megan. All the air seemed to go out of the room.

"My brother is gay," Megan filled in, her chin wobbling. "When he was in high school, a bunch of guys beat him up. They hurt him pretty bad too. He filed charges, and everyone in the school knew about it. So now, when people hear things about me, they automatically assume that it's true."

"That's messed up," Hazel replied.

"No shit," Megan spat.

"But why does Stephan pick on you? Why you and not Carolyn?" Hazel asked.

"Because Stephan wasn't dating Carolyn. He didn't feel betrayed by her," Megan said.

"Plus, it doesn't bother her," Ellen cut in. "She doesn't give them the satisfaction. So they leave her alone."

"So all this—tonight—it's my fault?" Megan sniffed. "It's my fault your boyfriend totally dissed me?"

Her shoulders sagged. Hazel knew she was *really* wasted.

"I need some Kleenex."

Ellen leaned over toward the white wicker nightstand and grabbed a box of tissues. She handed it to Megan, who blew her nose.

"Sylvia doesn't understand how much it hurts me," Megan said, frowning. "She could put a stop to it. But she doesn't. And she picks on me. Do you think she picks on me?"

Yes. Hazel considered. *I think she picks on all of you.*

"You guys are old friends," Hazel said. "Sometimes old friends can hurt each other the way new friends can't."

Megan smiled through her misery. "You're a new friend."

"Yeah."

"I think you're a good friend." Megan wiped her nose. Hazel reached over and gave her a hug. When they pulled apart, Megan asked, "Do I have any eye makeup left?"

"Not really." They laughed.

"Brandon should have defended you," Ellen said.

Megan nodded. "Yeah. Instead he laughed. That ass. He hasn't changed a bit."

Ellen looked down at her hands.

The door opened and Thom McDonald, a guy with a lot of piercings, poked his head in the room. "There's a call for you." He held out a portable to Ellen.

"Oh my God," she whispered. She took the phone and rushed through a door to the left of her bed, closing it behind herself.

Hazel looked questioningly at Megan, who shrugged and blew her nose again.

After a few minutes, Ellen returned. Her face was slack, her eyes huge. "It was my dad. I think he heard all the noise in the background. He's going to kill me."

"He didn't know about the party?" Hazel asked.

Ellen looked at her like she was insane. "Of course not. He'd have said no. But Sylvia wouldn't drop it." She started biting at her cuticle, pacing beside the bed. "He called to say he'll be gone an extra day. He's on a business trip."

"Don't tell Sylvia," Megan advised. "She'll make you have another party."

Ellen nodded thoughtfully. She turned to Megan. "Meggers, I'm sorry. I should have stood up for you better. I should have told Brandon he was a jerk."

"Oh, that's okay." Megan glared at her, picking up Monkey Boy's arm and giving it a shake. "After all, there was a guy involved, right?"

"Yeah, but we're PLDs," Ellen replied. "We stand up for each other. We're friends till the end."

Hazel gave a bitter smirk. She had believed that too. Sylvia had convinced her. But her picture of Sylvia was changing by the minute.

The bedroom door opened again. *Speak of the devil*, Hazel thought as Sylvia strode in.

"That bastard," she said. "We do not let guys treat any of us like that. *Any of us*."

Ellen hung her head as if she were personally responsible for Brandon's bad behavior.

"Yeah," Megan said. "Brandon totally dissed me, and she and Hazel just stood there."

"He's a jerk," Sylvia went on. She turned to Ellen. "You need to think about letting a guy like that get close to you."

"Everyone was drinking," Hazel said evenly.

She stared meaningfully at Ellen, trying to make her aware. Sylvia had another agenda, and it had nothing to do with protecting anyone but herself.

✢   ✢   ✢

INSTANT MESSAGE

YRSECRETPAL2PURPLEHAZE: U slut. Some1 should stab u 4 real. Cuz ur a total ho & u deserve 2 die.

"We all got the same message," Sylvia said over the four-way connection. "'You slut . . . stab you for real . . . you deserve to die.'"

"It wasn't just the one IM," Hazel replied. "I've also been getting text messages and phone calls. Cell phone calls."

"Me too," said Megan.

"Me three," Ellen added.

"It's Breona," Sylvia said determinately.

"But Breona doesn't have our cell phone numbers," Carolyn protested.

"Maybe she snooped around to get them," Sylvia sneered. "It would be just like her. She could have given the numbers to everyone she knows. Which is why I specifically asked you not to give it to anyone but us, Haze."

"I just gave it to Matty," Hazel replied.

"Matty seems very nice," Ellen said softly. "We can trust him."

"And we can all trust *your* taste in guys," Megan shot back. "Maybe Brandon pulled all this crap."

"Megan, don't say that!" Ellen pleaded.

"Brandon *has* shown his true colors," Sylvia decreed.

"I don't know," Carolyn said. "There are a hundred girls in school who would love to scare the PLDs. We're envied. That makes us targets."

"Are you sure it's not one of you, *mes petites*?" Sylvia hissed. "Because if it is, I am not amused. It needs to stop. *Now.*"

✝   ✝   ✝

PERSONALBLOG

HAPPY2BME

IT'S HYSTERICAL!

THEY'RE RIGHT TO BE AFRAID. I'M RIGHT HERE, BUT THEY CAN'T SEE ME. THEY'RE TOO CAUGHT UP IN THEIR STUPID

LITTLE LIVES. I LOOK LIKE THE REST OF THEM, BUT I'M THEIR WORST NIGHTMARE. THEY'VE HAD FAIR WARNING. NO MORE KITTY CATS AND HORSES. I NEED MORE. TIME TO MOVE UP THE FOOD CHAIN. IT'S SHOWTIME, GIRLZ!

CHAPTER NINE

"Do you guys mind if I eat with him today?" Hazel asked. She stood facing Sylvia.

This was a total break with PLD tradition, and she wasn't sure how the others would respond. But she needed some air—some time away from the group. Matty was the perfect antidote.

"Did something happen to your scrunchie?" Sylvia asked, squinting at Hazel's ponytail. "It's, like, faded or something."

Hazel's stomach tightened. It was her replacement scrunchie, and she'd had it for weeks. No one had said anything about it until now.

Sylvia turned to Megan. "Did you give her a bad scrunchie?"

Megan, who had been devouring a turkey sandwich, froze in mid-chew and said around her food, "What, bad? It was the only extra one we had."

"Don't talk with your mouth full." Sylvia made a motion of opening and closing her fingers like a sock puppet. "It's déclassé."

Megan blinked. Scowled. She looked at her plate and then at her sandwich, as if she were considering throwing it in a huff. Fuming, she swallowed and said, "I gave her the scrunchie *you* gave *me*."

"God, are you having cramps?" Sylvia asked. "You're so cranky, *ma petite*. I just asked you a simple question."

"I washed it," Hazel jumped in.

"Oh." Sylvia scrutinized it. "In what, bleach?"

"I don't know. Whatever we use at home," Hazel replied calmly.

"Well, what's done is done." Sylvia nibbled on her salad and studied Hazel as she chewed. "So now, Mattise . . . I think we can make an exception for amour." Her smile was generous and kind. "Go on and sit with him."

"Thanks," Hazel breathed, relieved to get away from Sylvia's scrutiny.

Her heart picked up speed as she walked to the table where Matty sat alone, waiting for the verdict. He looked wryly pleased as she came over to him, took off her backpack, and sat in the chair next to his.

"So the queen bee gave you time off for good behavior?" he drawled, taking her hand.

"I had to pay her a dollar," Hazel said. When she saw that he believed her, she snickered at him.

"I'm going to go get some rolled tacos. Want anything?"

"Yeah, I want something, but it's not on the menu." He gave her hand another squeeze. "When you get back, let's talk about homecoming, okay?"

Homecoming? *Oh my God!* It was only a week away, so that had to mean . . .

Hazel maintained. "Okay."

She could feel his gaze on her as she headed for the serving area. Sylvia gave her an encouraging nod, looking genuinely pleased for her.

You have no idea! Hazel wanted to tell her.

Homecoming! She wondered what to wear. She wondered where she'd get the money to buy a dress. She had finally paid off the phone. Maybe she'd be able to afford something nice.

"Rolled tacos with guacamole," she told the cafeteria worker, a wizened Asian woman with the requisite hairnet.

"Chicken or beef?" the woman asked, grabbing a plastic plate and a pair of tongs as she ranged over a large metal tray.

"Chicken, and—"

"Ellen, just listen!" Hazel turned. It was Brandon, shouting, causing a commotion.

Ellen had risen from her chair at the PLD table. Brandon was about a foot away from her, reaching out his arms. Sylvia looked placidly on.

"No," Ellen responded. "It's over, Brandon. Just leave me alone."

The cafeteria fell into dead silence as Ellen ran for the exit.

Hazel left the food line to intercept her. She caught up as Ellen disappeared inside the girls' room. Hazel entered and heard Ellen sobbing, locked in one of the stalls.

A freshman girl stood at the sink, applying her lipstick. Hazel gave her a look. "Can you go, please?"

The freshman frowned, obviously disappointed that she was

not going to get to watch the fireworks. She touched the side of her mouth, popped her lipstick into a hobo bag, and sidled out. The door shut behind her.

Hazel checked below the doors of the other stalls. No feet. She and Ellen were alone.

"El? It's me," Hazel said, knocking gently on the door. "What happened?"

"He . . . he's not good for me," Ellen wept.

Hazel waited. Ellen kept crying; the toilet paper roll rattled. She blew her nose. "Sylvia convinced me. He . . . the PLDs come first."

My God. Sylvia did this. She played her.

"No. No, Ellen," Hazel argued. "Brandon really likes you. You don't have to choose."

"He—he dissed Megan," she sputtered. "If he doesn't respect my friends, he doesn't respect me."

"Ellen, let me in," Hazel said.

Ellen pushed back the stall lock and the door swung open. Her face was pure misery.

"I should have broken up with him that night when he didn't defend Megan," Ellen said. "It would have shown my loyalty. But I was so *pathetic*—"

"No, it wasn't like that," Hazel said. "Everyone was drinking. And Sylvia—"

The door to the bathroom swung open, and Sylvia strode in. She reached out her arms and gathered Ellen up.

"Oh, sweetie," she cooed. "Poor little El. You'll do better. I promise you. Remember, El, we train people how to treat us." She pursed her lips sadly and looked at Hazel. "Right?"

"Right," Hazel said slowly.

Ellen went to the nurse, gave the standard girl excuse that she had cramps, and went home. She turned down Hazel's offer to come over.

"I just need some downtime," she said on her cell. "But thanks."

After school, Sylvia told the others she wanted to watch football practice, so they went up into the bleachers on the opposite side of the field from Breona and the cheerleading squad.

"Go, Brookhaven, uh, uh, uh!" the cheerleaders chanted.

"They are such total sluts," Megan muttered.

Hazel wanted to say something to them all about Ellen and Brandon, but she wasn't sure how to broach the subject. She couldn't believe that Sylvia would be so underhanded. Especially after preaching about their fellow PLDs coming first.

Coach Marano blew his whistle and the team ran through a play. The boys rammed into each other with such brutal force that it made Hazel wince. Brandon was really slamming into the other guys. He was also ignoring the girls up in the bleachers.

I don't blame him, she thought.

"Football is a savage, weird sport," Carolyn declared.

"Plus, boring," Megan said, yawning.

"*Mes petites,* be polite," Sylvia admonished them.

Meanwhile, the cheerleaders were making a pyramid, with Breona at the top.

Hazel watched, transfixed. Who was *really* the bad guy here? Sylvia or Breona? They both seemed so self-centered. It was hard to tell.

"Do you have any lip gloss?" Megan asked.

"Hold on." Hazel reached into her pack, found her tiny metallic purse, and unzipped it.

"What the hell is wrong with you, man?" Hazel's attention was yanked back to the field as Brandon shouted at Matty. He was holding his jaw. Matty held his fist as if he had just hit him.

"Oh my God!" Sylvia cried.

As Matty lunged for Brandon, Josh and another player grabbed his arms. Coach Marano stomped toward them, blowing his whistle, bellowing for them to break it up.

"You are dead!" Matty shouted at Brandon, struggling to get free.

"Come on, man, don't be such a wuss," Brandon taunted back.

"You try that again and I will *kill* you!" Matty shouted again.

Stephan came up beside Brandon and hollered to Matty, "Chill, Vardeman, it's a game! Don't get your panties in a bunch."

Matty took a swipe at Stephan, who narrowly ducked away.

"Hey!" Coach Marano stepped between them. He squared off against Matty, getting in his face. "What's going on?"

"He clipped me!" Matty shouted. "I told him I have a bad knee, and he—"

"No way!" Brandon yelled. "He just hauled off and punched me, Coach! For no good reason!"

"You tried to break my kneecap!" Matty lunged at Brandon.

Coach Marano held him back. Matty threw his body back and forth, pulling his left arm free. His features were so contorted with rage, he looked like someone Hazel had never seen before.

It was confusing. And a little frightening.

Matty made another fist and the coach bellowed, "You touch anybody else and you are out of this school, Vardeman!"

"My God. He is really losing it," Sylvia said. "Hazel, your boyfriend is acting like a total lunatic."

"No," Hazel replied. "Something happened to his knee. And Brandon and Stephan are ganging up on him."

"He looks like he's having a freak-out," Carolyn said, making a face. "That's what I call serious anger-management issues."

"I don't know, honey. I wouldn't want to find myself alone with a guy like that." Sylvia shook her head. "He's acting like a wild animal."

The coach ordered Matty off the field. As he left, he turned to Brandon. "This is not over!"

"Let's go," Sylvia suggested, rising. *"Allez."*

Hazel rose reluctantly and the PLDs filed out of the stands. Hazel gazed over to where Matty was sitting on the benches. He gave her a pleading look. She shrugged and followed the others.

They were due at Charlie's in an hour. Sylvia had ordered an emergency soiree—just the PLDs. No one was going to the game now.

When Hazel got to the Pollins house, Ellen was there— already on duty.

Her eyes were swollen from crying; she barely listened as everyone discussed Matty's *outré* lapse of self-control.

"I thought he was going to tear Brandon apart," Sylvia said as they waited in the kitchen for their microwave popcorn. "Didn't you, Haze?"

Hazel took a deep breath.

Ellen turned away, pouring a glass of wine. Her shoulders were tight, her movements stiff and unreal.

Hazel knew Sylvia was trying to blow things out of proportion. She'd broken up Ellen and Brandon—and Hazel had the distinct feeling she was trying to do the same to her and Matty.

That was not going to happen. Hazel wasn't going to give in to Sylvia's little power trip. She just needed to figure out the best way to get Sylvia to lay off.

The microwave dinged and Sylvia pulled open the door. She plucked the hissing bag out by its top and continued. "We're going to have to keep an eye on him, *mes petites*. Better to find out if there's something wrong with him now than to get your heart broken later." She gestured silently toward Ellen, who still had her back turned.

"Hate to agree," Carolyn murmured as she got the popcorn bowl out of the cabinet.

Megan nodded. "Sylvia's right." She placed a comforting hand on Hazel's arm. "It happened to me—and it happened to Ellen."

"You need wine," Sylvia said, in the same voice someone at a funeral would use to comfort the bereaved. Hazel had to struggle to keep from rolling her eyes.

Sylvia poured a glass and handed it over with a sigh. "Oh, Scrunchie Girl, so stressed. Don't give up on him yet. We don't know what happened. He may have had a perfectly good reason for trying to beat up Brandon in the middle of football practice." She smiled broadly and changed the topic. "Now, let's talk about homecoming. There's lots of planning to do and—"

"I'm not going," Ellen cut in.

"What? What do you mean, *ma cherie*?" Sylvia chirped.

"I'm not going to homecoming," Ellen growled. "Brandon is up for king and I can't deal."

Sylvia shook her head. "Well . . . fine. I can set you up with a job that night, if that's what you really want."

"Whatever," Ellen mumbled, leaving the room.

Megan raised her brows. "Someone's in a pissy mood."

"She's just upset," Sylvia snapped, turning her laser glare on Megan. "If you ever felt the way she did—*about a boy*—you would know what she's going through."

Megan's mouth dropped open; she blanched as if Sylvia had just slapped her.

Hazel couldn't suppress a bitter smirk. There it was. Sylvia's way of keeping everyone in line. No one's secrets were off-limits. At least, not to her.

Sylvia smiled and busied herself putting another bag of popcorn in the microwave.

The girls carried the popcorn and bottles of wine into the living room, and everyone started finding places. Sylvia had decreed that they would watch *The Ring*—a little horror to keep their minds off things.

Hazel shuddered. *The Ring* had given her nightmares for weeks, and with all the strange stuff going on lately, it was bound to give her a few more.

Ellen was in Charlie's room, tucking him in for the night. While they waited for her to return, Sylvia whispered to Hazel, "Be extra nice to Ellie. I'm afraid this is going to do her in."

Hazel raised an eyebrow. "Oh? What makes you say that?"

Sylvia bit her lip, as if reluctant to go on. "Ellen's very fragile. She's had some *bad spells* in the past."

Hazel wasn't sure what that meant—if it was real or another one of Sylvia's overstatements. She was going to ask when Ellen came into the room.

Sylvia patted the empty space on the couch beside her. "Saved you a spot."

"Thanks," Ellen said. She flashed Sylvia an anxious smile as she sat down. Sylvia handed her one of the bowls of popcorn.

When the movie ended, the girls packed up to leave.

Hazel carried the popcorn bowls into the kitchen. Megan washed out their wineglasses. They both looked up when Carolyn and Sylvia tiptoed in, giggling, and gestured to follow them.

Sylvia led the way back into the living room. Ellen sat on the sofa, picking popcorn out of the upholstery.

Sylvia then raised her hand toward the TV. Hazel could see that she was holding the remote. She counted silently to three. Carolyn flicked off the lights.

The TV strobed on. Ellen screamed!

Sylvia, Megan, and Carolyn burst into laughter. Carolyn turned the lights back on.

"Gotcha!" Sylvia cheered as she flipped the TV off. "You thought that girl from the well was coming to get you!"

"Oh God, you guys!" Ellen cried, smoothing back her hair and trying to look cool. "I almost wet my pants!"

"What's wrong?" a tiny voice asked.

It was Charlie, poking his head out of his room. He wasn't wearing his glasses, and Hazel wondered if he could even see them.

"It's nothing, kiddo. Just a joke," Hazel assured him. "We didn't mean to wake you up."

"Is someone hurt?" he persisted.

"No, no. We saw a creepy movie and we were scaring each other. Go back to bed."

"You're not staying?" he asked. His eyes were squinty and his face was pinched.

"Not tonight. But I'll be back soon."

Charlie retreated into his room.

"Okay, time to go," Sylvia announced, suddenly standing at the door. "Better lock up, Ellen. And if that weird chick climbs out of the TV? Just tell her you're going to make a copy."

Ellen didn't bother to pretend that she thought that was funny. She stood in the doorway as the others left, her arms around herself.

"You take care," Hazel murmured, giving Ellen a hug. "It's going to work out."

"I know," Ellen said unenthusiastically. She closed the door, and Hazel and the others headed for their cars.

They were about halfway down the front walk when Sylvia stopped short.

"Wait," she said. She pulled her cell phone out of her purse and dialed a number. As she put the phone to her ear, she pointed to the living room window. Though the drapes were pulled, Hazel could still see Ellen's shadow as she crossed back into the room.

The phone rang inside the house. It rang again. Then it stopped as Ellen picked it up.

"Seven days," Sylvia croaked. Then she hung up.

Last year, Hazel had gone to homecoming with Joy and the girls in a big group. It had been fun, even though they didn't know any of the kids who were up for court. They'd dressed up and danced with each other and a couple of guys who were just friends.

But homecoming was very different if you were a PLD.

If you were a PLD, your girlfriends spent hours with you at the mall, making sure you had the most perfect dress you ever owned. Sylvia put it on her Visa and told you that you could worry about it later. They worked with you on the shoes, the hair, the makeup. They spent hours on you, and you did the same for them.

And when you walked into the gym, heads turned. Because PLDs shone.

Hazel knew they looked like movie stars as they entered the gym—decorated tonight as an enchanted forest. Fake flocked

Christmas trees and a sweet candy cottage from a student production of *Hansel and Gretel* stood on either side of the basketball court. Strings of delicate twinkle lights hung above yards and yards of gauzy, midnight blue fabric. The floor was strewn with fake snow.

A fairyland, and four fairy princesses glided into the magical setting, basking in the admiration of everyone else. They all wore black, with accents of purple—purple buds in her hair for Sylvia, a purple sheen to Megan's dress, purple swirls of beads on Carolyn's shoes, and Hazel had a purple wrist corsage.

In the days leading up to the dance, Hazel worried that wrist corsages were passé. Sylvia reassured her: if a PLD wore one, they were hot again.

Hazel felt the glow; she saw it. She couldn't help but love it.

She spied Matty across the floor. He was dressed in a sharp black tux, very simple, very elegant. Their eyes locked, and he made his way to her through the crowd.

"Don't forget," Sylvia whispered, never losing her bright smile, "he may have apologized for freaking out, but he's still on probation."

"Right," Hazel said through her own clenched teeth.

Matty *had* apologized to Hazel for his freak-out—in the cafeteria, in front of all the PLDs. He'd explained that he was in pain and he'd temporarily lost it. Brandon understood that. It wasn't a big deal, but he was sorry if he scared her. It was a guy thing, nothing serious.

Sylvia approved of this pandering and hadn't said anything against Matty since.

Matty reached her and took her hands. He gazed at her admiringly.

"Whoa." He said simply that. Hazel didn't need anything more.

She pulled the purple rose boutonniere she had bought for him out of its box. Matty leaned over so she could pin it on his lapel, and when she was finished, he stayed down so that Hazel could give him a peck on the lips.

Then Josh and Brandon showed. Brandon silently scanned the knot of PLDs.

"*Bon soir*, Brandon." Sylvia grinned.

Brandon remained silent. His gaze rested momentarily on Hazel.

She knew what he was asking: was Ellen going to be there? She gave her head a quick little shake. He sighed and moved off without glancing Sylvia's way.

"Sylvia. You look amazing," Josh gushed.

Sylvia turned and focused on him; she bent her finger in a come-hither way. Then she opened a floral box and brought out Josh's boutonniere, identical in every way to Matty's.

"Be careful or I'll hurt you," she said to Josh as she pinned it on the lapel of his tux. "Ah, *mais tu es tellement beau.*"

"*Merci, ma belle,*" Josh said.

The PLDs settled into a table that Sylvia had gotten someone to save them—Hazel wasn't sure how, but it was the kind of thing she was so good at.

The four girls were on high alert for Breona Wu. So far she

hadn't shown—but no way was the head cheerleader skipping homecoming. The strange texts and phone calls Hazel had been receiving had slowed, but Sylvia was convinced that Breona was involved and that something big was going to happen with her tonight.

The long notes of a slow song poured through the speakers. Hazel wished it would never end. Matty drew her into his arms. She leaned her head on his chest. She could hear his heart, beating so fast. He smelled amazing.

"Hey," he said.

"Hey," she answered, contented.

"Are you having fun?"

Hazel gazed into Matty's deep brown eyes. "It's the best homecoming ever."

"I'm glad." He paused. "I just hope that nothing ruins this."

"Why would it be ruined?" Hazel asked.

"It's just—it feels like we always have to worry about *them*." He glanced over his shoulder at the PLDs. "Sometimes I wish we could just be alone."

Hazel stopped dancing. "As far as I'm concerned, we're the only people in the room."

Matty stooped to kiss her. Her eyes fluttered closed.

"Excusez-moi."

Hazel's eyes flew open. Sylvia was standing next to her. The expression on her face reminded Hazel of a cat about to pounce on a bird.

"C'mon," she said to Hazel. She held out her cell phone and gave it a shake. To Matty, "We'll be right back."

"I'm sorry," Hazel whispered.

Matty shot Hazel an annoyed look but let her go. Megan and Carolyn were already waiting by the door.

Sylvia grinned as they scampered outside. Hazel began to shiver in the chilly night air. Fog was swirling in the parking lot. She thought of her first night at the Darlings' and a little shiver crept up her spine.

"Okay." Sylvia punched in a number. "This is going to be great."

The other three grouped around her. Hazel could hear a distant ringing, then Ellen picking up.

"Seven days," Sylvia croaked. "Tonight you die!"

She clicked off as Megan cracked up.

"Recycled prank. She'll know it's us," Carolyn groused.

"God, you guys. The Duvaliers' house is in the middle of nowhere," Hazel said. "It's freaky out there. Why don't you just leave her alone?"

"Oh, please," Sylvia drawled. "If we didn't prank our Ellie, how would she know how much we love her?"

"I've got an idea. Why don't we *really* prank her?" Carolyn suggested.

"You mean, something stroke-inducing? Like our masterpiece with Hazel?" Megan asked.

"Yes! The ultimate prank!" Sylvia nodded. "It's the perfect way to get Ellen's mind off that loser. So—everybody think about it, okay? I want your best ideas on Monday."

Back in the gym, Hazel found a much bigger crowd. The band had kicked it up a notch and the dance floor was filled. Everyone seemed to be in high spirits, dancing and singing along.

Through the crush, she caught a glimpse of Matty. Anxious to rekindle the mood, she shouldered her way across the floor.

"Hi, Hazel!" someone squealed. It was Lakshmi. She was wearing lavender chiffon—probably in hopes of resembling a PLD.

Sadly, she looked more like a bridesmaid. Hazel gave a quick wave and kept moving.

She had nearly reached Matty when she froze.

A girl's hands were wrapped around Matty's neck. He was locked in an intense kiss.

Hazel felt like she'd been punched in the stomach. He was kissing another girl. But who?

When the two pulled apart, Hazel saw the girl's face.

Breona Wu.

She was wearing a low-cut red dress and had drowned her face, chest, and arms in iridescent sparkles. She was so drunk she was stumbling, and her lipstick was severely smeared.

Matty turned and found Hazel. She stared at him—immobilized, like a deer in headlights.

"Hazel," he began.

"Hey, baby," Breona slurred, teetering back on her red heels. "Happy homecoming. Give your date another kiss."

She grabbed Matty again, and his face contorted with anger. "Leave me alone, you psycho!" He grabbed her by the shoulders and pushed her down, hard.

Breona slammed to the floor.

"What the hell are you doing?" she screamed. Everyone in the gym turned to face her.

"Stay away from me. Not only are you a slut, but you're a whack job!" Matty continued, his voice mean and low and scary.

Hazel searched his face. His rage made him unrecognizable — like that day on the football field.

"Matty, c'mon, baby," Breona slurred, pawing toward him.

"Matty?" Hazel asked.

Breona seemed to notice her for the first time.

"You *bitch*!" she shrieked at Hazel. "You PLDs! You think you're all so hot! But all you do is steal people's boyfriends and do shit that gets them *arrested*! You are so freaking evil! All of you!" She lunged toward Hazel.

Matty stepped between them. He grabbed Breona by the arm and squeezed—hard. "You touch her and I swear to God, I'll kill you," he growled before letting her go.

He took Hazel by the hand. "Let's get the hell away from here."

"Don't you turn your back on me!" Breona shrieked. "I'll tell her everything! Does she know about us, Matty? Huh? Does she?"

"What is she talking about?" Hazel asked.

"Nothing. Someone should just put her out of her misery," Matty muttered.

He strode out the back entrance of the gym, dragging Hazel with him. When he got outside, he put his hands on his knees and sucked in big, deep breaths.

"God." He shook his head. "This is unreal."

"Matty, what happened in there?" Hazel demanded, her body vibrating with worry. "Why was Breona calling you her date?"

Matty stared at her for a moment, then began. "I didn't think I should tell you. I didn't want you to worry."

"Worry about what?" Hazel urged.

"When I first got here. Breona and I. We kind of fooled around," Matty confessed.

"*What?*" Hazel asked, incredulous.

"It was way before you and I hooked up," Matty clarified, "before school even started. It wasn't a big thing. It lasted, like, a week. I told Breona it was over, but she just wouldn't let go. She started calling my house at all hours, hanging up. I couldn't exactly prove it was her, but who else would it be?"

Hazel studied Matty. She peered deep into his eyes, searching for even the hint of a lie. He gazed back—nothing but honesty.

His story, Hazel thought. *It sounds so much like Sylvia's. Breona being psycho, unable to let go.*

It couldn't just be a coincidence. Could it?

Matty loosened his tie. "Let's get out of here for a while," he suggested. "Get some air. Maybe go for a drive?"

"Fine by me," Hazel agreed.

At that moment, Sylvia, Carolyn, and Megan burst out of the gym.

"Hazel!" Sylvia called. "Are you okay?"

"I'm fine," Hazel snapped, whirling around. "Not now, okay?"

"Okay." Sylvia stopped short. She held up her cell. "Just . . .

keep in touch." She shot a glance at Matty. Obviously, she didn't trust him.

After that display, Hazel couldn't blame her.

She nodded, said her cell was in her evening bag, and followed Matty to his car. He opened the door for her and helped her pull in her skirt.

He climbed in. Before starting the car, he took Hazel's hand. "I'm sorry you had to go through that," he said.

"It's okay," she replied, giving his hand a squeeze.

"I wanted tonight to be perfect," he said.

"It's fine—let's just go." Hazel gave him a quick smile and pecked his cheek.

They pulled out of the parking lot and Hazel caught a glimpse of the moon through the trees. The dance and Breona began to fade as they drove over Brookhaven's two-lane roads into a dark landscape of stables and fields. Hazel smoothed her satiny dress and admired Matty's profile as he concentrated on the road.

They ventured up a bit into the hills, and fog curled around the windows. Matty slowed, taking a left toward San Pasqual, then slowed as the mist hung around the car like a white blanket.

"Damn," he muttered. "We'd better stop. It's getting hard to see."

She nodded. "It'll probably let up in a little bit."

Matty put the car in neutral and set the brake. He reached into the backseat and pulled out a six-pack of hard lemonade. "I wanted to get some champagne," he told her.

"This is fine," she assured him.

He opened hers and handed it to her. They clicked bottles. "Here's to the weirdest homecoming ever."

Hazel laughed. "Here's to the weirdest cheerleader ever."

"Seriously," Matty said. He took a sip and rested the bottle in the cup holder. "What is the deal with Brookhaven? Is there like a hellmouth under school or something?"

"You have no idea." Hazel laughed, shaking her head. Then she turned serious. "You know, I owe everything to the PLDs, but sometimes all the drama is too much to take."

"You cold?" Matty asked softly. "The heat's as high as it will go."

Before she could answer, he pushed back his seat and unbuckled his seat belt, taking off his jacket.

"Oh no, I'm fine," Hazel murmured as he put the jacket over her shoulders.

With a gentle sigh, he kissed her. She pulled him closer and kissed back. She felt her cheeks flush with warmth as he wrapped his hands around her waist. She ran her fingers through his hair.

Then her cell phone went off.

"No," Matty groaned.

She answered it.

"Where are you?" Sylvia demanded.

"Matty and I went for a drive," Hazel said defensively. "It's foggy. We had to stop."

"Well, come back. There's news. Clancy totally saw Breona acting trashed, but she was out the door before he could do anything. He's probably going to suspend her for good this time."

"I can't come back now." She cleared her throat. "I'm busy."
Matty had moved back to his own seat, and he was drinking his
lemonade.

"Oh God, Hazel. Please don't do it in his car. That's something a sleaze like Breona would do. Besides, after that incident
over the summer, don't you think you should be more careful?"

She glanced over at Matty. The memory of her mistake
flashed through her brain. Then an image of Matty's face, filled
with rage. She tried to make out his expression but couldn't see his
face. He was cloaked in shadow.

Hazel frowned. "Okay, going now."

She hung up.

"What happened?" Matty asked, with mock sorrow. "Was
your permission to leave with me revoked?"

"Breona split," Hazel said, changing the subject. "We can go
back now. Everything's fine."

"Breona. That psychotic bitch." His voice was leaden. "A
raging hangover will be too good for her." He settled his bottle
between his legs and stared out at the fog.

Hazel reached over and caught up his hand in hers. "Let's forget about Breona for now."

She let him kiss her again. Ripples fanned from her stomach
to the ends of her hair. She felt dizzy and thrilled.

Stop, a voice inside her urged.

"You smell so good," he whispered.

Stop, the voice insisted.

Then Sylvia's words, echoing in her head: *After that incident over the summer, don't you think you should be more careful?*

"Matty, I . . . we can't do it here," she said bluntly. She shut her eyes tightly against the flood of mortification. "I mean . . ."

He started to laugh.

"What?" she asked, but she started laughing too.

"You're right," he told her. "Tonight was a total train wreck. This is not how I wanted it all to go."

"Thank you," she breathed.

"We'll slow down. But we don't leave until the fog clears," he suggested.

She nodded. "Agreed."

Long before the fog cleared, Sylvia called again to say they were leaving the dance. Matty drove Hazel straight home, promising to call her tomorrow.

Hazel stumbled through the doorway. It was late. She felt so ungodly tired.

Thankfully, her mom hadn't stayed up to ask her all sorts of inane questions about the dance.

She padded upstairs and had closed the door to her room when her cell buzzed. Hazel grabbed it and connected the call.

"It's me," Ellen said. "Sorry to call so late."

"That's okay, I'm still up," Hazel replied.

"I figured you would be." Ellen sighed. "So, was the dance fun?"

"Not exactly," Hazel assured her. "I left early and went for a drive with Matty."

"Did you talk to Brandon while you were at the dance?"

"No," Hazel said gently. "He didn't really hang with us."

"What did he wear?"

"His tux was black. He had a maroon cummerbund."

"Flowers?"

"He was there alone," Hazel said.

Ellen was quiet for a moment. "Did he get king?"

"We left before the announcement. I'm sorry."

"No, it's okay." Ellen sounded wistful. "Listen. I'm calling for another reason. Those weird messages—"

"What about them?" Hazel asked.

"Well, I got all that 'seven days' crap tonight," Ellen said, slightly annoyed. "But that was obviously you guys."

"Yeah," Hazel admitted. "Sylvia's dumb idea. Sorry, El."

"Don't worry about it," Ellen said. "It wasn't *those* messages that bothered me."

"Was there something else?" Hazel ventured.

"I got one of those texts, from a blocked sender. It was kind of vicious."

"What did it say?" Hazel asked.

"'I'm ready now,'" Ellen read from her cell's screen. "'Tonight someone dies. Guess who?'"

"Oh my God. Breona really is out of control," Hazel said.

"Maybe." Ellen paused. "What if it's not Breona?"

"Who else could it be?" Hazel reasoned. "She was acting like a total nutcase tonight."

Ellen let out a frustrated sigh. "You're right. It probably is her. Just be careful, Hazel. I know Breona is mad at you. We don't know what she's capable of."

"I hear you," Hazel told her. "And don't worry. I'm safe and sound—locked up tight."

"Good. I'll see you Monday, then."

"Um, Ellen," Hazel ventured, feeling sorry for her friend, "we're only juniors. Next year, homecoming will be different."

"God, I hope so," Ellen said. "I should go. My dad's knocking."

"Okay. 'Night."

"Bon soir."

Hazel hung up. She plugged her cell phone into the charger, and it buzzed again. A text message had come in.

YRSECRETPAL2PURPLEHAZE: TAG! UR DEAD!

HAPTER
TEN

The pretty Little Devils chat room

THIS IS A PRIVATE CHAT ROOM FOR INVITED MEMBERS ONLY

Members in chat room:

PLDSLY

PLDEL

PLDCARO

PLDMEG

PLDHAZE

PLDSLY: My voice system's full of these messages. El, did U do it 2 get us back?

PLDEL: No! I got them 2. Like every 5 mins. TAG! UR DEAD!

PLDMEG: Whoever did it, not funny, OK?

PLDCARO: Hearing it!

PLDSLY: Haze? What about U?

PLDHAZE: Same thing. TAG! UR DEAD!

PLDSLY: All right, *mes amies*. I've had about enough of this. It's freaking me out! We need to get to the bottom of who's leaving these messages, like *now*.

It was raining on Monday morning, suiting Hazel's mood. The creepy texts and e-mails had continued all weekend. And she hadn't heard from Matty all day Saturday or Sunday.

She couldn't figure out why he hadn't called her, especially after he'd said he would.

Now, hurrying to school, she was cold and frazzled; to make matters worse, she had worn a long skirt and the hem was soaked from getting into and out of her car. Like most Southern Californians, she had forgotten an umbrella, and she was getting drenched.

Students in hoodies carrying books above their heads hurried from their cars through the gates of Brookhaven High. Security guards flanked vice principal Clancy, who was standing on a platform as he spoke through a bullhorn.

"First period today will be a mandatory assembly. File quickly and quietly into the media center auditorium."

"What's up?" Megan asked as she found Hazel in the hallway.

"Not much," Hazel answered. "How are you?"

"Fine, considering the craziness that was this weekend." Megan yawned. "Want to find the others before assembly?"

Hazel nodded. Together they caught up with Sylvia, Carolyn, and Ellen.

The five friends took the balcony. People were hooting and throwing wadded-up pieces of paper. Sylvia sat in the middle and gathered them toward her.

"All right, ladies, what is the deal with this assembly?" she asked. "Did you see how freaked Clancy looked when he was out front?"

Ellen nodded. "Seriously. It was like he'd seen a ghost."

"I just hope this is not about the kids who showed up drunk at the dance," Sylvia said, rolling her eyes. "If I have to sit through a lecture aimed at trash like Breona, I am going to scream."

The microphone on the stage squealed loudly. Principal Kim came out from behind the curtain. With his dark blue suit and combed-over hair, he looked uncannily like a game show host.

He was flanked by his enforcer, Mr. Clancy, and a dour-looking woman with no makeup. Her light gray raincoat washed her out even further, Hazel noted.

"Take your seats," Principal Kim ordered above the din. Clancy took a step forward, as if he could intimidate everyone into obeying.

It took a few minutes for everyone to settle down. Then Mr. Kim scanned the crowd.

"I have some very difficult news to give you all this morning. This may come as a shock to many of you, since we know she had many friends at BHS." Mr. Kim looked down for a moment, gathering himself.

"Oh my God! This is it!" Megan whispered excitedly, tugging at Hazel's sleeve. "Kim is going to tell us that Breona's expelled for good!"

Principal Kim cleared his throat. "I'm sorry to have to tell you this, but one of your classmates, Breona Wu, passed away over the weekend."

There were gasps, shrieks. Someone started sobbing. Hazel turned to the other PLDs in utter shock. They stared back.

"Drunk driving?" Carolyn asked.

Sylvia nodded. "No doubt. What an idiot."

"This is Detective Charlotte Fullerton from the San Diego Police Department," Principal Kim continued, gesturing to the woman in the gray raincoat. "I want you to listen closely to everything she has to say."

Hazel sat forward. So did the others.

"Hello," Detective Fullerton said. "I realize that that is a great shock. We of the department extend our sympathies to the entire student body." She paused, then leaned closer to the microphone. "We are looking for information that might help us in our investigation. We're specifically interested in talking to anyone who saw Breona after she left the dance. There will be a reward for any information that leads to arrests."

"Oh my God," Sylvia said slowly. "Arrests . . . That means they're looking for suspects. Which means Breona was *killed*."

Hazel felt numb. A girl her age—someone she knew—had been murdered.

When the assembly ended, everyone went to their second-period classes, but no one did any work. The death of Breona Wu was all anyone talked about. Rumors were flying. Hazel felt like she couldn't escape people's stares.

After all, she was a PLD. The PLDs hated Breona Wu.

And everyone—*everyone* knew it.

At lunch, Hazel bought some ramen and a milk. Her stomach had been churning all day. The bland noodles were about all she could handle.

Hazel pocketed her account card, and Lakshmi pounced.

"Hazel! I heard some police officers talking about Breona in the office," she whispered urgently.

"Oh?" Hazel glanced over at the PLD table. They were watching her.

She gave them a weak smile and returned her attention to Lakshmi.

"The police," she continued. "They said Breona was *ripped to shreds*."

"What?" Hazel asked.

"At first they thought it was a couple of mountain lions. But they're doing all those tests. . . ." Lakshmi waved her hand excitedly. "Forensics stuff. It was a *person*."

Hazel couldn't make sense of what Lakshmi was saying. "What was a person . . . ?"

"A person ripped Breona to shreds. It took them hours to make a positive ID."

"Oh my God," Hazel said.

"Yes." Lakshmi's eyes glittered. "It's terrible. Tell *them* I found out for you."

Hazel had no idea what to say. She bobbed her head and headed for the PLD table.

"What did she want?" Sylvia demanded. "You look like you're going to throw up."

Hazel told them everything.

"Ripped to shreds?" Sylvia said contemptuously. "Where did she hear this? From Mommy?" She leaned sideways, peering over at Lakshmi. "It sounds ridiculous to me."

"She said there are police investigators all over the office," Hazel explained.

"No doubt. First a horse. Then a cheerleader. Next it'll be a human being," Megan drawled.

Ellen gasped. "Megan! Please! Someone is dead."

Sylvia gave Lakshmi a little wave. She looked like she'd die from happiness.

"And Mrs. Sharma just happened to hear them talking about a highly confidential police investigation?" Sylvia asked. "No way. Lakshmi's bluffing. She's just trying to be the center of attention."

The others nodded vigorously.

"I heard it was hit-and-run, just like we thought," Megan said. "You can have suspects in a hit-and-run. It's a form of murder, just an accidental one."

"Well, bad things happen to bad people," Sylvia said mildly. She glanced down at Hazel's tray. "Your ramen looks good. I'm going to get some too."

Hazel watched her walk to the serving line. She looked down at the plastic foam cup brimming with noodles and pushed it away.

"She could have had mine," she said to the others. "I can't

eat." She noticed the untouched food around the table. "I don't know how she can."

"Well." Carolyn picked up her fork and moved some pasta around her plate. "She does really hate Breona."

"Past tense," Megan murmured. "She hated Breona. Although I guess you can still hate someone if she's dead."

"Ever since the assembly, people have been staring at us," Ellen said softly. "And not in the usual way. I'll bet you anything they're saying we did it."

"God, that's sick," Hazel said. "I don't know how anyone could think *that*."

"I do," Megan said, her voice very low. She glanced over at Carolyn.

"I know what you're thinking, and don't even say it," Carolyn snapped.

Hazel and Ellen both tensed. "What?" Hazel asked.

"Megan, don't," Carolyn warned.

"PLDs don't keep secrets, Carolyn, remember?" Megan turned to Hazel. "It's just that . . . we all split up. Sylvia said she'd meet us at her house later, and then she went off with Josh. I went home and changed."

"So did I," Carolyn said.

"Then we met up and drove to her house. But we had to wait forever for her to show," Megan concluded.

"*So?* She was with Josh," Hazel said.

"So . . . she *wasn't* with us." Megan raised her brows. "How do we know where she really was?"

"Oh my God, you are not even going there!" Hazel cried. "You're saying that *Sylvia*—"

"I'm saying we all know how much Sylvia hated Breona."

"Shh, here she comes," Ellen whispered.

"There," Sylvia said, putting down her ramen, sitting down, and picking up a plastic fork. She twirled some noodles around the fork and popped them into her mouth. "Greasy, but tasty."

The others exchanged glances. Ellen picked at her cuticle. And Hazel sat in a daze.

The rest of the school day was surreal. Kids were taken out of class to be questioned by the police. Some returned. Others didn't. Rumors flew, including one that Breona had faked her own death so she could leave town and start over, afraid to show her face again after having so thoroughly humiliated herself at the homecoming dance.

As chance would have it, Megan, Carolyn, and Sylvia all had sitting jobs immediately after school. Everyone air-kissed in the parking lot, promising to be extra careful.

Hazel and Ellen walked together toward their cars. Ellen sifted through her bag, looking for her keys. She swore, then rummaged some more. She came up empty and stopped dead in her tracks.

"What is it?" Hazel asked.

"I'm sorry. It's just—I am so entirely freaked," Ellen confessed. "You know what I realized?" Ellen looked at Hazel with wide eyes. "If Breona is dead, that means she wasn't the one leaving all those messages all weekend."

"You're right. So who's pranking us?"

"Hazel, Breona has been murdered and we've been getting tons of threatening messages. I don't think this is just a prank."

"We don't know if Breona was murdered," Hazel said more calmly than she would have thought. "All we know is that she died."

"But Lakshmi said—"

"Lakshmi wants to get status by telling us things." Hazel cut Ellen off.

"You have a point." Ellen picked at her cuticle again. It was bloody and raw. "Um, you want to hang out together? I don't really want to be alone, you know?"

"Yeah." Hazel put an arm around her friend. "I know."

Ellen hugged her. Then her body went rigid. "Oh God, Hazel. Look."

Hazel turned and followed Ellen's gaze.

A black-and-white San Diego Police Department squad car was parked just outside the entrance gates, its red lights swirling.

Mr. Clancy was standing off to the side with his arms crossed. An officer was beside him, talking to a student.

Hazel looked closer. Dark curly hair, the letterman's jacket— it was Matty!

A second officer got out of the driver's seat. He told Matty to get in the car.

Matty shook his head. He looked red-faced and very angry.

"It's not my problem!" she heard him yell. The officer grabbed Matty by the arm and stuffed him into the back of the police car.

"Why are they taking him?" Ellen asked. "Hazel, why would the police want to talk to Matty?"

Ellen's father wasn't due home until after seven, so they went to her house. Hazel called her mother and said she would be studying late.

Ellen turned on the gas logs in the fireplace, and they sat for a long time—sipping cocoa, not talking much, not studying at all.

They turned on the news. Breona's death was at the top of the local broadcast.

"Police are investigating the grisly death of Brookhaven High School's beloved head cheerleader, Breona Angelina Wu," the news anchor announced.

Hazel realized that Lakshmi's report had been one hundred percent accurate. Someone had killed Breona in brutal fashion.

And the police had taken Matty away for questioning . . .

"Matty didn't do it. He couldn't. He was with you," Ellen said, reading Hazel's thoughts.

"He wasn't with me all night," Hazel said. "Maybe until two-thirty."

"Haze, you know him," Ellen insisted. "He's just not that kind of guy."

Then why did the police arrest him? Hazel wondered.

She buried her face in her hands.

"When he freaked out on the field, I thought Sylvia was overreacting." Hazel took a shaky breath. "But maybe she was right. Maybe he has problems."

"Stay calm," Ellen said, giving Hazel a reassuring pat on the back. "Brandon told me their fight was totally not a big deal."

"Brandon told you?" Hazel looked up. "You guys have been talking?"

Ellen's eyes went wide for a moment. "Don't tell Sylvia!" she squeaked.

Hazel rolled her eyes. "I think she has bigger things to obsess about right now. So, you know that she was just being manipulative, right? Trying to break you guys up?"

"Of course." Ellen shook her head. "But what else is new?"

"Wait. I don't understand. If you know about it, why do you guys put up with it?" Hazel asked.

Ellen picked up her mug. "The thing is, Sylvia has helped all of us at one time or another. We owe her. And besides . . ." She took a sip of her cocoa. "What would any of us be without the group? The PLDs as a whole are greater than the sum of its parts."

Hazel could barely believe what she was hearing. It was clear that Sylvia had them all under her thumb.

Was she as trapped as the rest?

"Listen, Ellen," Hazel said. "There's something else you should know."

Ellen cocked her head innocently. "What?" she asked.

"Sylvia and Brandon—they were hooking up for a while."

Hazel watched Ellen's expression. For a moment it looked like she was about to crumble.

"I hate to say it, but I'm not surprised," Ellen whispered.

"Really?" Hazel asked.

Ellen shook her head. "Brandon has always been kind of weird around Sylvia. And the truth is, she does this kind of shit all the time." She paused. "That doesn't make it hurt any less."

Hazel put a comforting hand on Ellen's shoulder. "I don't think you have to worry about it now. Brandon put an end to it. He really likes you, El."

"Really?" Ellen gazed up, hopeful.

"Absolutely," Hazel reassured her.

"It's just—it's weird that he never mentioned anything about it. Like he wanted to keep it a secret or something."

"He probably just didn't want to hurt you," Hazel said quickly.

Ellen gazed into the distance, thinking. She frowned. Seconds ticked by in silence. "It's okay," she finally decided. "I know where his heart really is."

Hazel smiled. "You know he—" She was interrupted by the ring of her cell phone. She rummaged through her purse, pressed talk, and put it to her ear.

"Haze," Sylvia said. "I heard."

"Heard what?" Hazel asked.

"About Matty. The police. A bunch of kids saw it happen." Hazel heard typing in the background. "There's something you should read," Sylvia continued. "It's in the student files. I'm e-mailing it to you *now*."

"I'm out," Hazel said, throwing Ellen a glance.

"Well, you need to get home," Sylvia said. "You need to see this. Now."

"But—"

"Look, just do it," Sylvia said curtly. "It's important."

"What did she want?" Ellen asked once Hazel had hung up the phone.

Sylvia's words echoed in her head. *Real friends tell each other everything.* She wondered what Sylvia could have found out about Matty.

"She left me an e-mail," Hazel said. "I—I should go home anyway. My parents will be wondering."

Ellen shrugged, like she was a little hurt, but she didn't press. Hazel grabbed her keys.

Hazel entered her house and let the front door slam.

"Hi, honey," her mother called from the kitchen. "We're having that chicken you like so much."

"Great," she said flatly, heading straight for the stairs. "I have homework."

"Okay. I'll call you when it's ready," her mother replied cheerfully.

She must not have heard about Breona yet, Hazel thought. *She wouldn't be so calm otherwise.*

She trudged up the stairs and down the hall. Corey was in his room, but she didn't say hello. All she wanted to do was slip under the covers and try to forget everything.

After changing out of her wet clothes and throwing on a pair of jeans and a sweatshirt, Hazel sat down at her computer. She powered it up and logged on to her e-mail.

From: PLDSLY@hotmail.com

To: PURPLEHAZE@hotmail.com

Subject: I THINK YOU NEED TO READ THIS

Hazel took a breath and clicked on the subject line.

Hazel, this is from the school files. It's about Matty. I know this will be painful for you, but I figured you should know before it's too late. I had a bad feeling about him and there's no denying it now—it's all in the files. Call me later, *mon petite*, and we'll talk about everything.

xo, Sylvia

Hazel braced herself and scrolled down. Part of Matty's file had been pasted in the e-mail.

VARDEMAN, MATTHEW

". . . Matthew violated the temporary restraining order taken out by his girlfriend's parents prior to leaving for Brookhaven. . . . Matthew is prone to violent outbursts and physical aggression . . . serious anger-management issues. . . . We recommend continued counseling upon arrival in Brookhaven . . . as he will encounter additional stress with this transition, outbursts can be confidently predicted. . . .

Hazel read it again.

. . . violent outbursts and physical aggression . . . serious anger-management issues . . .

Hazel remembered Matty's explosion on the football field. His anger on the night of the dance. She shuddered. She'd been alone with him in the car after that. How could she have let herself trust him?

"Hazel . . . Hazel, did you hear me?" Her mother was calling her.

"What, Mom?" she yelled back, trying to keep her voice from cracking.

There were heavy footsteps on the stairs.

"I said, you have company," her mother hollered.

Hazel shot bolt upright as her bedroom door slowly swung open.

Matty. He was *here*.

He was dressed in black, his hair dripping from the rain. His chest was heaving. Hazel saw a wild, desperate look in his eye.

. . . *prone to violent outbursts* . . .

Matty came toward her. She stood up to cover the e-mail on-screen, then clicked off the monitor.

She turned to face him, her shoulders tensed. "What do you want?"

"Just hear me out." He held his hands out in front of him but continued into the room. "It was no big deal. They asked me some questions and let me go. They didn't have any *proof*." He smiled wryly. "So they had to release me."

Hazel stared at him. Mute.

"I saw you in the parking lot as the police car was pulling away," he explained. "I know it looked bad. But they let me go, Hazel. I had nothing to do with it."

He came closer, reaching his arms out to touch her. Hazel stepped to the side, slowly backing away.

"I was going to call. But I had to get to you. I was freaking out." He took another step toward her. "I found out how Breona died."

She took a breath and stepped back again; she was nearly against the wall.

. . . restraining order . . .

"Someone stabbed her," Matty said, his dark eyes boring into her. "Hundreds of times."

"You. Need. To. Go." Hazel forced the words from her frozen chest. *"Now."*

Matty scowled. "What? Why? You think *I* did it? Are you crazy?" he demanded, growing louder.

"Get out of here," she rasped. "Please."

He gave her a long, hard look, then turned and stomped back down the stairs. She heard the front door open, then slam shut.

Hazel sank onto the bed, exhaling. It was all so confusing. She knew Sylvia was a manipulator, but it was all right there in Matty's file—and in the angry expression she'd seen on his face. What was happening? Matty couldn't have killed Breona—could he?

✝   ✝   ✝

PERSONAL BLOG
HAPPY2BME

ALL SENSE OF TRUST HAS BEEN COMPLETELY TRASHED. I'M SICK OF BEING TREATED LIKE A DOG. HAZEL IS PLAYING WITH FIRE. SECRETS AND LIES—SOON THEY'LL ALL SEE WHERE IT GETS THEM. THEY'LL ALL PAY.

HAPTER ELEVEN

There were officers all over Brookhaven High. Some wore khaki San Diego Police Department uniforms. Others wore street clothes. Those were the detectives—or so Hazel assumed. Her life had become a crime-scene television show—only there was no sound track, and no one seemed to know who'd done it.

Walking down the hall, she scanned the crowd for Matty.

She pushed her way through the crush. Everyone seemed to be swept up in a swirl of tension—all tight, scared faces, hunched shoulders. Some people were talking too loudly; others were silent. School as they had known it was over forever.

Hazel paused a moment in front of her locker, remembering the day she caught Matty taping his green carnation to her door.

She thought of his smile . . . how flustered he had been. Was that the face of a brutal killer?

Then she thought of Breona's freak-out.

Breona, who was gone.

Hazel's cell phone went off, ripping her out of her heavy thoughts. She checked the ID—Sylvia.

"Yes?" Hazel answered.

"Did you do this?" There was a brief silence, then . . .

Bad babysitter. It was a metallic voice, just like the chip on Charlie Pollins's door.

"No!" Hazel cried. "What is it? Where is it?"

"In my locker. It goes off when I open the door."

"Oh my God." Hazel stared at her locker. She hesitated for a moment, then she worked the combination and pulled.

Bad babysitter!

It was a harsh, rough voice. The same one from the prank calls? Hazel backed away.

"This isn't your prank, Hazel?" Sylvia demanded.

"No!" Hazel cried, her eyes still glued to the open door.

"Then who did it?" Sylvia demanded.

"Why are you asking me?" Hazel asked.

"Because Charlie Pollins does this kind of thing. With those chips," Sylvia said impatiently. "It had to be one of us. Who else would have access to Charlie?"

Hazel didn't have to think hard. Only one other person she could think of had access to Charlie. The same person who had made his missing-pet posters. The same person who played video games with him till late at night.

Matty Vardeman.

✚   ✚   ✚

Everyone bought chicken noodle soup for lunch, as if solid food were too much to deal with. It was salty, and Hazel couldn't shake the image of huge vats of chicken feet simmering away in a factory someplace. She put down her spoon and sipped a bottle of water.

Sylvia looked around their table. "The voice chips. Give it up. Who did it?"

Everyone stared at everyone else.

A ripple went through the cafeteria as the doors by the diversity mural opened. Three police officers, Detective Fullerton, and Clancy strode in.

"It had to be one of us, right? Who else has our locker combinations?" Megan whispered.

Hazel watched as the authorities slowly made their way through the lunchroom.

"Those wouldn't be hard to get," Sylvia answered without turning her head. "There's a list, right? Of all the combinations? People like Mrs. Sharma have access to them. She probably gave the list to Lakshmi—who sold our combinations to the highest bidder."

"Maybe Lakshmi did it herself," Megan ventured.

"No, she's not that smart," Sylvia said contemptuously. "Whoever did this used Charlie's voice chips. So if it wasn't one of us, it was someone close to us." Sylvia's voice dropped to a low growl. "Attending our parties . . . pretending to be our friend."

Hazel remained silent.

The PLDs turned as one of the detectives strolled by their table.

"They're going to ask us about the drugs in Breona's locker,"

Ellen whispered, her voice high and nervous.

"Why? No one asked us about the drugs before," Sylvia pointed out.

"They're going to talk to us eventually," Carolyn agreed. "Someone is going to tell them how much we hated her."

"So?" Sylvia said. "We didn't kill her."

"We talked about payback," Ellen ventured.

"To each other, hello?" Sylvia sounded extremely irritated, as if she couldn't believe how dense Ellen was. "We didn't kill her, Ellen."

"True." Ellen exhaled slowly. "So why do we all feel so guilty?"

Sylvia turned a cold eye on her. "*We* don't." She looked at the others. "Do we?"

Hazel spoke up. "Whoever killed her was a total psychopath."

"A psychopath. Like someone who had a restraining order taken out on them?" Sylvia asked, giving her a look.

Hazel's stomach clenched. Beads of sweat collected on her forehead.

"We should tell them about the voices in our lockers," Ellen said, eyeing the police officers. "Show them."

Everyone looked at each other, then at the cops.

"Okay, okay, I confess," Carolyn said, half raising her hand. "I did it."

Everyone stared at her in total disbelief.

She grimaced at her soup and pushed it away. "The voices in the locker. I planned it forever ago, and Charlie called me and told me they were done. I already paid him, so . . ." She shrugged.

"That . . . is in *amazingly* poor taste," Sylvia said icily.

"Dude, you have totally got balls," Megan said. "I swear, that is one of the greats!"

"You're nuts," Ellen said. "It was so inappropriate!"

"That's what makes it so fabulous," Megan argued. "It's *so* wrong!"

Sylvia sighed like a mother of wayward children. "You never cease to amaze me, *mes petites*."

"Hey, we're not the pretty little *angels*," Megan said. She turned to Carolyn. "So, the scary phone messages, the e-mails? That was you too?"

"No." Carolyn's smile faded. "I just did the voice chips."

"Well, it's time to confess," Sylvia told the group. "The game is over. Prank caller, come out, come out, whoever you are!"

There was dead silence.

The detectives retreated from the cafeteria, done with their intimidation.

The lunch bell rang, and the PLDs pushed back their chairs.

As they walked into the quad, Josh appeared out of the crowd. He gave Sylvia a quick kiss. Hazel noticed rings under his eyes.

"Hey," he said. "I just left Kim's office. The police wanted to talk to me, but my parents said no, not without them and a lawyer present."

"Good," Sylvia told him, reaching up and tousling his hair. "Smart."

He frowned. "But doesn't that make me look guilty?"

"No," Sylvia replied. "It makes your parents look like

they're not idiots." She took his hand, swinging it back and forth. "Everyone is acting like they killed her. Why would they ever think it was you?"

"Sylvia," he protested, then sighed and shook his head, reddening. "You know why. Because of . . . the three of us. You know."

Sylvia stared at him. "Oh my God, you're kidding," she said. "They think you killed her?"

"I don't know," he said, his voice shaking. "But if they talked to me, chances are they're coming for you too."

Hazel wondered, Would they? Would they question Sylvia Orly? And if so, what kind of skeletons would they find in *her* closet?

Hazel kept her eyes out for Matty again as she walked to chemistry lab. She concentrated on putting one foot in front of the other—on breathing, on not falling apart.

Lakshmi was waiting for her just inside the door.

"So what's up? Did Sylvia say anything about the info I gave you?"

Hazel couldn't believe her ears. With everything that was happening, Lakshmi *still* hungered to be in with the cool kids. It was twisted, and it mortified Hazel; she didn't want to be a person of this much importance anymore.

"Lakshmi, I—I need to sit down."

"The police are questioning everybody," Lakshmi announced, following Hazel to her lab stool. She looked pointedly at the empty chair that had been Breona's. "I heard that the policeman who found her body vomited on the spot."

"God!" Hazel cried. She raked her hands through her hair and put her elbows on the lab bench. "How can you even go there?"

"I'm only telling you what I heard," Lakshmi whined.

"Why?" Hazel asked.

Lakshmi blinked rapidly. "*You* know," she replied.

"Take your seats, please," Ms. Carpentier called to the class.

Lakshmi went back to her own table. Hazel sat down and opened her textbook, but she couldn't listen to Ms. Carpentier's instructions. She just fuzzed out . . . stopped.

She had no idea how long she stayed there, just staring at the chalkboard. The next thing she knew, Ms. Carpentier was beside her.

"Hazel, do you need to talk with someone?" the teacher asked in a whisper. "The school counselor, perhaps?"

Hazel licked her lips, trying to decide how to reply.

"This must be so difficult for you," Ms. Carpentier said. "I know you had words with her, but you must not blame yourself under any circumstances."

The teacher went to her desk and opened a spiral book. She wrote something down and tore off a slip of paper.

She returned with a slip that said, COUNSELING REFERRAL.

"I'm going to recommend that you talk to Ms. Clasen. A lot of the students are going to her for grief counseling. Just go down there and make your appointment. They'll give you a tardy pass for your next class."

She handed Hazel the form. "Do you want someone to go with you?" she asked. "Maybe Lakshmi?"

"No," Hazel said quickly. She wouldn't be able to stand it. "I'm fine. I'll go alone."

She hurried into the hall, hanging a right to get to the administration building, and walked across the quad by the front gates of the school. She thought she could see people staring at her, and she kept her eyes down, imagining their whispers.

There goes a PLD. They hated Breona. They wanted her dead.

Hazel found Sylvia waiting for her at her locker.

"I'm calling an emergency meeting at Carolyn's," she said. "No one's home, so we'll have some privacy."

Hazel rubbed her forehead. "Sylvia, please don't tell them about Matty's file."

Sylvia examined her manicure pensively. "I *do* have a bit of a dilemma," she said. "It's important information."

Hazel gave her a pleading look.

"Well, they already know he's under suspicion. I guess we don't have to tell them the rest," Sylvia agreed.

"Thank you, Sylvia." Hazel's voice cracked and she let out a low sob.

"Don't cry." Sylvia pulled her into a tight embrace. "We're here for you. I'm here. I won't tell them, all right? Forget the meeting— we'll keep it between us for now."

The next morning was another rainy mess. Hazel had forgotten her umbrella again, and this time she had no defense against the weather. As she passed by the front entrance, something caught her eye. She stopped.

Piles of rain-soaked flowers, candles, stuffed animals, and notes had been left by students. The ink was running down the largest note, which read, WE LOVE YOU, BREONA. A lot of the tributes were signed by people trying to wrangle some social cred—pretending they loved and missed someone who never even knew they were alive. There were photos of Breona in her cheerleading outfit and dressed for a formal.

"She had a dog," Hazel murmured to herself, studying a shot of Breona with her arms around a tiny Yorkie. She thought of Sylvia's dog, Asterix, and frowned. Something about this picture confused her.

Something about it didn't make sense.

At lunch Hazel was the first to arrive at the PLD table. She set her stuff down and went off in search of hot soup. She wasn't hungry, but she was getting shaky from not eating. She had only picked at her food at dinner, and everyone had been too busy talking about the murder to notice.

As she reached the serving line, she felt someone's gaze on her and turned her head. Across the room, Matty was standing against a window, staring at her.

She looked away.

Tight-lipped, she got her soup. She set it on her tray and managed to pay for it and get it to the PLD table without losing her mind.

By that time, the others were there. Sylvia looked from Hazel to Matty and back again; she reached across the table to squeeze Hazel's fingertips as she sat down.

"You're okay, Haze. You're fine. We're here."

Ellen said sweetly, "You need a spoon. I'll get you one."

Hazel thanked her. When she looked back at the window, she saw that Matty was gone.

Lunch ended; she swam through the day. The classrooms were steamy and smelly from the damp weather, chemistry lab failed to engage her, and she blew off Lakshmi's attempts to be friendly without even realizing that she was doing it.

The rain poured down all afternoon. Parts of the school roof began to leak. Buckets sat in corners, and the steady *drip-drip-drip* got on Hazel's nerves.

It wasn't until she was halfway to her car at the end of last period that she realized she had left her makeup bag in the gym bathroom. She hung a U, sighing as she shouldered past the crowds headed the other way.

Watery overhead lights illuminated the gunmetal gray lockers and cement floors of the girls' locker room. The class of 2002 had painted a mural of ancient Greek Amazons carrying shields, spears, and swords on the far wall. Still, the gym was dreary and dark, just like the day. The Amazon figures seemed shadowed and ghostly.

She walked along the first row of lockers, bisected down the middle by long wooden benches. She scanned for her bag, hoping no one had taken it. She had just gotten a ton of new Hard Candy makeup.

There it is. She saw it lying at the far end of the bench, beneath an Amazon carrying a spear. She smiled, and her face felt like it was cracking; she hadn't smiled all day.

She picked up the bag, unzipping it to see if everything was there. The reassuring shapes and smells were a source of comfort.

There was a sort of buzz.

And the room fell dark.

Oh, great.

Hazel stood where she was, waiting for the lights to blink back on again. It was probably just a janitor flicking the wrong switch—or a temporary short. While she waited, she felt in her bag. Lipstick, blush, her little jar of sparkles for her cheeks. Eye shadow, mascara . . .

The lights didn't go back on.

"Hello?" Hazel called.

No one answered.

"Um, hello?"

Footsteps echoed toward her from the end of the room. "Over he—" she began, and then she clamped her mouth shut.

Stalker. Murderer.

A wave of panic shot through her; she inhaled slowly and tried to think what to do.

More footsteps. Slow. Deliberate.

Cold fingers tiptoed up her spine. Goose bumps broke out across her body; her hair stood on end.

She took a step backward, trying to remember the layout of the locker room. How many times had she been in here, how many hundreds of times?

Step. Step. Closer.

Hazel moved faster. She backpedaled—and slammed against a locker.

The noise echoed in the frigid silence.

Oh my God. He knows exactly where I am.

She clenched the makeup bag with all her might. The blood was roaring in her ears. Her heartbeat pounded in double time.

Closer now.

She held her breath.

Someone knocked against the wooden bench at the far end of her row. They were maybe twenty feet away from her. If they ran at her with a weapon . . . would she be able to get away?

Lakshmi had said the cop who found Breona threw up. . . .

She had never been more terrified. *This is really happening. Someone is in here and they're stalking me.*

She tried to swallow, but she couldn't. She heard herself whimper.

Then there was a clatter of footsteps, moving away from her.

A few seconds later, the lights came on.

"Who's in here?" It was Coach Hart, with her familiar short hair, little gold earrings, and Brookhaven sweatshirt.

"Oh God," Hazel said in a rush. She hurried toward the coach. "Someone was here, someone was creeping around—"

"I'm here now," the coach said. "Don't worry, Hazel. I'll have a look around—"

They walked together, exploring the locker room in silence,

until the coach said, "You probably just heard me, coming to see why the lights were out."

"But who turned them off?" Hazel asked.

"Faulty wiring. It happens all the time when it rains. Or when the wind blows. Or when the sun shines," the coach replied, with a wry expression. "But I'll contact the police, just in case."

She walked Hazel to the exit, opened the double doors, and stopped, watching the rain. "Hold on," she said.

She ran back to her office and returned with an umbrella. It was yellow with pink polka dots—ironically cheerful.

"Bring it back tomorrow," the woman ordered.

"Thank you," Hazel said.

"Sure." Coach Hart headed back toward the lounge. Hazel opened the umbrella and walked into the rain. She looked left, right, and saw a cluster of drama kids in black clothes as they headed for the media center theater.

Feeling very alone, Hazel half walked, half ran to her car.

☦   ☦   ☦

PERSONALBLOG

HAPPY2BME

NOW SHE KNOWS WHAT IT'S REALLY LIKE TO BE POPULAR. EVERYONE WANTS A PIECE OF YOU. AND SOME PEOPLE WANT YOU IN PIECES. I HAVE NO PROBLEM WITH THAT. I'M READY FOR ANOTHER KILL. THIS TIME I'LL LET EVERYONE JOIN IN ON THE FUN!

HAPTER TWELVE

"What is *this*?" Sylvia shrieked.

Hazel had just come from her locker to get her chemistry lab workbook. She hadn't slept well again.

And now . . . disaster.

Sylvia had one hand wrapped around Lakshmi's arm. The other one clutched the purple scrunchie Hazel had given her.

"I found it," Lakshmi said miserably. But it was clear even to Hazel that she was lying.

"You stole it!" Sylvia shrieked.

"No!" Lakshmi said.

It was a bizarre redux of Breona and the carnation. Hazel was aware of people stopping, watching. Eyes widened, mouths broadened into eager smiles.

A strange thought crept into Hazel's head: was *Breona* the crazy one in the cheerleader-PLD dynamic? Or was it someone else?

"It's just a scrunchie," Lakshmi said.

"Oh, don't even pretend with me." Sylvia sneered. "I know you'd sell your soul to have one of these."

"Leave her alone," Hazel spoke up. "It's not her fault. I gave it to her."

"You what?" Sylvia stared at Hazel. She shook the scrunchie in her face. "Doesn't this mean anything to you? Don't you know who your friends are?"

Hazel stood there, silent. Sylvia threw the scrunchie down, turned on her heel, and walked away.

At midday, Hazel trudged across the quad. From the corner of her eye, she caught Sylvia approaching with Megan and Carolyn in tow. Hazel braced herself for another onslaught, but Sylvia's expression was kind.

"We need to talk," she said softly. "Come on."

They walked past administration to the ROTC building.

"Listen. I'm sorry for before. We're all going crazy with everything that's happened," Sylvia said as they turned a corner. "But what I meant to say was—"

"What the—" Megan stopped short, and everyone followed her gaze.

Brandon was dead ahead, standing with his thumbs in the loops of his jeans.

He was talking to Ellen.

They were both smiling. And standing very close together.

Sylvia marched up to the two of them, her pale, perfect complexion growing red. "Brandon! What the hell do you think you're doing? Why don't you give it up? Ellen has had it with you."

Brandon looked from Sylvia to Ellen.

"Um, Sylvia is right," Ellen said, staring at the ground. "We're through. So go away."

Brandon reached out a hand. "Ellen, you don't have to do this. Why don't you just tell them the truth?"

Ellen looked shocked; she glanced over at Sylvia.

"Tell them," Brandon urged. He whirled to face the PLDs. "We've been dating for weeks. She's been keeping it a secret because you're all completely messed up!"

"Get the hell away from her!" Megan said, taking Ellen's arm. "She doesn't want you!"

"I swear to God, Megan. You'd better let her go." Brandon's voice shook with fury. He glared at each one of the PLDs in turn, his gaze finally resting on Sylvia. "You are so manipulative. So insane. Why can't you just leave us alone?"

"Because you don't deserve her. Because you're just like your friend Stephan," Megan argued.

"That's not true! I—"

"Enough," Sylvia said in her most composed tone. "Megan, Brandon's right."

"What?" Megan asked, wide-eyed.

"It's not my business. I'm washing my hands of this entirely." She regarded Brandon and Ellen coolly. "You two do whatever you want. I won't interfere."

Ellen's face lit up. "Oh my God. Really? Are you serious?"

Sylvia nodded. "I'm serious. If you want him, Ellen, go for it. You two deserve each other."

"Sly," Ellen whispered, her voice full of emotion, "thank you."

"No problem." Sylvia turned to the rest of the group and motioned for them to follow her. Hazel fell into step next to her and heard her mutter, "No problem at all. Just don't come running to me when this whole thing turns into a car wreck."

Hazel got in her car and drove. So much was happening—so many thoughts swirling through her head. She couldn't go home. Not yet.

She cruised down the streets of Brookhaven, through downtown and past Avenida Escondida. All the while, she wondered about Sylvia. There were times when she seemed like two people at once—the one who cared for her friends and did her best to protect them and the other Sylvia, the one who manipulated everyone for her own gain and amusement.

Which was the real one? Hazel wondered. Which was the stronger one? Which one would win out in the end?

This afternoon—with Ellen. Was it a victory for the caring Sylvia? Or was it another manipulation? One the rest of the PLDs had yet to figure out?

Hazel hoped it was the former—for Ellen's sake.

She drove back around the avenue and looped toward the park.

The park—where two police cars had pulled in and left their lights flashing. Where three cops were standing in a loose semi-circle around a tree.

A tall policeman had someone pushed up against the tree and was forcing him to stand still while a gray-haired officer patted him down. . . .

Matty, Hazel realized.

The gray-haired cop cuffed him. Then the other policeman walked him over to one of the police cars and opened up the back.

"Oh my God," Hazel said. "They're arresting him!"

✢   ✢   ✢

YOU HAVE ENTERED
The pretty Little Devils chat room
THIS IS A PRIVATE CHAT ROOM FOR INVITED MEMBERS ONLY

Members in chat room:

PLDSLY

PLDEL

PLDCARO

PLDMEG

PLDHAZE

PLDSLY: OK, it's been confirmed. Matty's been officially arrested and held.

PLDCARO: They must have more evidence this time.

PLDMEG: We knew he was a psycho.

PLDEL: O, Haze, I'm so sorry!

PLDSLY: Ellen, RU *folle*? Arresting a killer's A Good Thing.

PLDMEG: It's just so freaky. Haze was his GIRLFRIEND. How scary is that?

✢   ✢   ✢

A week had passed and Hazel hadn't heard a word from Matty. She knew that he probably couldn't call her. That he was waiting for her to contact him somehow, but she couldn't bring herself to do it. She just didn't know what to think.

Her heart told her that Matty couldn't be the killer. He couldn't. But there was his file—and there was the arrest. It didn't help that along with the police, the rest of the PLDs were convinced that her boyfriend was a murderer.

This morning, as Ellen had done for all the days since Matty's arrest, she picked Hazel up and they drove to school together. The town Christmas decorations were going up—holly and bells mounted on the streetlights.

"The Winterfest dance is coming," Ellen said. "I can't believe I'm actually going with Brandon."

"Yeah," Hazel muttered. She stared vacantly out the window. "That's great."

"Oh, Haze!" Ellen stopped short. "I didn't mean—"

"It's okay," Hazel reassured her.

Inside, she couldn't help but hurt.

Just a few weeks ago, she was at homecoming with Matty. Just a few weeks ago, she was falling in love. How could it all have changed so quickly?

"So guys—no calls, no wacky e-mails, no text messages for the past week and a half." Sylvia stabbed a sliver of lettuce. "The same amount of time Matty has been in custody. I think the police got their man."

"I think we're lucky he didn't hack any of us up," Megan muttered.

"So," Sylvia said cheerfully, "it looks like things will blow over just in time for my birthday party."

Hazel knew Sylvia's party was the next big event on the PLDs' social calendar, but she just couldn't find it within her to care. Things were getting back to normal at the speed of light. At least, that was how it seemed. Meanwhile she was stuck. Frozen by what had happened. Beyond devastated.

Sylvia had noticed and had been especially nice to Hazel since Matty's arrest. Hazel was excused from sitting but got a share of the money anyway. Sylvia took her to the movies. And for pedicures. The PLDs played poker and Hazel was pretty sure Sylvia let her win.

Still, Hazel knew it would take a lot of time to get her back to her old self. Could there be a worse way to break up?

They planned Sylvia's birthday party. It was going to be catered by the same chichi company the Duvaliers used. Everything that could be purple would be purple.

As Sylvia kept reminding everyone, it was going to be amazing.

"Hey, sexy ladies," Josh greeted the table. Brandon approached with him.

"Hi," Ellen chirped.

"Got some sugar for Monkey Boy?" Brandon asked. He stood behind Ellen and threw his arms around her.

Hazel noted Ellen's expression. It was pure bliss. *I guess she really doesn't care about his past with Sylvia,* Hazel thought.

Megan and Carolyn snickered, as if Ellen's happiness were somehow uncool.

Mercifully, Ellen didn't notice. She pushed back her chair. "That pudding looks good," she said, pointing to Megan's bowl. "Come on, Monkey Boy. Let's get some."

"You can have some of mine," Megan offered, lifting the bowl off the table.

"No, it's okay." Ellen giggled. Brandon grabbed her around the waist. He tucked her under his arm and hooted like a baboon. "We'll get our own."

Brandon carried Ellen away to the serving area.

Sylvia regarded them coldly. She gave Josh's hand a pat. "I'm so glad my boyfriend has class."

"Hey," Josh joked. "I could be up for a little walk on the wild side."

Sylvia smiled seductively. "Patience, Josh." She planted a long, passionate kiss on his lips. "Now go away. We have business to discuss."

"Okay," Josh said, giving Sylvia another kiss. "Au revoir."

He took off.

Sylvia glanced toward the cafeteria line. Hazel followed her gaze.

Ellen and Brandon were fooling around near the fruit bowl— Ellen pretending to offer her Monkey Boy a banana.

Even Hazel couldn't help but smile a bit at the sight.

Sylvia leaned in closer. "So, Haze. Now that everything has calmed down for a while, we've decided to do one last prank."

"The four of us," Carolyn clarified. "Because it's so good—"

"And because it's *symbolic*," Megan cut in.

Sylvia nodded. "One last prank says we refuse to let everything that's happened this year get the better of us. We are still strong. We are still the PLDs."

"And," Carolyn added, "it is really, really good."

"It's going to be our grand finale, and then we're done," Sylvia concluded.

"You think that's a good idea?" Hazel asked. "I mean, doesn't it still seem wrong?"

"Here comes Ellen," Sylvia said, ignoring Hazel. "Tonight we'll finalize the plan." She smiled as Ellen returned to the table, carrying her pudding and grinning naively.

✣   ✣   ✣

PERSONALBLOG

HAPPY2BME

THEY THINK THEY'RE SAFE! THAT MATTY'S GONE, SO IT'S ALL GOOD. THEY THINK THEY CAN KEEP THEIR SECRETS. THEY ARE SO WRONG. I'M STILL HERE. AND I KNOW EVERYTHING. ALL I NEED IS THE PERFECT MOMENT TO POUNCE.

YOU HAVE ENTERED
The pretty Little Devils chat room
THIS IS A PRIVATE CHAT ROOM FOR INVITED MEMBERS ONLY

Members in chat room:

PLDSLY

PLDMEG

PLDCARO

PLDHAZE

PLDSLY: OK, let's talk about the big prank. Meg?

PLDMEG: KK, here it is. On the 27th, a Sat., Charlie Pollins is going to movies w/friends 4 a bday party. Mr. P. is working late, needs someone to watch Charlie after he's dropped off. While he's at movies, we get Ellen over early, tell her to meet Charlie there to sit after movie.

PLDSLY: We get there ahead of her. We put Monkey Boy doll in study. Hide out. Turn off all the power.

PLDMEG: Then we prank-call. Tell her to go to the study.

PLDSLY: There is Monkey Boy, in the chair! She sees shadow, freaks. Thinks—*intruder!* We turn on lights, just the dumbmonkey.

PLDHAZE: Scare her bad? I don't like.

PLDMEG: No! We don't let it go on too long. If she gets scared, we stop!

PLDCARO: It works only cuz of Monkey Boy.

PLDMEG: *Exactement!* It'll be cool. Wait & C!

✛   ✛   ✛

YRSECRETPAL2BRANDOG: Hi, Brandon! Im at Charlies 2nite. Rendezvous @7:15 PM! Park far. Come in thru study. Wait 4 me.

BRANDOG: El? Hey! Sounds good. Ill B there. Hasta!

✛   ✛   ✛

Hazel's phone vibrated at a little after seven. She was in Charlie's room, messing with his Game Boy, and the jiggling against her hip startled her.

"Okay," Megan murmured in her ear. "The prank is ready to go. Monkey Boy is in the chair."

"Okay," Hazel whispered back. Ellen wasn't there yet, and it was probably all right if they spoke in normal tones of voice. Still, the whispering added to the stealthy vibe of the last and greatest PLD prank.

Ellen was due at seven-thirty, and Carolyn was on duty in the front room. Her job was to watch out the window and call Megan when Ellen was at the door.

"I want to come see," Hazel said.

"No! Stay where you are," Megan insisted. "No unnecessary movement. She might show early. You can see afterward."

"Carolyn will let us know when she's here, right?" Hazel asked.

"Yes," Megan replied. "And remember, we don't want there to be any shadows on the curtains. So when I say go, get in Charlie's closet."

"I don't really get why I have to be *inside*—"

"In case she doesn't go to the study right away. What if she checks Charlie's room? She's not supposed to know we're here, Haze."

Well, duh. Hazel felt minorly insulted. "But we're not going to draw this out, right? Because it wasn't very funny in the locker room—"

"Haze, chill. It's our last prank. El will be cool with it. She's got a backbone. You've just never seen it."

"Okay." Hazel still wasn't convinced.

"Sylvia's in the hall closet closest to the study," Megan said. "She's got the cordless from the kitchen. When the phone rings, you grab the portable in Charlie's room so you can listen in."

Hazel had the extension on her lap.

"I'm going to be in the basement so I can turn off the power right after she gets here," Megan reminded her. "So actually, you might as well get into the closet now. Don't forget your flashlight."

What if I'm the one being pranked? Hazel thought.

Hazel had been secretly worried about that ever since the plan was set.

She wouldn't put it past the PLDs to concoct some elaborate hoax—to throw her off balance just to scare the heck out of her.

Maybe they wanted her to hide in the closet so they could turn off the lights and ditch her? Or maybe someone was already hiding in the closet, waiting for her?

"Hazel?" Megan said. "Are you in the closet?"

Hazel hesitated. She picked up her flashlight from Charlie's dresser. Then she walked to the closet and peered inside. No one there. She rummaged among Charlie's things to see if she could find a speaker or a voice chip, some other kind of electronic special effect set up to spook her. Still nothing.

"Hazel?" Megan repeated.

"Yes," she said quickly, before Megan could ask again. "I'm in here." She switched the portable to her other hand.

"Okay, I'm getting off my cell now so Carolyn can call me when she sees Ellen. I might be able to warn you with a vibrate-only call, but don't answer it again. And remember, when the portable rings, wait for Ellen to answer the phone and then connect."

"I'm good to go," Hazel assured her. She pulled the closet door partway shut and braced herself for the power to go out. She considered sitting cross-legged on the floor. Then her cell vibrated.

She took a breath; Ellen had arrived.

The prank was on.

CHAPTER THIRTEEN

The front door opened. Hazel could hear the jangle of keys and the rustle of Ellen taking off her coat. She had been told that Charlie would be dropped off a little after she arrived, so the empty house made sense.

Hazel listened hard, trying to keep track of Ellen's movements. Then the landline let out a shrill, startling ring. Hazel jumped, dropping it. It smacked her foot.

She grimaced, bending down to squeeze her toes.

Then the light in the closet went out. Megan had turned the power off.

Hazel felt around on the floor, trying to figure out where she'd dropped the portable. She found the phone and picked it up. The prank call was in progress.

". . . have them tied up," a very hoarse voice whispered. "Call the cops and they're dead."

"Who . . . what . . . ?" That was Ellen. She sounded terrified.

"I'm the same guy who killed that slut." Hazel knew it was Megan, but all the same, her voice was chilling.

This wasn't what we agreed to, Hazel thought. *It wasn't going to be Breona's killer inside the house. Just an intruder.*

"Now I'm gonna kill the little boy."

"I'm calling the police," Ellen said. "Right now."

"Call and he's dead. I'll be out of here before they come. I'll leave the way I came. No one will see me. And you'll be dead too."

"Oh God, oh my God . . ." Ellen trailed off.

God, Megan, be more obvious, Hazel thought.

There was a muffled sound. It was Sylvia in the hall closet; Hazel figured the noise would draw Ellen toward the study instead of the kitchen.

It worked. Hazel heard Ellen in the hallway and on the phone as well, a strange combination of natural voice and metallic, like a poorly mixed sound track.

"Don't you hurt him!" Ellen's voice was high-pitched, shrill. There was a loud banging, more shouting, only it was a different voice.

"Hey!" It was a guy's voice, familiar. Who was that?

Hazel's first instinct had been right: this was a bad prank. It wasn't funny. She was putting a stop to it—right now.

She shouted into the phone, "Ellen? Ellen, wait!"

Then she heard a sound she couldn't identify—a loud thud.

And then screaming.

Hysterical screaming.

Hazel threw open the closet door and raced out of Charlie's room. She ran into the hall. "Ellen?"

A light flared on the wall; Sylvia emerged from the closet with her flashlight. "What's going on? What happened?" she demanded.

The door to the study was open and so was the door beyond it, leading outside. Sylvia pushed past Hazel, raced inside the study. "Oh my God!" she cried.

Hazel ran in after her.

Sylvia's flashlight beam sliced through the shadow, giving Hazel tiny glimpses of the scene.

Ellen sprawled on the floor, gasping.

Charlie's baseball bat at her feet.

"Megan, turn on the lights!" Sylvia bellowed.

The lights switched on.

Hazel covered her mouth with both her hands.

Monkey Boy, with his hideous, laughing face, sat untouched in the study chair. Behind him lay Brandon, sprawled on his back. He didn't move.

Hazel ran to him, crying, "Brandon? Are you okay?"

Sylvia came with her. Hazel fell to her knees. There was no blood, but there was an angry red mark spreading around Brandon's right eye. Hazel cautiously reached out and touched his shoulder; he was still.

She looked at Sylvia, who paled. Hazel carefully raised Brandon's head.

His eyes were open but vacant.

"Brandon?" Hazel called. She looked at Sylvia. "Oh my God. Is he breathing?"

"Oh God, oh God," Sylvia murmured. "Brandon, can you hear me?"

He didn't answer. Ellen was hunched in the corner, whimpering and crying.

Footfalls thudded down the hallway, and Megan burst into the room. "What's going on?" Her eyes grew wide with terror when they fell on Brandon's body.

"Sylvia?" Megan said in a trembling voice. "How did he get in here?"

Sylvia shook her head, too stunned to speak. Carolyn was standing in the doorway, her arms wrapped around her body, hugging herself.

Megan rushed over, bent down, and said, "Brandon?" She touched his forehead. Then she moved her fingers under his nose. "Oh my God. You guys, he's not breathing!"

"What was he doing here?" Carolyn suddenly demanded. "How did he get in here?"

"He's not breathing," Hazel repeated steadily. Then her voice rose as everyone stared at her. *"He's not breathing."*

The next few moments were a blur. Someone was holding on to her and crying. She snapped out of her stupor to find herself with her arms around Megan. Sylvia and Carolyn were wrapped around Ellen and holding her tightly.

He's dead. He's dead. The thought repeated in Hazel's mind. But how could this have happened? How could their prank have gone so horribly wrong?

Carolyn took a deep breath. She looked at Ellen. "What did you hit him with?"

Ellen was beyond answering. Her body shook with deep, soul-crushing sobs.

"Charlie's baseball bat," Megan filled in. She reached for it.

"Don't touch it," Carolyn said. "They'll need to dust it for prints."

"What?" Hazel said. "Fingerprints? What are you talking about?"

Carolyn took a long, ragged breath. "Ellen killed him," she said calmly. "We have to call the police."

CHAPTER FOURTEEN

Ellen killed him.

There was a long silence as everyone processed that.

Then Sylvia said, "Charlie's going to be home soon."

"Oh my God." Megan stared at the others. "What are we going to do?"

"We have to tell the police," Carolyn said.

"No! No, please," Ellen begged. She could barely speak. Her eyes were red and swollen and her face was wet with tears. "It was an accident! I didn't mean to—"

"Besides, this is our fault." Sylvia looked at each one of them in turn. "If we hadn't planned the prank, this never would have happened. We can't let Ellen take all the blame."

"But what's *he* doing here?" Megan cried, pointing toward Brandon's body. "How'd he get in?"

"He must have let himself in through the study door," Sylvia said. "Ellen, did he know you were going to sit Charlie?"

Ellen shook her head. "I . . . I didn't tell him." Her eyes

widened as she looked at the group. "How did he know? Which one of you told him?"

No one spoke.

Sylvia took a deep breath, exhaling. She stood up straight and raised her chin, reasserting her command. "Okay. We are *not* going to the police with this."

Everyone looked at her in shock.

"We all had a hand in this. We're all guilty," Sylvia said.

"It was an accident," Hazel argued.

"No, it wasn't," Carolyn said. "Someone told Brandon to come here."

"Who?" Ellen bellowed. "Who did this?"

"Shut up," Sylvia snapped. "We were all in on the prank. We're all involved now." She paused. "Don't you see? Even if it was an accident, they can still send us to jail—*all* of us—for manslaughter."

Hazel stared at the others. She found a look of horror on each of their faces—an expression that must have reflected her own.

"I can't let that happen," Sylvia decided. "I'll take care of this." She whipped out her cell phone and dialed.

"Sylvia, that's ridiculous." Megan grabbed her wrist. "What are you doing?"

Sylvia stared at her coolly. "Let go of my hand," she said in an almost conversational tone. "You go head off Charlie. Pick him up at the movie, take him to the diner, and wait till we call you." She looked at Hazel. "Get Ellen out of here. Get her something to drink."

Hazel put her arm around Ellen, supporting her. "Come on," she said gently.

Ellen rose with her, lurching forward. Together they shuffled into the kitchen. On the way, Hazel glanced at the walls, the bookshelves, the gray carpet—a photograph of Charlie and his parents.

Everything felt close and foreign, as if all these strange objects might just collapse in and suffocate them.

In the kitchen, Ellen leaned her back against the counter. She ripped at her cuticle. Blood pooled around the moon of her thumbnail.

Hazel sat down beside her. She gave Ellen a glass or two of wine. Then Hazel switched her to water.

After a while, Carolyn peeked in on them from the doorway. She had a bedsheet clutched in her hands. "What is that for?" Ellen asked, her voice taut with grief.

"Don't worry about it. It's going to be all right," Carolyn said gently, as if Ellen had a terrible disease. She disappeared into the study again. ·

Ellen looked at Hazel and sobbed, "Why was he here?"

"I don't know, El."

They sat on the floor. Hazel had no idea how much time passed. She heard noises, then talking. There were sounds in the backyard. She got up to see what was happening.

Sylvia came out of the study, blocking her way.

"What's going on?" Hazel asked.

"Go back into the kitchen. Don't leave Ellen alone," Sylvia said firmly.

"But—"

"Do it," Sylvia ordered her.

✛　　　✛　　　✛

After a while, Carolyn called them into the living room. "I'm going to drive you home now," she told Ellen.

"But . . ." Hazel couldn't say what she was thinking. *What about Brandon?*

Carolyn wiped her forehead. She was sweating. "Josh was here. He and Sylvia took Brandon away. I'm going to handle Charlie tonight. That's all you need to know."

"What?" Hazel said as Ellen stirred beside her. They both stared at Carolyn as if she were speaking a foreign language.

"Brandon is gone. I'm taking the baseball bat and burning it. We're going to get another one. It's going to be all right."

"But . . . it's just a prank," Ellen cried. "He's really alive and we're all going to laugh over this later, right?"

"No," Carolyn replied firmly. "It's not a prank. He's dead."

Ellen let out a loud wail. Carolyn knelt beside her and caught her chin in her hand. "Ellen, listen to me. Listen. We can't tell anyone about this. We have to stay silent. PLDs hang tough. We hang together. Got it?"

Ellen sobbed, then she hiccupped a few times and took a ragged breath. "Where . . . where is he?"

"I don't know," Carolyn answered. "Sylvia and Josh took him away."

✛   ✛   ✛

From: YRSECRETPAL@hotmail.com

To: PLDEL@hotmail.com; PLDMEG@hotmail.com; PLDSLY@hotmail.com; PLDCARO@hotmail.com; PURPLEHAZE@hotmail.com

Subject: Surprise, surprise!

I told him to be there. I knew what would happen. You killed him, but I made it so. I'm just warming up. One of *you* is next.

✛   ✛   ✛

On Monday, Megan, Hazel, and Ellen met early in the school parking lot. Ellen looked like she hadn't slept in days.

"I talked to Sylvia," Megan said.

"Oh God. Where's she been?" Ellen asked.

"I don't know. She started to say something like, 'I'm sorry,' but then she caught herself and she said, 'I'm so tired.' Which didn't make any sense in our conversation."

Ellen looked stricken. She glanced from Megan to Hazel.

"Maybe she's just stressed," Hazel suggested.

"Maybe," Megan agreed.

Ellen cleared her throat. "What about Carolyn?"

"She would barely speak to me. Maybe saying anything over the phone freaked her out." Megan touched Ellen's shoulder. "Be careful what *you* say today, El. Stay calm."

Ellen said, "I should go home. I'm not going to be able to handle being here."

"I'm here," Hazel told her.

"We both are." Megan regarded them both. "All this time, I've been such a wiseass. But this is serious. Someone called Brandon. Someone let him in. I'm scared to death."

Everyone at school was buzzing about Brandon Wilde. The police had declared him missing.

His parents had already been on TV, begging someone, anyone, to come forward and tell them where their son was. The news made Hazel's stomach churn with guilt.

The police were back on campus. Swarming like insects. Pushing hard for kids to be interviewed.

Sylvia sent everyone a text.

Sylvia, who no one had heard from since Friday.

Sylvia, who had buried Brandon's body.

Meet 3rd fl. bathroom b4 lunch

She was leaning against the sinks with her arms crossed, waiting for them. When they had all trickled in, she said, "Josh is being questioned."

Hazel gasped, but Sylvia was quiet and calm as she continued. "He's being questioned, but he's refusing to answer unless he's charged. He's strong. Like we have to be. And we are, right?"

The group nodded like trained dogs, although Ellen's nod was the weakest. Sylvia saw it and pounced.

"Ellen, people are going to assume you're messed up because you're *folle* with worry. But after a while, they're going to take a closer look at you. You have got to pull yourself together."

She pulled out a plastic vial, glanced furtively around, and popped it open. She held out a small blue pill.

"These are tranquilizers," she said. "Perfectly legal in France. I want you to take one. Now."

"Oh my God, Sylvia, she could get expelled," Carolyn said.

Sylvia smiled wryly. "Don't you think that's the least of our problems?"

"But—what if she gets high? What if she starts spilling her guts?" Megan asked. "Not a good idea."

"The pills aren't that strong. They'll just take the edge off." She smiled kindly at Ellen. "I know this is hardest on you. You loved him. Even though he was a dirtbag."

The word hit Hazel like a slap to the face.

Brandon was dead. What purpose did it serve to talk about him that way?

Ellen teared up. Without a word, she took the pill from Sylvia's palm. She grabbed Hazel's bottle of water and swallowed it down.

"Good." Sylvia put the vial back in her purse. "Now listen. I gave this a lot of thought. We have to continue with my birthday party."

"Um . . . poor taste much?" Megan asked, astounded. She glanced at Hazel as if to say, *Can you believe this?*

"We have to act normal," Sylvia reminded them. "Otherwise it looks suspicious. We didn't go into mourning when Breona was killed, did we?"

"That's too much to ask, Sylvia," Megan argued. "We should just stick together and keep a low profile."

"Keep a low profile . . . you mean, *act guilty*?" Sylvia's face was hard, her gaze harder. "I went the extra mile for this group. Josh and me both. The least you can do is give me some backup."

Ellen moved her fingers to the destroyed cuticle on her left thumb. Sylvia smacked her hand, hard. "For God's sake, stop that!"

"I'm sorry! I just—I'm sorry!" Ellen ran out the bathroom door.

Sylvia wearily rubbed her eyes. "Hazel, please go get her. She listens to you."

Hazel found Ellen at her locker, fumbling with her combination. "Ellen," she called.

It took her three tries to work the combination. "Hazel, I'm never going to last," she said as she rummaged through her things.

"You have to last," Hazel said. "It's going to work out, Ellen."

"How?" Ellen grabbed something and brought it against her chest. It was a picture of Brandon and her, standing together with their arms around each other. "His parents deserve to know. They're going to be haunted for the rest of their lives. . . ."

Hazel couldn't argue with that. She didn't know what to say, what to do.

Ellen began to cry; Hazel felt a confusing rush of impatience, fear, and empathy.

She was there too. She was just a little better at hiding it.

Then again, she hadn't been the one with the bat.

She drew Ellen into her arms, soothing her, saying, "It's okay, Ellen. We'll figure out what to do." The minute the words were out of her mouth, she regretted them. They had already been told what to do. Had already agreed to it. "Hang in. Just hang in and maintain."

"I don't know if I can, Hazel," Ellen whispered. "I don't think I can."

The week dragged on. Tuesday slid into Wednesday and then Thursday. Sylvia was still determined to have her party on Friday night.

Ellen was on the edge. Hazel knew she wasn't far from it herself. She sat in chem lab, staring at Ms. Carpentier's scribbled notes on the whiteboard. She couldn't make sense of any of it. Her brain was too full of questions.

All this hiding, all this secrecy. Why is no one thinking about the biggest question of all?

Who told Brandon to be at Charlie's house?

Who sent the e-mail to all of us afterward?

Sylvia kept saying they were all responsible, but the real culprit was the person who set them up.

Who did it? Who would want Brandon dead?

Mr. Clancy entered the room. He spoke with Ms. Carpentier in a hushed whisper. Ms. Carpentier looked first at Mr. Clancy and then at Hazel, her face cold and serious.

"Hazel?" she called. "Would you come here, please?"

Everything ground to a stop. Only one thought played in Hazel's mind.

They know.

She felt a strange sense of relief. It would all be over soon.

But at the same time, she couldn't move. She was frozen, rooted. She couldn't even blink.

"Hazel?" Ms. Carpentier repeated.

Keep it together, she coached herself. Heads turned as she slid off her stool and walked as steadily as she could to Ms. Carpentier's desk.

"Would you come into the hall with me, please?" Mr. Clancy requested. "We have some important questions to ask."

Hazel looked down nervously at her hands, following the vice principal out of the lab.

After the interrogation, Hazel walked in a daze to her car.

There was a note stuck under the windshield wiper blades. Hazel unfolded it and read it. CALL!! S.

She pulled her cell phone out of her backpack and held it in her hand for a moment. Then she dialed Sylvia.

Sylvia answered on the first ring. "Where are you? Where'd you go? Why didn't you answer your phone? Lakshmi said they sent you to the office."

Hazel said, "Detective Fullerton was there."

"*What?*"

"She asked me what time I was with Matty on the night of the homecoming dance."

"And that's all?"

"That's all," Hazel confirmed.

"But she can't do that. She can't question you without your parents' permission."

"No. She can if it's not going to incriminate me. I'm not suspected of anything."

"She didn't ask you anything about Brandon? Didn't hint . . . ?"

"No. Just Matty."

Hazel felt dizzy. She had been surprised. The detective's questions had turned out to be so harmless.

"You should have refused to answer any questions without your parents," Sylvia chided her. "They might take what you said and twist it around. Breona went off on you at the dance. They might say you have a motive."

"What?" Hazel's heart pounded against her ribs. "What are you saying?"

"Just that what they *tell* you they want to know and what they're looking for may be two very different things."

"Oh God."

"So next time, tell them no," Sylvia said. "We have to stick together. Come over after school. People are here to decorate for the party."

Hazel couldn't believe she was serious. "Sylvia, I have to go home," she said. "I'm freaking out."

"You really should be with us." Sylvia's voice was kind. "Do what you think is best. But *don't* talk to them anymore."

Hazel drove home and crawled into bed. She lay huddled under her blankets. Eventually she began to doze and dreamed of . . .

. . . absolutely nothing.

She woke up in the dark to her computer beeping. Someone was sending her an instant message. She got up, feeling stiff all over, and shuffled to the keyboard. The time readout was nearly 9 p.m.

It was Matty. Sucking in her breath, she accepted his message.

MATTY2PURPLEHAZE: Haze, please read. I'm cutting & pasting this 4 U:

http://www.sandiego.gov/police/index.shtml

Hazel clicked on the link.

County of San Diego, Dept. of Medical Examiner

Investigator's Narrative

Case Number: 200X-07948

Decedent: WU, BREONA ANGELINA

. . . based on physiochemical and temperature readings, estimated time of death was between 9 PM and 2 AM

MATTY2PURPLEHAZE: They let me go. I did not kill her, Hazel. I wuz w/you.

PURPLEHAZE2MATTY: I know. Police asked me about it today. I told them the truth. I'm so glad U R OK. I'm sorry I didn't call. I was so scared.

MATTY2PURPLEHAZE: I want to see you.

PURPLEHAZE2MATTY: It's late. My parents.

MATTY2PURPLEHAZE: Please, Haze. I need you.

Hazel waited at the window. Matty's PT Cruiser rolled up thirty minutes later.

She peeked out in the hall. Corey was in his room and her parents were in theirs. Their TV was on. The house was dark.

Her heart pounding, she snuck down the hall and out the door.

She opened the passenger-side door and was greeted by Matty's familiar smile. She got in. Just the sight of him made Hazel want to throw her arms around him. Instead, she held herself in check. After all they had been through, would he still want her?

"Matty, I'm so sorry," she blurted. "I should have just gone to the cops sooner. I should have tried to clear your name."

But Matty cut her off, pulling her into a tight embrace. "It's okay," he whispered.

Hazel hugged him back. She felt tears welling in her eyes.

"I—I should have believed you," she cried. "I know that now. But you lost your temper and Sylvia . . . she showed me your restraining order—"

"Restraining order?" He held her at arm's length, regarding her suspiciously. "What are you talking about?"

"In Virginia," she said slowly. "Your girlfriend . . . You had a counselor who said you were violent and aggressive. . . ."

She trailed off, silenced by the look of shock on his face.

"Hazel, no one had a restraining order against me. I never saw a counselor in Virginia."

"But it was in your permanent record. Online."

He stared at her. "And you read this . . . when?"

"Sylvia. She hacked in." Hazel stared at the floorboards, ashamed. "After they arrested you that first time, she showed me the file. That was why I was scared of you."

"Oh God." He closed his eyes and leaned back in his seat. "Sylvia has been messing with you, Haze. With *us*."

She shook her head. "I don't understand."

"Show it to me," Matty insisted.

Together Hazel and Matty tiptoed upstairs to Hazel's room.

She logged on to her e-mail, found the message from Sylvia, and clicked on the link.

A message flashed on the screen: access denied.

"Sylvia hacked in and made up a fake file," Matty insisted.

"But why?" Hazel wondered aloud.

In her head, she knew the answer. *To have control over me.*

But was there more? Megan had mentioned that the PLDs were separated during the time of Breona's murder—and that Sylvia was late in meeting them afterward.

Was Sylvia trying to put suspicion on someone else after Breona's death?

Tell him, she urged herself. *Tell him all of it.*

"It's all right, Haze. I'm here now." He kissed her again. And again. "It's all right."

But it wasn't all right. Everything was a mess.

After Matty left, Hazel knocked on her parents' door.

The sound on the TV went down, and she poked her head into their bedroom.

"I'm going over to Sylvia's," she said. "I put the number on the breakfast bar."

"It's ten o'clock. Isn't that kind of late?" her father asked.

Hazel shook her head. "I'll be back by midnight. I promise."

"Call us when you get there. Be careful. Lock your doors," her mom ordered her.

"I will," she told them both.

And I won't come back without my questions answered.

CHAPTER FIFTEEN

Hazel clutched the steering wheel until her knuckles were white. She sped toward Sylvia's. Sylvia couldn't get away with this.

Hazel pulled up to the curb and stared at Sylvia's house. It was a huge Tudor mansion with a high wall and rosebushes lining the facade.

Before Hazel could pull open the driver's-side door, she heard music blaring from Sylvia's house. There was a glut of cars parked along the sidewalk. Hazel strode up the stairs and through the front door with determination.

There was a crowd blocking the foyer, and it carried through to the living room. Hazel didn't say a word to anyone. She stormed through the kitchen and out to the backyard.

Stephan Nylund had a beer in one hand and a cigarette in the other. He was babbling to a group gathered around him.

"Yo, someone saw Brandon in LA," he slurred. "He's just hanging out there. Living like a rock star. Getting all kinds of booty."

Hazel pushed past and glared at him with disgust.

Farther on, she saw Megan and Ellen sitting together. Ellen was cradling a drink and swaying unsteadily.

Hazel marched up to them.

"Haze," Ellen slurred. Her eyes were glazed.

Megan regarded Hazel cautiously. "Where have you been?"

"Megan, we have a problem," Hazel began.

"What is it?"

"It's Sylvia. I found out something tonight. Something really important. I think she faked a file after Breona's murder to—" Hazel stopped short. Sylvia's voice blared from inside the house.

"This is not funny! Who did this? Who did it?"

Hazel strode back into the house, following the sound.

The large room connected to the parlor was cast in darkness. A handful of kids were grouped around the television set; on the screen was a bird's-eye view of trees shimmering in a night wind, and children were singing an eerie chorus as an orchestra played a frightening counterpoint.

Sylvia's silhouette blacked out the images as she punched the player open and yanked out the DVD.

"Hey, that was *Diabolique*!" a guy curled on the couch pointed out.

"I know what it is!" she yelled. "I want to know who put it in there!"

No one spoke.

Sylvia charged out of the room with the DVD in her hand.

"What the hell is her problem?" someone muttered.

"All she does is talk about that damn movie," another one said.

Carolyn came up behind Hazel; she gestured for her to follow. They walked out the back door together, through the noise and laughter. Carolyn drew Hazel aside and said, "Sylvia is seriously losing it."

"I know," Hazel said. "And I think I know why. It's guilt. She faked school files about a restraining order out on Matty."

Carolyn smirked. "I'm not surprised. She's a total hacker, you know."

"She is?"

"Didn't you know? She can hack anything."

Hazel's mind whirled. The text messages from an unknown address, the e-mails from the same address. The altered voice on the phone. Breona, who she hated, dead.

Brandon, who scorned her in favor of Ellen, also dead.

She grabbed Carolyn's arm. "Can we talk?"

Carolyn nodded. "Sure."

"Good. Come with me. And don't tell Sylvia a thing."

They gathered in one of the guest bedrooms in Sylvia's immense mansion. Ellen was nervously twisting a lock of hair around her fingers and rubbing her eyes.

"I can't believe she's doing this," Ellen said hysterically. "I can't believe there's a party going on after everything that's happened. How can she be so cold?" she demanded, tears flowing from her eyes. Megan and Carolyn put their arms around her, trying to hush her.

"That's why I wanted to talk to you guys," Hazel said. "We're not going to let her get away with this."

Ellen wiped her tears away and looked up at Hazel. "What do you mean?"

Hazel knew it was time. The others might not like what she had to say, but they had to get to the bottom of all of this. She couldn't stand another moment of guilt—another second of uncertainty.

She took a deep breath.

"I need you all to think back to the days after Breona's murder. Remember what you said to me in the cafeteria? About the night of homecoming? The night that Breona died? Megan said Sylvia was missing for a while that night."

"I did," Megan answered slowly. "So?"

"So Matty's been let go by the police," Hazel explained. "He's cleared of the murder. It couldn't be him, because he was with me when Breona died. That means someone else killed her."

"Wait—Sylvia was MIA for a few minutes and you automatically think she did it?" Carolyn argued.

"No, there's more. Right after the murder, when the police were asking questions, Sylvia showed me a file from Matty's permanent record. It said he had violent tendencies—and it was completely fake."

"So you think Sylvia faked it," Ellen filled in.

Hazel nodded. "She saw Matty's blowup on the field, and it gave her an idea—a chance to divert suspicion . . . from herself."

The others were silent.

"She was the only person in school with a real reason to want

Breona dead," Hazel told them. "Sylvia and Breona may have had bad blood for years, but when Breona tried to steal Josh over the summer—"

"Sylvia lost control of her boyfriend for a few months, and she couldn't stand it," Megan chimed in quietly.

Hazel nodded. "She wants to control everyone around her. She needs it. You all know that. She tried to control us too. She couldn't stand the thought that Breona broke her little spell. And that's why she killed her."

"Wait," Carolyn interrupted. "Even if that's true, why would she arrange for Brandon to be there the night of our prank?"

"Because he wanted me instead of her," Ellen said in a low voice. "She couldn't stand the thought of Brandon choosing to be with the lamest PLD over her—the queen bee."

Carolyn and Megan shared a look of surprise. Ellen kept her head down, studying her massacred nails.

"Ellen, you *knew* that they used to fool around?" Megan said incredulously. Ellen looked up at Hazel and gave a small, sad nod.

The girls were silent for a while. Finally Hazel said quietly, "We need to go to the police."

"What?" Carolyn countered. "No, we can't!"

"We have to," Hazel argued. "Think of Brandon's parents."

"Think of *yours*," Megan replied. "Think of all our parents. When they hear that we killed someone—"

"But we *didn't* kill someone," Ellen pointed out. "Sylvia is responsible for all of this. If we tell the police about it, *she'll* be the one to go to jail. *She'll* be the one they blame."

"Besides, do you want to carry this secret around for the rest of your life?" Hazel asked.

Carolyn shook her head. So did Megan.

They knew they couldn't get away with it. Not forever.

"Okay," Megan finally agreed. Carolyn nodded. "We'll go."

Hazel didn't sleep at all that night. They had decided to meet early—before school, by the big rock behind the media center where the drama clique hung out. They'd go in and talk to Mr. Clancy and Detective Fullerton as a group.

Hazel rose from her bed more times than she could count—to go to the bathroom, to splash water on her face, and to wander down the hall to stand in front of her parents' room, her hand poised to knock.

She didn't knock, but she looked in on her brother. His room smelled like rotten food. Game cartridges and DVDs were strewn all over the floor. She saw him in his bed, wrapped up in his covers, snoring.

She almost woke him but decided not to.

The hours dragged by; she was swaying on her feet. Sheer adrenaline was keeping her awake. She tried to distract herself by deciding what to wear.

By six she was ready to go. She paced her room, exhausted and hungry. Her family was stirring; her dad usually got up first, to make coffee. She heard him pad down the hall. She stayed in her room because if she didn't, she would probably tell him what was going on. She had told a lot of lies already. She would just rather not tell them all over again.

Then it was six-thirty, and then it was seven. Time to leave.

Hazel grabbed her keys, took a breath, and left the sanctuary of her room. She studied it for a moment—the purple bedspread with blue and green flowers, the matching curtains, the poster of Jude Law.

Will I ever see my room again?

She passed the kitchen. Her stout, balding father saw her and gave her a just-a-sec wave. "Hazel, do you mind very much lending Mom your car today? We had to take hers in yesterday."

She blinked. "What? What happened?"

He smiled quizzically. "*Nothing happened*, Hazel. It just needed a tune-up."

"Oh. Sure," she said. "No problem."

"Do you need a ride to school, or can you get one from a friend? You don't have to leave until eight, right?"

Hazel touched her forehead. "I can probably get a ride."

"Right." He chuckled. "Because getting a lift from your old man wouldn't be cool."

Oh, Dad, you have no idea. "Cool" is the last thing on my mind.

She retreated to her room and called Ellen's cell.

There was no answer. She figured Ellen was talking to her father, trying to get out of the house. She rang Carolyn instead.

"I'll be there in fifteen minutes," Carolyn said. "Meet me out front."

"Well," Hazel said with a sigh, "I guess this is it." Carolyn had pulled into a spot in front of the school.

"I guess so," Carolyn replied. They sat in silence, just staring at the empty school for a moment before grabbing their bags and getting out of the car.

"There's Megan," Carolyn said as they came around the corner of the media center. Her back was turned to them, but they recognized her by her purple hoodie. She was leaning sideways against the rock, her head down.

"She looks upset," Hazel whispered.

"We're all upset," Carolyn replied.

"Megan," Hazel called out. Megan didn't respond.

"You okay, honey?" Carolyn said softly as they approached. Megan didn't say a word.

"Hey, Meg?" Hazel reached out and put her hand on Megan's shoulder. Her friend collapsed under the weight, slumping onto the ground.

"Oh my God!" Carolyn screamed.

Hazel crouched down beside Megan. She turned her over.

A pair of blue eyes stared blankly up at Hazel.

Megan was dead.

CHAPTER SIXTEEN

"Megan, Megan!" Hazel yelled, shaking her by the shoulders. The hood of the sweatshirt fell away. Megan's neck was marked with deep purple bruises.

"She's been strangled!" Carolyn exclaimed.

Both girls were suddenly startled by a loud cry. They whirled around to see Ellen, one hand covering her mouth, the other shakily clutching her car keys, tears gushing out of her eyes.

"No, please, no," Ellen whimpered.

"Ellen!" Hazel said.

Ellen let out another sob and then tried to wipe her tears away. "Oh my God. Is she dead?"

Hazel's mind raced. *Did Sylvia overhear us planning to go to the police? Or did someone tell her about it?*

Just then her phone let out a sharp beep. Hazel cautiously pulled the phone out of her bag. New text message.

YRSECRETPAL2PURPLEHAZE: Tattletales. Careful who u talk 2. U might end up like her.

✢   ✢   ✢

"Hello?" Hazel said hesitantly into the phone.

"Hazel," Sylvia said. "I've been trying to reach you ever since I heard." Her voice sounded hoarse, like she'd been crying.

"Since you heard?" Hazel said slowly.

"Since I heard about Megan. I still can't believe it," Sylvia said. "How could this have happened, Hazel? What was she even doing there?"

"I don't know," Hazel replied. "None of us know. That's what we told the police, Sylvia. We don't know how it happened."

"I'm so devastated, Hazel," Sylvia went on. "The funeral is Saturday and I'm not going to school for the rest of the week. I just can't."

"Yes. It's awful. An awful shock," Hazel said stiffly.

The funeral was horrible.

The smell of incense and dying flowers made Hazel's throat close up. Her eyes began to water.

There were huge arrangements everywhere. The church was freezing, which was surprising, given that it was overflowing with high school students.

Megan's casket was closed, and Hazel tried hard not to imagine her lying inside that box—all cut up from the autopsy, filled with embalming fluid, and held together with big stitches.

She thought of Brandon then and tried even harder not to picture what his body must look like, two weeks later.

The girls hadn't let on about Sylvia to anyone. The police had riddled them with questions when they showed them Megan's body, but the PLDs all remained silent. Partly because of their shock—and partly because they weren't sure what Sylvia would do if they implicated her.

The chubby, weak-chinned priest droned on, talking about what a wonderful girl Megan had been, what promise her young life had shown.

"But God in his infinite wisdom saw fit to take her to his kingdom," he declared.

Sylvia let out a pained sob. She'd been in tears for the entire service. The other PLDs sat beside her in stony, fearful silence. If Hazel hadn't been so stunned by fear, she would have been disgusted by the irony.

Finally, they packed into cars and drove to the cemetery. As Hazel watched Megan's casket being lowered into the ground— secreted away—she finally did break down. Her mother squeezed her shoulder and Hazel only cried harder.

Then there was a reception at Megan's home. The house was filled with morose, darkly clothed adults, clutching glasses of wine and huddling in small groups, sharing dismayed whispers. *How could something like this happen in Brookhaven?*

Hazel's parents stayed only a few minutes. They took Corey home after she assured them she'd get a ride. Hazel gritted her teeth as she watched Sylvia approach Megan's mother. She gave her a long embrace, brushing more tears out of her eyes as they separated.

Crocodile tears, Hazel thought.

It was clear that Megan's room was off-limits, so the PLDs gathered in the rec room. There were just as many reminders of Megan there—her collection of horror movies sat on the shelf by the television and photo-booth pictures of her, Sylvia, Ellen, and Carolyn from fifth grade were pinned to a bulletin board.

Carolyn had smuggled a bottle of wine down there. They sat on the floor around the coffee table and passed the bottle. Hazel took tiny sips; her stomach was clenched with anxiety and the wine tasted bitter to her. The others were gulping it down and getting wasted fast.

Hazel's heart was pounding. Sylvia had killed Megan. She was coldhearted. Ruthless. She'd had too much power for too long.

I am sitting with a murderer, Hazel thought over and over.

"I'm going to miss her so much," Sylvia whimpered, reaching for Carolyn's hand.

"You don't need to say that," Carolyn said sharply, pulling her hand away.

"Carolyn, what's wrong with you?" Sylvia demanded.

"You didn't give a crap about her," Ellen blurted. Hazel was surprised. It seemed like Ellen hadn't recovered from her stunned daze since the Brandon incident.

"You loved to torture her," Ellen went on. "You wouldn't let her forget about hooking up with Carolyn. You held it over her head every chance you got."

Sylvia blinked at her. "Ellen, now is neither the time nor the place."

"She's right," Carolyn cut in. "You told the whole school about it. It's your fault Stephan still won't let it go."

"How dare you?" Sylvia shouted. "Who got Stephan Nylund's digital camera before he could upload the photos?"

"But who kept the photos?" Ellen cried. "You did! You threatened her with them ever since. You wouldn't let it die."

"Shut up!" Sylvia screamed.

"No!" Ellen yelled back. "You do it to all of us. You are an evil, controlling bitch, Sylvia Orly."

"Whoa!" Hazel put her arm around Ellen. "Calm down. We're at Megan's funeral."

"Brandon didn't even want you," Ellen said, brushing Hazel off and pointing her finger in Sylvia's face. "He wanted me, not you."

"That's enough!" Sylvia shouted, getting to her feet. She advanced on Ellen.

"Yes, it *is* enough!" Ellen said. "We are done. All of us. The PLDs are over."

"Oh? *You've* decided that?" Sylvia's voice was dripping with contempt.

"Yes!" Ellen shrieked at her. "I have." She took Carolyn's hand. "Come on. Let's get the hell out of here."

"Why? So you can go wring her neck and blame it on the rest of us?" Sylvia asked.

Ellen froze. "What are you saying? That *I* killed Megan?"

"Why not you? You've always been the weird one, Ellen. A weird little freak," Sylvia spat. "If it wasn't for me, do you think *anyone* would be your friend? I made you who you are."

Ellen narrowed her eyes. "Don't try to pin this on me. Three people are dead, and you had reasons to be mad at all of them. Brandon liked me better than you. Breona Wu totally dissed you. And Megan—you killed Megan thinking she was me. We were going to tell. And *you* were the one who was going to go down for it. We all know it was you, Sylvia. We all know it!"

"Really? Where's your proof, Ellen?" Sylvia cried. "You have none. Because you know it wasn't me."

She turned to Hazel. "You don't believe this . . . this *merde*, do you?"

"*Merde*, like you dish out?" Hazel replied. "You are a total user, Sylvia. Ellen's right. We're through."

Carolyn took Ellen's arm. Without another word, the two left the room.

Hazel followed them toward the door.

"Come back here!" Sylvia shouted. "Come back here if you know what's good for you, you pathetic losers!"

Hazel kept going.

"You are so going to regret walking away from me! You are all going to be sorry!"

Lakshmi was delighted to take Hazel home. She yakked all the way to the Stone house.

"Is it true she was buried with her scrunchie and her Claddagh ring?" Lakshmi asked.

Hazel said not one syllable in reply.

It was not a Movie of the Week moment. She was not going to discover that Lakshmi was her actual true best friend. Real life didn't work that way.

"I hope you feel better," Lakshmi said by way of parting, obviously disappointed that Hazel hadn't talked or, better yet, invited her in.

Her parents had waited for her to return. Hazel was blandly noncommittal about what she and the other girls had done at the reception.

"I just hope you're okay, honey," her mother said, worry lines creased around her eyes. They sat down at the kitchen table together, and Hazel let her mother make her some tea. Watching her mom putter around the kitchen, getting out jam and butter for toast, Hazel finally did have some kind of a moment. Maybe her mom wasn't the smartest or most interesting or most sophisticated person. But she was kind. She loved her children.

Hazel's mom trusted her. More than Hazel ever should have trusted her so-called friends.

Hazel excused herself and went up to bed. But her thoughts wouldn't let her sleep.

She took a shower. As she leaned against the tiles, her tears mixed with the water.

Ellen was right. Sylvia was evil. But there was no way to prove it.

Hazel felt lost. She needed a sane voice. Someone to lean on.

She got out of the shower and called Matty. He was there in

minutes, holding his arms out as before. She didn't kiss him. She kept her distance.

"Matty," she began. "I . . . I have to tell you something awful." She took a deep breath.

In a rush, she told him everything. The big prank. Ellen. The baseball bat. Brandon dead on the floor.

"Oh my God," he breathed. "He was killed? And you knew that and *didn't say a word*?"

She stared down at her hands. At some point, she had started biting her nails, and she hadn't even realized it. They looked awful. She felt ugly. She couldn't believe Matty was sitting with her when she was so repellent.

She turned to him, searching his face. "It was unreal, Matty. For so long I didn't know what to do. I didn't know what to think. But then I started putting the pieces together. It was Sylvia. We were going to the police—Carolyn, Ellen, Megan, and I. We were going to tell them everything. But then . . . we found Megan."

"Oh my God." He stared at her. His shock reflected her own worst thoughts. She felt herself beginning to panic. "Sylvia," he said. "She's been right there with you all along." She held on to both his hands and took deep breaths, willing herself not to shatter.

He wiped her tears with his fingers. "I'll help if you'll let me. I'll keep you safe tonight. I'll stay in my car out in front of your house until the sun comes up."

"No way," she protested, amazed that he could be so kind. "You won't be safe out there. You can sleep in here . . . on the floor."

"Your parents won't mind?" he asked.

"They won't notice. Don't worry."

While Matty settled into the blankets she'd laid out on the floor, she picked up her cell phone and checked for messages.

There was one voice mail—from Ellen:

"Oh my God, Hazel! I was attacked! I was at Carolyn's and I was freaking out so much I went for a walk, and someone jumped out of a car and tried to knife me! I ran back into her house. We don't know what to do! Call me back as soon as you get this."

Her heart pounding, Hazel called back. There was no answer. She dialed Carolyn's cell phone.

"Oh my God. Where have you been?" Carolyn asked. "There's a huge cut on Ellen's arm! I'm so scared, Hazel. Someone is out to get us."

"We have to go to the police," Hazel said.

"And tell them what? About Brandon?" Carolyn asked, panicking. "It's like Sylvia said. We need some proof."

Ellen grabbed the phone from Carolyn. "We can't go to the police, Hazel! Sylvia will get us."

"Listen," Hazel said. "Stay calm. We'll meet up in the morning and talk this over. Matty is here. He's going to help us."

"I can't believe this is happening." Ellen sighed. "Just stay on the phone with us. Carolyn will get on the other extension. We're so scared."

"I just had a thought," Hazel replied. "Sylvia got me this phone. Is there some way she can listen in?"

"God, I don't know," Ellen said. "She is a total hacker. She showed us all how she got into restricted sites and spied on private chat rooms. It's not such a stretch to think . . ."

"Let me call you back on my landline," Hazel replied.

She got the portable and called back. She, Carolyn, and Ellen stayed connected the entire night, dozing, talking, comforting each other.

☩　　☩　　☩

PERSONALBLOG

HAPPY2BME

SLEEP TIGHT, LITTLE DEVILS. YOU CAN RUN BUT YOU CAN'T HIDE. IT WILL ALL BE OVER SOON—FRIENDS TILL THE END. THE VERY END.

☩　　☩　　☩

The next morning the PLDs converged on Matty's house. The place was shabby and messy. Denise, his sister, was working a double shift.

They stuck to Matty's room. It was like being in a bunker. There was a poster of *LA Confidential* on one wall and a poster for *Collateral* on the other.

"I still say we ask Josh," Matty said. "For all we know, he's just as eager to get out of this mess as you guys."

Ellen and Carolyn disagreed.

"Josh can't be trusted," Carolyn said. "He's Sylvia's little puppet."

"He'll tell her we're going to the police," Ellen said. She took a breath. "The same thing that happened to Megan could happen to us."

"What we need is proof," Matty said, lowering his voice. "We need to find Brandon's body. That way, it's not your word against hers. They'll have no choice but to take her into custody."

"But nobody knows where Sylvia and Josh took it," Carolyn said.

"We have to think," Hazel said, casting her thoughts back to that night. "Maybe Sylvia let something slip." She looked into the faces of the others and saw horrible regret—the need to go back and undo that night.

In that moment, Hazel hated Sylvia with every bit of her being. She clasped hands with Carolyn and Ellen. "We're in this together," she said.

"Finally," Ellen said. "All this time we talked about being there for each other. This is the first time it's ever really been that way."

"You all seemed so close," Hazel said. "Like such good friends."

"Haze, I'm so sorry you got mixed up with us," Carolyn replied. "You had some pretty decent friends. They weren't ultra-cool, but you were doing okay."

Hazel squeezed Carolyn's hand. "I didn't know I was doing okay," she confessed. "I wanted to be a PLD."

"Everyone wanted to be a PLD. But what were we?" Carolyn sighed. "I'd give anything just to be a regular person."

"Too late," Ellen said.

They fell silent. Thinking. What could Sylvia have done with Brandon?

Hazel's gaze moved to the movie posters on Matty's walls.

"Hey," she said slowly, "Sylvia was always going on about *Diabolique*. Then she totally freaked when someone put it in at the party . . . after Brandon died and the night before Megan—"

"Original or remake?" Carolyn interrupted.

"Who cares?" Ellen said. "It's the same movie, right?"

"It was the original," Hazel told the group. "The one in French she was always saying we should watch. Then finally someone put it on and she went crazy. Why?"

"I've seen it," Matty offered. "It's a classic. There's a great scene with a swimming pool. That's where they dump the body."

"Well, it's not like Sylvia dumped the body in *her* pool," Carolyn said. "I think someone might have noticed that."

"In the movie it wasn't just a regular pool," Matty added. "It was an abandoned pool. It was filled with leaves and junk. Very cool in black and white."

Hazel shook her head. "Abandoned pools . . ."

There was a long silence, broken at last by Carolyn.

"Oh my God!" she exclaimed. "There was this old, abandoned house. . . ."

"Where?" Ellen looked interested.

"Deep in the woods behind Sylvia's house. We used to go out there when we were kids. Sylvia was completely obsessed with the place."

"It had a pool?" Hazel asked her.

"Yes. We used to go out there all the time, and then one winter it burned down."

"It did? How?" Hazel asked.

"I don't know, but part of me always suspected Sylvia set that fire."

Hazel thought back to the night at the Darlings'. Sylvia telling her what a strange child Breona had been. How she'd gotten Hazel to talk about her deepest secret.

Sylvia was the strange one all along, Hazel realized. *How could I have trusted her? How could I ever have been so stupid?*

"Is the house still there?" Ellen asked.

Carolyn nodded.

"Then let's check it out," Ellen suggested.

"I know the way," Carolyn said.

Matty looked at Hazel. She swallowed. "Let's do it. You drive."

HAPTER
SEVENTEEN

The hills were black. There was no moon, and a hot, dry wind rustled through the trees. It was called the Santa Ana, and it was giving Hazel a headache.

She sat with Matty in the front of his Cruiser, her hand on his thigh, as they barreled down the two-lane strip of highway that led to Sylvia's house.

Carolyn navigated them down a back road so they wouldn't have to cut past Sylvia's to get through the woods. "Okay, up this driveway."

Beneath the branches of several overgrown pepper, eucalyptus, and acacia trees was a steep, shadowy strip of blacktop. Hazel doubted that the casual driver would have noticed it. Some of the trunks were still blackened from the fire Carolyn had mentioned; the wind whipped them hard, and they bobbed and dipped as if they might break in half.

"We're not that far away," Carolyn announced. "Cut the engine. We can walk from here."

Matty turned off the ignition and killed the lights. He had found only one flashlight at his house; he turned it on now and aimed it at the ground. The wind tossed leaves at them as the four walked up the steep driveway.

"The pool is to the right," Carolyn said.

Hazel nodded, taking Matty's hand. They continued walking.

The wind blew again, and a thick stench wafted toward them. Hazel retched. There was only one thing in the world that smell could be—the smell of death.

"We're here," Carolyn announced.

They were hovering at the edge of the deep end of a half-full swimming pool. The smell radiated from it. Matty's flashlight shone down on a suspended blanket of brown, desiccated leaves.

They all stood quietly, staring.

"We know he's there," Hazel pointed out. "Can't we just tell the police?"

"No." Ellen cleared her throat. "We have to be sure."

"I'll do it," Matty volunteered. He fanned the flashlight back and forth, then found some concrete steps leading into the pool's shallow end. He turned to Hazel and kissed her quickly.

The wind howled through the ruined trees and blew the leaves on the surface of the pool. Hazel's eyes watered.

The flashlight beam moved ahead of Matty as he reached the bottom of the pool. He walked forward, moving his flashlight back and forth, scanning the area in front of him.

Then he stumbled. He swore; the flashlight beam jittered. There was a splashing sound . . . and darkness.

"Shit," Matty exclaimed. "I lost it. I can't see a thing." He knelt down, reaching into the leaves and muck.

"Come back," Hazel pleaded.

"No, wait!" Ellen said. "We can't just leave!"

Hazel turned. There was a rustling in the foliage.

"Oh my God," Carolyn said. "Who's there?"

Silence.

Then something hard rammed into Hazel, knocking her to the ground. Ellen screamed.

Hazel tried to get to her feet, but someone was holding her down. Hazel turned her head and bit down, hard. The attacker flinched and Hazel jumped up.

"Get to the car!" Matty shouted. He dashed up the steps and grappled with the attacker.

Someone grabbed Hazel's wrist and pulled her up.

"Come on!" It was Ellen. They ran together back down the driveway.

"Call 911!" Matty shouted.

As they ran, Hazel felt in her pocket. Her phone must have fallen out. She was about to say so when Carolyn began speaking into her own cell.

"Please help! We're on Descanso Road, by the abandoned house. We're being attacked!"

"Matty!" Hazel yelled. She reached the car, fumbled with the door, and turned on the headlights. Their harsh, yellow glare lit up the scene, exposing Matty—and Josh.

Looking stunned, Josh backed away slowly, putting his hands up.

"What are you doing here?" a familiar voice demanded. The

girls turned to see Sylvia, glaring, her hands on her hips.

"You killed Breona and Megan. You set Brandon up. Now you want us dead too," Hazel accused.

"That's not true!" Sylvia insisted. "Someone sent me a text. . . ."

In the distance the wail of approaching sirens rose.

"You set me up," Sylvia said, backing away. "One of you did this!"

Sylvia shoved Hazel out of the way and jumped inside Matty's cruiser. The keys were still in the ignition.

"Sylvia!" Josh cried. "Wait!"

Matty tackled him before he could move, pinning him to the ground.

Tires squealed as the car shot backward.

"No!" Hazel cried. Sylvia couldn't escape. Not after everything she'd done.

Sylvia gunned the engine. The car ran over a jagged tree trunk. She shifted into drive and pressed the accelerator. The tires screamed and smoked, but the car didn't move.

She revved the engine again. But the car was immobilized— held in place by the burnt remnants of the tree.

Red and blue lights flashed over the driveway as the police approached.

"I didn't do it!" Sylvia screeched, putting her head down on the steering wheel. "I swear I didn't do it!"

And then the police were there to take her away.

Epilogue

Months went by: juvenile hall, therapists' offices, social workers' cubicles, police stations, courtrooms.

The charges against Hazel, Carolyn, and Ellen—conspiracy, obstruction of justice, and dozens of others—had been dropped in return for their testimony against Sylvia and Josh.

Brandon's body wasn't found in the swimming pool. But he had been buried in a shallow grove near it. Sylvia swore on the witness stand that she had received a text message: **I know where Brandon is; I'm taking U down!**

She said she had panicked, and that was why she and Josh were there—to move him so no one would find out the truth.

"But that's what they wanted me to do!" Sylvia insisted. "They wanted to frame me!"

The jury didn't believe her for a second. The police had found no trace of the message in question. In possession of the most damning physical evidence—Brandon's body—Sylvia had been convicted of a laundry list of crimes, and Josh had been convicted of many of the same.

She was also charged with the murders of Breona and Megan, her trial pending for each of them.

But Sylvia's testimony at the first trial seemed destined to damn her for the rest.

"I didn't kill them!" she screamed. "They turned against me.

They thought they could take me out. But they can't. No one can. I'm the reason the PLDs exist! Without me, they're nothing!"

And in a way she was right.

Christmas went by in a blur, and soon it was time to go back to school. Most of the students avoided the surviving PLDs.

The absence of Sylvia Orly was like the elephant in the room that everyone could see but no one wanted to talk about.

"So, tacos again today?" Lakshmi asked Hazel. She set her tray down beside Matty's and pulled back her chair.

They were together again, the lesser lights and Hazel.

The PLD table had been taken over by some jocks.

Ellen and Carolyn didn't sit together anymore. Carolyn had joined a group of totally out lesbians and, to Hazel's surprise, wasn't getting very much flak over it.

"Yes, tacos again," Hazel said.

Matty kissed her cheek and showed her a sketch he'd been working on: a portrait of Hazel in charcoal.

"You look good," Lakshmi said. Her coolness Q had been upped by the return of Hazel, the notorious former PLD, and she knew it. She was trying hard not to act conceited about it, but she was clearly loving it. Much to Hazel's surprise, she and Stephan Nylund had even started dating.

Lakshmi looked up from the sketch and frowned slightly. Hazel followed her gaze. Ellen hovered on the distant perimeter of their table, in a new green poncho and matching green cropped pants. She had on silver heels. It was all very *over*.

"Got a minute?" she asked.

Hazel got up and followed Ellen away from the table.

"Um, I was wondering if you might like to hang out a little after school. My homework . . ." She shook her head. "Hideous mess."

"I'm sorry, but I have something to do," Hazel said.

Ellen took it hard. She swallowed, looked down. "You're lucky," she said. "You had backup friends. Brandon is gone. Carolyn's all with the lesbians and I'm . . . I'm stuck."

"I'm sorry," Hazel repeated. She didn't know how to explain. Ellen wanted—no, expected—things to go back the way they had been. Hazel couldn't go there.

"It'll be okay," Hazel lied. She doubted that it would ever be again. The best they all could hope for was to repair the damage and move on.

"Come on," Matty teased Hazel. "Just a little kiss?"

He grabbed her around the waist and planted his lips on the small of her neck.

Hazel squealed. "Quit it! That tickles."

They were at a small jock gathering in the park near Charlie's house. Hazel didn't sit for the Pollinses anymore. But she saw Charlie now and then. He had a new cat.

The party was nothing spectacular, just pizza and some beer. But it was nice to have been invited.

Slowly, slowly, things seemed to be returning to normal.

"Yo, we're going on a beer run," Stephan told Matty.

"You in?" He was holding hands with Lakshmi, who was blushing a little, still clearly overwhelmed by her own good fortune.

"Sure." Matty pulled out his wallet and handed Stephan ten bucks. Seeing Lakshmi with Stephan made Hazel feel awkward—especially when she considered how awful he had been to Megan. Carolyn couldn't care less, but Hazel knew that ever-loyal Ellen had not forgiven him for the rumors he'd spread about their now-dead friend.

She seriously doubted Ellen ever would.

Matty continued kissing Hazel's neck. He moved her behind a pepper tree, shielding them from view. He hadn't pressured her to hook up, but she knew he was waiting for her to give the word. Maybe it was time.

Hazel's phone vibrated; she had a text.

YRSECRETPAL2PURPLEHAZE: She's good enuff 2 B ur friend but I'm not? Not 4 long.

"No!" Hazel gasped, looking up at Matty. "It can't be!"

"What is it?" Matty asked.

Hazel held her phone up with a trembling hand. "This address. I haven't seen it since Sylvia went to jail. It doesn't make sense. . . ."

There was the squeal of tires. A bloodcurdling scream.

"Oh my God!" one of the guys yelled. "Someone call 911—Lakshmi's been hit by a car!"

Hazel's heart sickened. She had assumed she was safe.

But no one was. Not at all.

PERSONALBLOG
HAPPY2BME

SAYONARA, LAKSHMI! YOU TOTAL LOOZER!
I THOUGHT IT WOULD END WITH SYLVIA, BUT IT'S CLEAR TO ME
NOW THAT WAS WISHFUL THINKING. MY FRIENDSHIP WITH
HAZEL AND CAROLYN HAS DIED. AND SYLVIA WILL TURN 18 AND
GO FREE.

IT'S NOT FAIR. BUT IT'S OK. I'M STILL KICKING, AND THEY'LL GET
WHAT THEY DESERVE. MATTY WILL PAY FOR INTERFERING. THEY'LL
ALL PAY, SLOWLY. PAINFULLY. THAT'S WHY I'M

HAPPY2BELLEN!